"Though small the Lusian realms, her legions few,
The guardian oft by Heav'n ordain'd before,
The Lusian race shall guard Messiah's lore."

Os Lusiadas, Luis Vaz de Camoes, published 1572.
Translated by William Julius Mickle, Canto VII,
pp 197, London, 1877

We can be heroes just for one day

David Bowie, Alessandro Rodolfo Lindblad,
Brian Peter George Eno, Brian Eno

BEAUTY, LOVE & JUSTICE

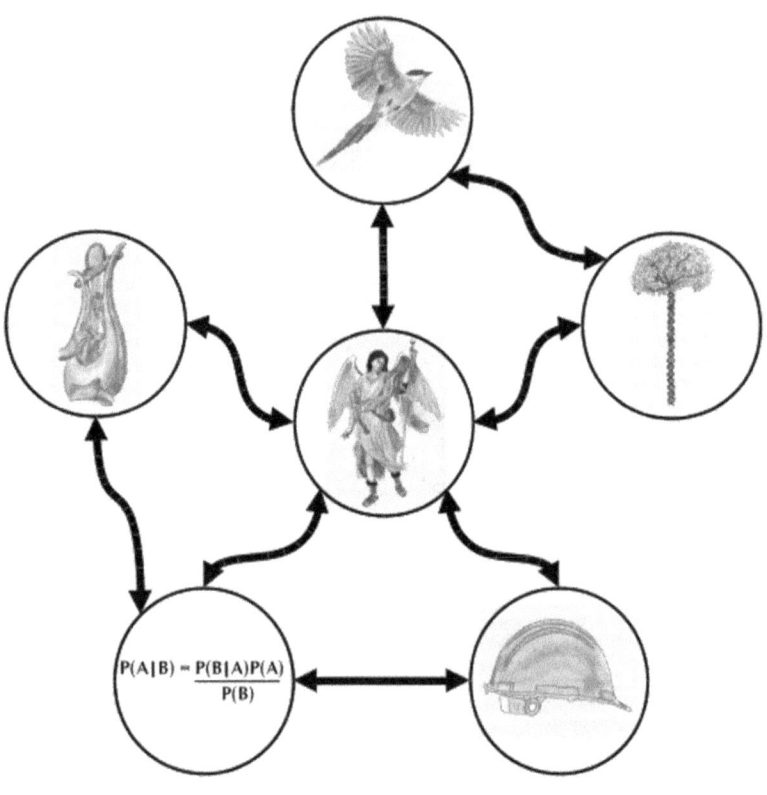

BEAUTY, LOVE & JUSTICE

A MODERN MORALITY TALE ABOUT OBSESSION,
DECEPTION, SACRIFICE, AND CIDER.

ALCINA FARADAY

urbanepublications.com

First published in Great Britain in 2015
by Urbane Publications Ltd
Suite 3, Brown Europe House, 33/34 Gleamingwood Drive,
Chatham, Kent ME5 8RZ
Copyright © Alcina Faraday, 2015

A CIP catalogue record for this book is available
from the British Library.

ISBN 978-1-909273-58-0
EPUB 978-1-909273-59-7

Design and Typeset by Julie Martin

Cover by Julie Martin

Printed by CPI Group (UK) Ltd,
Croydon, CR0 4YY

urbanepublications.com

To Vavatch, my inspiration.

$\mathcal{A}$CKNOWLEDGEMENTS

I am indebted to Matthew for his belief and encouragement, and to all the Urbanians for their support.

I'm also grateful to Greg Mosse, Jonathan Lee, Brian Burr and Ian Robinson for their helpful and frank feedback, and to IMR for his beautiful illustrations and tutorials on Bayesian Theory.

Cover image – *The Death of Hyacinth*, Benjamin West – 1771 – reproduced with the kind permission of the Philadelphia Museum of Art

All illustrations by

PART ONE

POLLINATION

CHAPTER 1

LUSITANIAN
LOVESTRUCK BLUES

Tiago had enjoyed a couple of drinks.

He started upstairs with caution, but by the third flight he was listing to port. He gripped the handrail and grinned, sober enough to know he shouldn't be here, unable to turn round and go home. On the dark landing he got his breath back, peered down the corridor, and saw the heavy oak door to Raphael's office. It was slightly open, a thin shard of light slashing the carpet red, spelling danger.

But Tiago wasn't frightened of anything right then. He swanned over to an old mirror to inspect his dark reflection, hoping the mottled glass would reveal the characterful face of the intriguing, brilliant young man he knew himself to be; deadly, incisive, the thrusting young turk of the trading floor, the undisputed *infante* of commodity derivatives, a merciless, cool and resolute pioneer, a new da Gama.

A baby seal stared back at him, big-eyed, cute, wavy-haired.

"Oh fuck. Please club me."

He licked his fingers, raked the hair back, looked at himself sideways on; better. He straightened his collar, shot his cuffs and tried three new looks; purpose, depth, decisiveness. After a while he nodded. Slightly flushed maybe, but good, sharp but understated, just the right amount of effort; perfect, in fact.

He stood back and nodded at his reflection; finally what he wanted to see, finally reality. It wasn't always this easy. Tiago's standards were exacting, so ditching fact for fantasy – once a necessary survival tactic – had become an addiction. The raw data sometimes happy-slapped him at three in the morning. Someone, possibly him, was orphaned at four, squandered his adolescence in religiosity, got his heart broken and his faith shattered at twenty-one when a first lover dumped him for Jesus, and spent two weird years in grubby clinches with faceless businessmen too cowardly to charge hotel porn to expenses. True, his losses had been trumped by academic, sporting and musical achievements, a stellar CV and a stack of fat (but untouched) annual bonuses – but success had only fed a habit for basking in personal glory while maintaining a deep inner conviction that all the shit things in his life were happening to somebody else, egging him on to censor his memories and daydream, shape-shifting to handle the world like the playmates of his childhood would. Such as a stark-liveried *salamandra do fogos* when guile was needed; *Cyanopica cyanus,* an azure-winged magpie for a quick getaway; or a hatching *Anax Imperator,* the Emperor Dragonfly, when only total transformation would do.

Tonight, however, the reflection was good. Tonight would be glorious, as long as his luck held. Still looking in the mirror, he took a gold coin from his pocket, flipped it, snatched it on the fall, and slapped it onto the back of his hand.

"Heads and we go in."

He lifted his hand and looked.

"Good."

He kissed the coin, put it back, and went over to the forbidding door. After a short pause he crossed himself, pushed it open and edged through the gap.

The office was shadowy. An old green, glass lamp shed fey beams that picked out a red velvet sofa, gilt frames around Raphael's favourite artworks, small bronzes, mirrored panels, and a brass clock on the mantelpiece. The darkness was a message – I'm working right now, this is my moody lair, my sulky den, no time wasters – but Tiago had seen it by day. It was one of the most unimproved rooms in Paris, aggressively analogue and outdated.

Raphael was sitting at his desk in the far corner, his forehead on his left hand, a fountain pen in his right. It was all very artfully composed; a glass of champagne on the desk, bubbles catching the lamplight and surging up like whirling diatoms; a cigar smouldering in a brass ashtray; and music playing quietly, taking the edge off solitude; a lascivious lute solo.

Tiago breathed deeply, taking in this thinner air, slowing himself, matching the pace of his quarry. He stalked around the door and closed it behind him.

"Good evening."

"Hold on." Raphael raised his left hand; a saint. "I'm so sorry. One second please." He underlined something and put the pen down. "Right. I'm all yours."

He looked up with an icy smile, and thawed. "Well fuck me.

It's O Senor Tiago."

"For it is he." Good start. Tiago leaned against the door. "Working late, Monsieur Davide?"

"Apparently. I thought you were one of those fuckheads from the party." Raphael leaned back in his chair. "It's been a long time young man."

"A year."

"No."

"Yes, a whole year." Tiago walked forward on air. "I'm sorry. You're still working."

Raphael stood. "No I'm not. Not now." He walked over, pulled up a metre away and offered his hand. "It's good to see you Tiago."

"It's good to see you too." Tiago took the hand and looked down, bemused by the phantom object in Raphael's grasp. It was someone else's hand, not his. His hand was being kissed, on the back, the palm, the inside wrist, and someone was saying *Enchanté*. Well, maybe not that.

What someone actually said was: "You look very well Tiago. This dark grey suits you."

"Tom Ford."

"Perfect on you."

Tiago stared at his mystic paw, took his time. An answer would mean being let go.

"Thanks."

Raphael let go. "You went back to Lisbon in the summer, didn't you? Someone told me." He put his hands in his pockets. "Lisboa, I suppose I should say. Where the Lisboans live."

"Lisboetas." Tiago put his hands behind his back. "Uh-huh."

"So when did you get back?"

"Monday."

"Really? I'm honoured."

"You are, rather."

"How was it?"

"Where?"

"Lisbon."

"Hot."

"Hot." A nod. "Good to be home again?"

A shrug. "Paris is my home now."

"I'd better welcome you home then." Raphael put his hands on Tiago's shoulders. "Welcome back to the City of Light, O Senor Tiago."

The two air kisses weren't quite what Tiago had in mind. He drew back and looked up, giving it both barrels, a killer beam of wide-eyed cuteness.

Raphael took a deep breath. "That welcome won't really answer, will it?"

Another shrug. "We Lusitanians are more expressive."

"I'll try again then, shall I?"

"Do."

The embrace was gentle, and formal, and of unimpeachable propriety; at least, it was until Tiago closed his eyes. Six years ago he had come to Paris, and two days later he had met Raphael, and that night he had gone back to his shiny new apartment, sat amid a small cardboard city of boxes and the smell of new paint, and written the acrostic in his Filofax.

```
    T
    I
R A P H A E L
    G
    O
```

And then he had studied the business card, and added more.

```
    T
    I     D
R A P H A E L
    G     S
    O     I
          L
      D A V I D E
          A
```

It was a perfect fit, an omen, a fluffy, mewling wolf cub dropped in his lap. His questionable past was forgiven, Jesus still loved him, Paris was a new start, and Raphael, this son of David, would be the mystical agent of his rebirth. And later that night, when the Raphael incubus came – masterful and winged like an angel, stirring him in sticky dreams – it had felt like fate. Yet despite such splendid augury, Destiny had taken her sweet time, and for six years, on dull days in front of the screens, on planes, in his white bed at home, or in far-flung beige hotel rooms, Tiago had lost himself in daydreams and fantasies. Raphael's love was coming, for sure; as profound as the faith of stained-glass martyrs, and as mighty as the passion of mad poets, immense and epic. When *The Love of Raphael for Tiago* came it would be deeper than the ocean, and more glorious than the sun, and stronger than death, a fitting compensation for all the setbacks of his young life. Every day he had to wait was merely foreplay, a test of his constancy.

The odd thing was that for all those six years Raphael had wasted his epic love on Martin Nelson, an overrated English academic who wrote mucky poetry and did a lot of lightweight arts TV, waving his arms around and talking sparky nonsense about Ovid and Catullus. Martin was lithe and mercurial and good-looking. Raphael worshipped him, and together they exuded an aura of contentment which, though modest, was still enough to make you throw up at ten paces. Tiago had faith, but after a party a year ago at which the "Nelson-Davides" (*ridiculous*) had left him feeling like a scabby mutt outside a locked shop, he'd gone back to Lisbon and settled for twin silver medals of promotion and a best friend's bed. Leaving Paris had been a good move. Staying away would have been smart too. But Tiago was clever, not smart. And so here he was, mortifying his flesh in the impeccably reserved embrace of the man he adored.

He breathed in the scent of Raphael's hair, glad to be here despite it all, brushing away imaginary fibres on Raphael's shoulders, staking a modest claim. "This is a beautiful suit. Did you have it made?"

"Yes. London." Raphael released him rather too easily and stood back, hands in his pockets. "Have you by any chance been drinking this evening, Tiago?"

"You know, I might have had a couple."

"You might have had a couple."

Tiago pointed at the ashtray. "Have you been smoking Raphael?"

"Possibly. The odd cigar."

"As well as or instead of?"

"Both."

Tiago shook his head. The room lurched a bit; it would probably be best not to do that again. "Weak man."

"I'm trying to quit."

"Again?"

"Yes, again."

"Weak man, a man of straw."

"I will this time."

"Really?"

"Yes."

Tiago took out a pen and wrote on his hand.

"What are you doing?" Raphael took Tiago's wrist and then dropped it. 'Exit all Phillip Morris positions'. What a cheeky little fucker you are." He went back to the desk, took a draw on the cigar. "I remember when you were such a nice, unspoilt young man."

"I've been corrupted by North Europeans." True enough, in dreams at least. Tiago went over to the mantelpiece, touched the cold brass case of the clock. "I like your nice new clock."

"Nice?" Raphael shook his head. "And do you like the drawing above it?"

"Your Apollo?" Tiago had seen it many times before; the handsome head, the young man insolent with all the power of youth, an expression of unmistakable purpose, depth and decisiveness. Easy for a fucking god to pull off, but not so easy for a mortal who'd drunk too much on an empty stomach. "I love it. You know I do."

"No. To his right."

It was new, a sketch of a young girl, looking to one side, half turned away. It had been lightly executed, dashed off in a few simple stokes, suggesting rather than revealing her.

"Yes, I do. She's coming to terms with things." He frowned at Raphael. "She's a bit Caravarra. A bit Cavaraggio. I mean Caravaggio."

Raphael came over and stood beside him. "Do you think so? I'd be very surprised. There's no record, no provenance. And she's not in any of the finished works."

"She looks calm." Tiago looked back at the picture. He'd read a lot of books about Caravaggio. He knew he was right, and Raphael was wrong. But this was not the time to have an argument about an artist whose name he couldn't pronounce, so instead he frowned in what he hoped was a clever way. "Tranquil."

"Tranquil. Good word. Well, don't fall in love with her. She's off tomorrow. To Canada, North Ontario. There's a town there. Anyway, she's going to a hospice for kids. They wrote to me, asked me if I could help. I thought she would be ideal. Beauty is important in places like that." He put his head on one side. "And I had that old frame knocking around."

Tiago was appalled. There was generosity, and there was folly. "You're just giving her to them?"

"No material value. No provenance."

"But she might be a." Tiago took a deep breath. "A Caravaggio?"

Raphael shook his head. "Oh, I rather think I might be the better judge of that, don't you?"

Tiago looked away. Being bested was one thing; being patronised was another.

"Right. Well, I'm amazed. I never knew there was a moral dimension to dealing in Fine Art." Big F, big A.

"There's a moral dimension to every job, even in whatever the fuck it is that you do."

"Right, yes, in raping the planet. Of course that's all down to me isn't it? Where do you think your fucking gold leaf comes from? Your fucking cigar?" Tiago snorted, angry with Raphael, angrier with himself, but too proud to cool down yet.

"Hey, come on." Raphael put his hand on Tiago's arm. "I wasn't criticising you."

"You were. But it's fine." It wasn't fine. He moved Raphael's hand away, turned away. "Some commodities companies are more responsible than others, but I don't have the luxury of choosing my fucking clients like you do. I don't get to set the moral compass. In fact I don't think there is one. My job is to make as much fucking money as possible. And fortunately I am fucking superb at that and my colleagues fear and respect me." He looked at the girl in the picture and recoiled. It felt as if he'd been swearing in church.

There was a long silence, and then Raphael's voice, in velvet. "So what are these fearful and craven colleagues like?"

Tiago breathed. An idol was an idol after all. "Actually, these colleagues are mostly dogheads."

"Mostly?"

Tiago wrinkled up his nose, stage-whispered. "Some of them are fuckheads." Possibly all of them. "They call me TJ." To his face anyway; worse stuff behind his back, no doubt.

"Got a lot of friends at work?"

"Not one."

"Bothered about that?"

"What do you think?" Tiago rubbed his chin. "I serve Mammon. I am his creature."

Raphael nodded. "Ah yes, Mammon, the great pagan deity of our times, and his soul-eating cult of corporate morality. It's very depressing. How on earth can you stand it?"

"They give me lots of money."

Raphael frowned. "You've got enough fucking money Tiago. Join the angels."

"Angels." Tiago shook his head. "I was going to be a priest, to join a mission in São Paulo, or Macau, or Goa." He stroked the clock case, amazed that he sometimes forgot this.

"Ah yes. I remember you telling me that once. I was rather intrigued."

Tiago nodded. Intriguing was good. Intriguing was ideal. "I suppose it is quite unusual." He looked at Apollo, wondered who the model was, what he'd been thinking while Raphael drew him.

"So what happened?"

Tiago turned. Raphael was looking into his eyes. It was too much so he looked back at Apollo. It was one of Raphael's ex-lovers maybe; there were probably loads of them, and they were no doubt all gorgeous. It was time to be a man of the world. "Oh, well, I met someone. I mean, I found someone."

"Not Jesus, clearly."

"No. Not Jesus. Rogerio. Though he did look a bit like Jesus, especially in the mornings." *Oh, for fuck's sake.* "No, I mean, after a while I began to fear that my faith was superficial, just the surface of ecstasy, I guess. Like when you're surfing, and a wave takes you, and it's only then that you know what the sea is." Tiago shook his head like a wet dog. No; not sex. He didn't want to make it about sex. "No. I just realised that I needed someone, a lover, a partner, a husband, and that I wanted to be a father, so being a priest was really rather a shit idea, wasn't it?" Better, but hardly brilliant; some hunter he was turning out to be. "I don't know what I'm saying. Fuck it."

But it was okay. Raphael was looking at the drawings. "Actually I think you express yourself very well. About the first person, the first time, how it makes everything different." He nodded. "You think people will look at you and notice you've changed. It happens to everyone." He touched Tiago's arm. "But you interrupted my lecture. About the angels."

"Right, yes." Tiago was a pretty good negotiator; he knew that when you didn't want to talk, you should just ask questions. "So, what would you do if you were me?"

Raphael folded his arms. "What, if I were bright, talented and driven, with loads of money and no moral purpose?"

"And working with dogheads, yes."

"Ah, I forgot them. I don't know. But I'd find something." The voice was low, confiding. "Anything, I suppose, that meant I was leaving the world a better place. That's why we're here, to make this world better, even if it's just with one little picture. But you're more glamorous than me. You could be Brave Sir Tiago."

He dubbed Tiago with an air sword. "Is that you, soldier?"

Tiago bobbed. "Sir, yes sir. That's me."

"So what's your quest? Think of something big."

Easy. "I will fight for more beauty in the world, and more love, and more justice."

"Excellent." Raphael nodded smartly. "And you've already gone into battle."

"How?"

"You're a musician."

"You've never heard me play."

"I have. I heard you after the party at the Spanish Embassy. You played Albeniz, an arrangement of *Jerez*, I think. It was really very good." It had been the Portuguese Embassy, and it was an observation, a school report, grudgingly complimentary; and Raphael was moving on. "And I can't imagine it's hard for you to find love."

"No, you're right. I've found love. I'm in love."

Raphael picked up the clock and put it down again. "Ah yes, with Rogerio, who looks like Jesus in the mornings. So it's only justice where we need to think it through." He looked again at the girl. "Justice. Where are you going next?"

"Cusco in May actually, for a meeting. A investors' conference, on copper and iron ore."

Raphael laughed. "Fuck. I would have thought there was endless scope there." He rubbed his chin. "But I suppose you don't get much time to plan your charitable works before you check out of the Hilton Suites Cusco and get your bullet proof Merc to the airport?"

"Not really, no." Tiago looked away. Actually it was the Marriott and a Lexus. And he did have a plan, a good one, something he'd been working on for years. But Raphael didn't deserve to know about The Church of Christ Economist right now; he would probably only take the piss, and have to be put right, and it really was too soon for another row.

Tiago wrinkled up his nose, sniffed the air, and asked himself the question any normal person would at a time like this. What would a salamander do in this situation?

...

Amelia liked salamanders, but preferred newts, and would never pretend to be either; because that would be a ridiculous way to carry on. Tonight she was swimming downstream a few miles away from the opulent office, sweeping the water aside with purposeful strokes. Her head torch was off because she was thinking deeply about cider, and sex, and how to get hold of money for her secret science projects, and although the Seine was turbid tonight her thoughts on the third matter were crystal clear; she'd identified a sponsor, a wealthy philanthropist, vain, weak, and crazy enough about art to be easily duped into paying for science. Best of all, at least according to university rumour, he was recently single and very eligible, likely to be snapped up pretty soon, swept off his feet and encouraged to splash cash.

Amelia smiled a tight-lipped smile and switched her on her head torch. Raphael Emmanuel Davide was a perfect choice. Now all she had to do was approach him.

CHAPTER 2

IT'S THE HOPE THAT
KILLS YOU

Tiago had softened in the face of Raphael's apology. It was after all the latest in a long series, and like all the others it had been swift, humble and charming.

"I'm sorry Tiago. You really should just tell me to fuck off. I'm such a fucking idiot sometimes. You must forgive annoying bastards like me because there's no hope of a cure for us."

"Naturally."

They stared at one another for a while.

Raphael frowned. "Are you chewing gum Tiago?"

"No." But he would next time; yes sir.

Monsieur Davide walked into the deserted art studio and closed the door behind him. "Ah, da Silva. You're here."

"Sir." Tiago stood up. Unlike the other boys he didn't fear the darkly stern new art teacher, but getting detention wasn't a smart move in your final year before grande école. "I'm sorry about the chewing gum sir. It won't happen again."

Monsieur Davide frowned and ran a hand through his raven hair. "The chewing gum?" He loosened his tie and unbuttoned his collar. "Ah yes. The gum." He smiled. "Actually, I wanted to speak to you alone. Tiago."

"Alone sir?"

"Yes." The young teacher came closer, eyeing him like a hawk eyes a young lamb. "Your work is exceptional. Your talent is phenomenal. Now you're ready to learn about form, human form. And I'm ready to teach you."

A seductive arpeggio wrapped around them. "Ah. Listen to this. You'll love this."

Tiago engaged brain, coughed, listened for a few seconds. "Not Mesangeau."

"No. The last one was Mesangeau."

"I know it was. It was the C major, the Sarabande." Tiago lowered his eyes, turned his head. "Not Bach. Weiss?"

"No." Raphael crossed his arms. A few intimate seconds passed.

Tiago nodded. "It's Kapsberger. A toccata. The third. Who's playing?"

"It's a friend actually. Well, a friend and business partner. Tomas Paul Gosele. He's the main financial backer for this gallery actually, but amazingly he's also a Professor, at Turing in London. Space stuff. Ballistics." Raphael droned on; Tomas Paul was, clearly, brilliant, a genius, not just a talented musician, and a shrewd collector of art, and a businessman, but also – 'incredibly' – an inventor with his own successful spinout company. He was a polymath, a Renaissance man, amazing.

Tiago hadn't come here to listen to another man's virtues. He yawned. "Amazing."

"Oh yes. I meant to tell you. I've got a sure thing for the Prix de Diane. Apparently Wastrel Banker is on very good form."

Tiago grinned. They'd made this game up during a boring concert a few years ago, passing notes to and fro like kids in the back row at school. He still had the programme.

"Really?"

"Yes, really. And I've also heard good things about Lusitanian Dandy." Raphael looked him up and down. "And Lisboeta Fop."

Tiago shrugged. "I'll probably back Bibulous Artist, or maybe Askenazy Flaneur."

"Very good."

"Though actually I've been rather taken with Parisian Sybarite."

"Sybarite?" Raphael frowned. "What happened? You swallow an encyclopaedia?"

"I know what it means. You taught it to me, at your spring party last year."

"Did I?" Raphael rubbed his chin. "How very patronising of me. Had I been drinking at all?"

"Maybe a little." Maybe a lot. Tiago let it flow back; Raphael leaving a group of friends to come over – charming, kind, urbane, funny – and the band striking up *Oye como va*, and the touch on his arm.

Hey, it's your song Tiago.

No. It's Spanish, actually. Santana is from Cuba. They speak Spanish in Cuba. I am from Portugal, where we speak Portuguese.

Oh fuck, sorry. But you'll forgive me, of course, because you know everything about everything, and I know fuck all about anything.

He'd said *Yes, of course,* but Raphael had said *Prove it* and taken his drink from him, and led him into the middle of the crowded dance floor like a lover would. *Put your left hand on my shoulder, and I'll take this one. Good. Now.* And then for five dazzling minutes he'd kept his eyes lowered in sulky forbearance while Raphael held him close and put torque across his arms and shoulders, gauging his strength, moving his body through the space, strong and fast, like a lover would; assessing the response of his slight frame, checking his turning circle, asking him smiling questions *Too fast? Too slow?* like a lover would. Casting a net, weaving a web, leaving him dizzy and turned on, for all the world like a lover would.

And then, disaster; Martin, late, in jeans for God's sake, still carrying his airport coffee, with his ludicrous electric blue headphones round his neck, his stupid, studenty rucksack over one shoulder.

Sorry I'm late Raphael. It's a fucking long way, is Chile, and my bag's in fucking Bogota apparently. Hello Tiago baby, don't you look cute. Someone will finally fuck you tonight, I shouldn't wonder. Late for you though, isn't it? Haven't you got a paper round in the morning little lambkin?

And Raphael had laughed, and dropped Tiago's hand, and clasped Martin close and kissed him full on the mouth, and held him, saying words loud enough for Tiago to hear; *Oh God I've missed you so Marty, a week is too long baby, I've been going fucking crazy without you.* And Raphael and Martin had danced all night, and whooped it up, because they were lovers; and Tiago had gone home, and stared miserably at the acrostic, and gone back to Lisbon, because he was a fantasist and an emotional fuckwit.

He looked at Raphael. Dashed hope and hurt flooded back. He was no Don Juan, no predator. Going back to Lisbon had been smart, and coming here tonight had been foolish. Well, he wouldn't be foolish anymore. He coughed and looked at his watch; time to go. "I think it was that night, at the party."

Raphael was frowning. "I am not a Sybarite; not at all. I just can't resist beautiful things. But you're lucky. I bet you have people queuing up to buy you beautiful things." He looked up and smiled, and his eyes caught the light like a cat's would, emerald green, spellbinding.

Tiago caught his breath. *You are out of your league. Get out of here.* "Actually, they're not." He looked down, planning his exit. "I mean, I'm not seeing anyone at the moment."

"Really?"

Tiago shrugged and shook his head. He had cash for a cab, and if he left now he could be in bed by one, playing out a more satisfactory version of this scene; the first embrace ending differently, the taste of the cigar, the sound of the music, what they might do on the red sofa, or on the desk. Or under it, maybe.

He looked up. "No, no one. Not at the moment."

Raphael studied him. "Well. All I can say is that the world's gone quite mad."

Or on the other hand, he could stay.

Tiago half-closed his eyes. "Maybe." Snakes and fucking ladders.

"And I haven't even offered you a drink." Raphael gestured

towards the sofa. "Come. Sit." He took a glass from a cabinet and asked what was the party had been like.

"Oh, you know. Boring." Tiago sat down. It felt surprisingly good. "I don't really like going to these things but the bank has to send somebody with languages. And I get tomorrow off."

"Is that all? I'd want a fucking week off." Raphael grinned. "I know it's for charity but really." He poured champagne and gave the glass to Tiago. "Drink this. Pol Roger. Churchill drank a bottle of it a day. Still beat Hitler." He leaned back against his desk and raised his glass. ""Cheers and fuck Hitler." As Churchill's parrot said."

Tiago smiled. Good; harmless fun. "Cheers and fuck Hitler."

Raphael put his head on one side, staring at the bubbles. "But as we know, Churchill was a genius, and Hitler was a stupid Nazi cunt. And lo, the angels did smite him. Ha ha."

"Angels one, Nazis nil. Yay."

Raphael laughed. "Yay indeed, although more than one-nil might have been better. But now you're joining the angels, who knows what's possible?" He raised his glass again. "Here's to Beauty, Love and Justice."

"Beauty, Love and Justice." Tiago smiled. "Actually I make excellent *pasteis de nata*."

Raphael pointed his glass at him. "You could do a cake sale." He smiled. "Unfortunately, I can't boil a fucking egg."

"You could do a sponsored parachute jump."

"I could, couldn't I? Without the parachute. Maybe the angels would catch me."

"Like Jesus." Tiago nodded. This was how he should have

played it, their familiar, casual flirty banter, safely married mentor and pert disciple. He'd been too ambitious, too impatient, expected too much from this first encounter after so long. He should enjoy tonight, then play the long game he'd played so well at for six years; the long hours, and cross country running, and long quiet nights at his flat with his books, his piano, his guitar. Long, quiet, celibate nights; well, nearly celibate. It depended on your definition of sex. He sipped his drink and looked Raphael up and down. What was his definition of sex? And what would he make of a romantically deluded twenty-nine year old virgin who jacked off a lot?

Probably not a lot, although right now Raphael was smiling contentedly. "The angels. Poor bastards." He toed the fringe on the rug. "But surely we're already among them. I mean, with my name, and well, you." He made a sweeping, hand gesture towards Tiago that meant *This is a very beautiful thing.*

"Thanks." Tiago flushed deep red. The sofa was low and his eyes were on the silver buckle of Raphael's belt, a dark glint roughly where the intersecting A of the acrostic was. He looked away and re-booted the daydream from this afternoon's boring teleconference with São Paulo; a yacht, Raphael's smoky lips on his tanned neck and chest. *Alone at last baby. Oh my Tiago. Oh my beautiful love.* A ripple of desire licked him. He moved his hands.

There were voices in the street outside, swearwords and shouting in out of town accents. Raphael laughed. "How marvellous. The jeunesse doree. Heading for the Champs Elysees. You should get out there Tiago. You might find someone to buy you beautiful things."

"Maybe." Tiago looked at his hands. In a heartbeat he'd gone from mildly aroused intoxication to flaccid, stone-cold sobriety. He looked up at his tormentor, and nodded to himself; he'd become prone, prey, a writhing beetle impaled on a thorn, and Raphael was the handsome, barbaric shrike, *Lanius excubitor*, looking down at him, wondering whether he fancied a snack now, later, or not at all.

Tiago drained his glass. He was a fool, in love with an old-fashioned flirt, and hope was killing him by inches. His little beetle legs flailed helplessly. And, unforgivably, he didn't even have a plan.

...

Amelia had plans coming out of her ears, but if you wanted to win the Nobel Prize for Chemistry, and you had to steal money and break every code of ethics to do it, you needed a few contingencies up your sleeve. So she drew up plans on planes, on buses, on trains, in any spare time she could find; even now, underwater, she was working up numbers, costs, and critical paths for two projects at once. She hadn't always found it this easy. At first she'd found it hard to set priorities; but inspiration had struck on her twenty-first birthday.

After a couple of mugs of home made calvados the four box model looked impressive on her tutor's whiteboard.

	GOOD	BAD
OLD	Restore	Ignore
NEW	Invent	Destroy

Restore, Ignore, Invent, Destroy. Tomas Paul Gosele had frowned. *Destroy? Like what?*

I'm going to start with unnecessary announcements on tubes, and buses. They annoy me. They interrupt my music. And anyone who gets on a train without knowing where it's going deserves to get lost.

Tomas Paul had shrugged. *Shouldn't you be at a party?*

This'll do.

Fair enough. Okay then. How?

The old-fashioned way.

And he'd laughed. *Yes. I can see you now, all furtive, like a little mole, with inky-nails and green-goggles, in your smelly skunkworks. So. Who's paying for all this?*

I'll get patrons.

Patrons won't fund your kind of science Amelia. Re-filling the mugs. *Are you sure you got all the methanol off this?*

Most of it.

Well, it's only temporary blindness. Tomas Paul had closed his eyes and sat back. *You'll have to deceive them Amelia. Think of something they'll fund. Something artsy. Charge them extra and spend the difference on Petri dishes.* Smiling a crooked smile. *What about that old dump grandpa left you? Isn't there something there that needs fixing up?*

She'd sulked for a few moments, chewing the wrong end of the board marker with green teeth. *There's a folly, a temple to Apollo and Diana.* It was a wreck, a blackened ruin in the overgrown orchard. Gloucester Old Spots nosed around it, scratched their wobbly haunches on the fallen columns, crapped on the slimy piers. *When I was a little girl I did my black magic there. I watered a Blenheim Orange with puppy blood.* Even then she'd known she was ahead of her time, putting trees first. Trees were cool; blossom in spring, bugs in summer, apples in autumn, songbirds in winter. Puppies just yelped, and widdled, and shat in your lap. Puppies were for kids.

Tomas Paul had smiled. *You have an original mind Amelia. You'll do well, if you don't get locked up.* Lighting a blue and gold cigarette. *Now all you have to do is find some silly rich fucker to fund your folly.* Toasting her. *Here's moths in your ermine, as the ladies say.*

She'd clinked her mug against his: F sharp. *Nunc et semper, magister.*

Nunc et semper, Amelia.

And now her silly rich fucker was in her sights. Amelia switched off her head torch, rose to the surface and dodged a bloated poodle to swim to the quay.

...

More dead pet than darting predator, Tiago knew how the Zig Zag girl felt. He ought to go, but alcohol had numbed the sting of the putdown, and all there was at home was an empty bed. He nodded to himself. He would stick around for a bit. He would give it one more year. Jacob had served seven years for Rachel, after all.

Outside the room two party guests walked past, noisy and drunk. Raphael laughed. "Fucking arrivistes. Says he." He gestured towards Tiago with his glass. "So, what should I be buying? Peruvian gold futures, derivatives of? Any money in those these days? Or did that all go when your lot wiped the Incas out? Poor little fuckers. "

"Not my lot. The Spanish." Tiago dug the coin out and flipped it across to Raphael. "Here."

Raphael caught it palm down and took it over to the lamp. "That is a pretty thing."

"Two escuts gold cob, Lima. Eighteenth century. Keep it."

"Really? You guys are superstitious. It's not lucky, is it?"

Tiago shrugged. It used to be. "Actually Peruvian gold is a good investment at the moment."

"Really?"

"No, not really."

Raphael looked at his watch. "Isn't it time you fucked off back to Lisbon?"

"I can't. No jobs. Haven't you heard? The IMF Troika is killing my proud country."

"So you're one of these economic migrants?"

"I prefer to think of myself as an ex-pat. At least, that's what my contract says."

Raphael put the coin on the desk. "Peruvian fucking gold." He smiled his usual boyish dazzler, but the lamp betrayed creases on his neck, dozens of feint grooves crisscrossing his cheekbones like Nazca lines, even traces of grey in his hair, white hairs among the black above the temples.

Tiago nodded. Fate had kept him in the room. *See this, Tiago?* She was over two metres tall, draped in shimmering russet silk, light-eyed and full lipped, pointing towards Raphael with a sinuous arm. *Summer is ending for Raphael. Time is running out for him. You're going to have to stick around, young man. Wait it out, and writhe on that thorn for as long as it takes. For this is to be your quest, loving this beautiful, diminishing man; comforting him, giving him a good life.* She smiled sadly. *And if that love is to be undeclared, and that good life is to be lived with somebody else, somebody unworthy, well, lucky you. It makes your quest more noble, does it not?*

Tiago nodded. "Lucky me."

Raphael looked up. "Sorry?"

"Sorry. Miles away." Tiago raised his glass. "Here's to your Englishman."

Raphael frowned. "My Englishman."

The clock began a silvery chime. Tiago talked over it. "Martin. How is he?"

The chime finished and Raphael looked up, his face bleak and vacant. "Of course, you've been away haven't you? That's why you don't know." He put his glass down on the desk. "Fuck." He folded his arms. "Fuck. I do so hate telling people."

CHAPTER 3

ALLEGRO NON TROPPO

Tiago's startled bunny eyes and angel fish gawp weren't doing much for him, but that didn't really matter because Raphael was staring into space, drawling unconvincingly in lazy clichés; they'd agreed to *call it a day* last summer, they'd *grown apart*, they'd *wanted such different things* from life.

"I wanted things to carry on as they were. And I wanted a Maserati Grancabrio in Rosso Trionfale." Raphael held the bottle mid pour and looked over, turning his head slowly like a mantis. "It's a car Tiago. It's an obscenely beautiful, very expensive motor car. V8 engine, four fifty bhp, nought to a hundred in five point five."

Tiago shut his mouth and nodded. "Right." The words were glancing past, raindrops passing an aeroplane window. He looked down at his hands. "That sounds, nice. Is it, nice?"

"Yeah, it is nice." Raphael put the bottle down. "And Martin… well…he missed England." He handed the glass to Tiago. "And when your mid life crises diverge like that…" He shrugged. "That's it. Time to call it a day. So he went back to Oxford."

"Thanks." Tiago moved the glass from one hand to the other. Champagne spilled in his lap.

"You okay?"

"Sure." His heart was beating against his ribs with jerky spasms, a fat moth fretting in a lampshade. What was wrong with this picture? He wasn't in it. Dismay gave him stupid words to say. "Why didn't you call me?"

Raphael half smiled. "Oh Tiago, I would hardly call you to tell you that. But it's kind of you to ask." He put his hand on Tiago's shoulder. "Are you all right? You're very pale."

"Yes. Sure. I missed lunch and I had a few drinks at the party. This is my fifth or sixth or something." Tiago touched the back of the hand. "I'm okay."

Raphael sat beside him. "Tiago, look." He put an arm around him, the wrong kind. "Just because Martin and I are finished, that doesn't mean it can't be done. You'll find someone of your own, of course you will. And you'll be much happier than we were. You're so kind, thoughtful. We were always pretty selfish really."

Tiago got up, shaking Nice Uncle Raphael off. "I'm not scared of being alone. I'm used to it." He went across to the mantelpiece. "I'm just sorry for you."

Raphael snapped. "Well don't be. Do I look like I'm fucking falling apart?"

No he didn't. And apparently Raphael's life was just peachy. He was fitter than he'd been for years, running and riding, great cross country rides in England that winter with his brother-in-law Rob. And the business was thriving with all the extra work he was getting done. Tiago turned away, looking for the prompter. Raphael didn't know his part; he was playing the happy-at-being-single-person, the once-broken-hearted-but-on-the-mend-survivor. Soon he would be the ready-to-love-again romantic lead, looking for that-special-somebody-who-heals-the-wounds-and-makes-life-worth-living-again co-star.

And it didn't seem that Tiago was going to share the billing.

He felt for the coin. *Shit.* It was on the desk. *Fuck.* He was on his own. He took a deep breath and closed his eyes, thinking what to say first, what to offer, what to demand, how to shape it. He felt a touch on his arm.

"What is it Tiago? What's wrong? Tell me."

He closed his eyes more tightly. This loving and gentle voice from his fantasies wasn't helping, leading as it usually did to Raphael taking him to bed. *What is it Tiago? What's wrong darling? Tell me. I can make it better baby.* He turned away, clearing his head. The man of his dreams was back on the market. This was no time to think about sex.

"Tiago?"

Tiago looked down. "Look, Raphael. It can't be possible that you don't know. Not even if you're trying not to know."

"Right." Raphael nodded, took Tiago's hands in his own. "Look. Tiago."

Tiago's heart ramped to sprinting speed. It would have been unbearable anywhere but in the home straight; but hey, maybe he was in the home straight. "Yes?"

"Look. If there was something between you and Martin, it really wouldn't matter to me. It wouldn't have been your fault. I know he could be very compelling at times."

Or maybe he wasn't even out of the blocks.

Tiago mouthed a silent no, winded by the sudden slide onto the thorn that split his shining carapace in two; but he was James, a Son of Thunder, resilient in the face of Life's Unbelievable Crapness, so he breathed deep and found a voice, a cybernetic, elevator pitch sound, designed for numbers, and clarity, and spelling things out to people who, despite their manifold perfections, were rather slow on the uptake. It didn't quite match the Elysian beauty of his love, but it would have to do. And he'd have to cheer up. Moody desperation wasn't alluring. He smiled. It went okay.

"Look, Raphael. I really need you to listen to me. Okay?"

"Sure." Raphael put his hands on Tiago's shoulders. "Good. This is better. This is more like you Tiago, much better." He took his hands away again.

Tiago looked down. "I need to know I have understood, you see."

"Okay."

"You're on your own?"

Raphael shrugged. "Yes I am."

"And there's no one else you want?"

"No. No one." Raphael shook his head slowly. "No one at all."

"Right."

They were a foot apart. The sound of a football match rose up from a car radio on the street; PSG were ahead and the fans were whistling, wanting it to be over.

Tiago waited for the noise to die down. Time for route one football. "So what about me, Raphael?"

For a long while there was just the sound of the clock.

"What about you." Raphael like an automated ticket line *Sorry, I didn't quite catch that.*

Tiago looked up, shrugged. "You're alone. I'm alone. What about me? What about us?" He tried another smile. It went okay; maybe not quite as well as the first one. He stepped forward, placed his hands on Raphael's lapels. "We could be a power couple."

There was another long silence. "Tiago."

"Yup?"

Raphael put his hands on Tiago's shoulders. "Tiago, you're beautiful, and I'm very flattered."

"Don't say that. People only say that when they're about to say no. And you're not going to say no. Because you're too smart." Tiago smiled again, still looking down at his hands. The clock was dragging this out, a singer slowing down an accompanist.

"Tiago." Raphael smiled, but only with his eyes; okay, it was a wince. "Tiago, for me it needs to be love."

"No problem." Tiago smiled and meant it. "No problem at all. It is love. It's been love for years, for six years, more than that. We met in February 2006. February 17th. It was a Friday. It was snowing." He smoothed Raphael's lapels with his fingers. "It snowed in our champagne." He beamed. "So love is here. Love is no problem. Love is a done deal."

Raphael closed his eyes and took his hands away.

Tiago looked down, smiled. "I know you've always liked me Raphael."

He looked up. Raphael was observing him, unsure. Maybe he

was playing it too cool, too nonchalant. He should show his cards a little, his feelings; not too much, not too soon.

"I've wanted you for years, Raphael. I can't believe you didn't know. I've dreamed about you." Too much. "Nobody compares to you. No one." Better. "You're everything I've always wanted. You're perfect. I can't believe you didn't know." He'd said more than he intended, but it felt okay. "You must have known."

Raphael sighed. "Tiago, I had no idea you felt like this." He put his hands over Tiago's as if to move them, but didn't move them. "Had I known, I would have been more guarded, perhaps."

"No, Raphael, listen." He took Raphael's hands and held them. "This is the best offer you'll ever get in your life. I mean it. Give me the chance. You won't regret it. Just think of us together." They would get there. Raphael just couldn't believe his luck. That was what it was. "Just think of us together, Raphael. Together, in bed."

Raphael closed his eyes. And then he shook his head. "No, I'm sorry, Tiago, but no."

Tiago stared at him. It almost sounded like he meant it. "No, you don't mean that Raphael."

Raphael opened his eyes. "Tiago. You are so beautiful. And I'm very flattered, and..."

And nothing.

Tiago frowned. Anger was welling inside him. He was losing it, but he knew he wouldn't be able to stop himself. "Look, Raphael. It's not a fucking crush, okay? It's love. I swear it is. My love is deep, Raphael, and I'm strong. I swear I'll be so fucking good to you. You'll feel you've never been loved before, because I'll be so devoted, and faithful, and loving, all my life, for all of our life, together. I won't be selfish. We'll never grow apart. We'll grow together."

He closed his eyes. His throat was stinging, tears coming. All of a sudden he felt empty. What else was there to offer? He turned away, his face in his hands. "Oh god Raphael. I can't believe you don't fucking want me. You must do, you fucking must do!" He shook his head. "I mean, sweet fucking Jesus. We're both on our own. Surely I'd be better than nothing?"

The final words hit him hard, but he didn't cry. He wasn't that kind of person. Instead he shook, and shuddered, and prayed for the ground to open. But it didn't, and after a few seconds he felt a hand on his shoulder.

"Tiago, please. I'm really not worth it."

"You fucking are." But he let Raphael turn him and hold him, a kiss off without the kissing, knowing that even the joyless, consoling hug coming his way would chase away the nightmares forming a disorderly queue behind his eyes, the wing beats, the denuded trees, the phone ringing in the empty hallway, the unopened letters addressed in his best handwriting, the appraising stare of Benjamin fucking Franklin. He clung and swallowed hard, fighting panic the way Rogerio had shown him. *Utqueant laxis, Resonare fibris, Mira gestorum, Famuli tuorum, Solve pollute, Labis reatum, Sancte Johannes. It's all right Tiago, You're with me. Nothing can harm you.*

After a few minutes the waves of pain abated and stillness came to him.

"Jesus. I'm so sorry Raphael. I'm so sorry. What a fucking idiot you must think I am." He tried to draw away.

Raphael held him more tightly. "You cry it out if you need to."

"I'm not crying. I don't need to." But he let himself be held for a few more moments, listening to Raphael's heart, thinking how close he'd come. "*Basta.* Enough."

Raphael's voice was a murmur. "Shall I let you go now?"

"Yes." Six fucking years.

"Promise you won't fall over?"

"Promise." Raphael would never let himself be alone with him now. This had been his chance. He'd blown it.

Raphael gently pushed him away. "Right. Come and sit down before you fall down."

They sat on the sofa, side by side, like unwanted subs on a bench. The silence could have run forever, but Tiago was a quick thinker. He knew what to do. He would make light of it. A brave, detached attitude would get him through the next few minutes, and one day they would laugh about this. He managed a smile, a half laugh. "Hey, look. I'm sorry about that. I freaked out. I've drunk too much."

But Raphael was still off the script. "My god, Tiago. Your heart must have been full. I've never had such a selfless offer of love. Never in my life."

"Right." Tiago couldn't help himself. "An unwelcome offer."

Raphael turned towards him. "I couldn't say that. That wouldn't be true, and after what you've said I owe you the truth."

Tiago looked over, racking his brain for words, finding few safe to say. "Which is what?"

Raphael filled the silence. "Oh come on Tiago. Don't be so fucking stupid." Harsh words said tenderly. "You're about the most beautiful thing I've ever seen, even with ink on your fucking nose." He smoothed blue away from Tiago's face. "Come on. You must know."

Tiago held his breath. "Assume I know nothing. Assume I'm a complete fuckhead."

"Well, you're perfect, aren't you." It was a statement, not a question. "I'd love to make everything better for you. Of course I would. I'm only human. But it wouldn't be right." Raphael looked down at his blue finger. "I mean, Christ, Tiago, how old are you?"

"Twenty-nine. Last month." Fuck, was that all? Tiago looked up. *Was that really all?*

"Really? I thought you were much younger."

"What, do you want to see my fucking ID?"

"Hey." They sat quietly for a few moments. "Don't get angry Tiago. It won't help."

Tiago shook his head. "I'm sorry. I'm so sorry."

"It's all right. It's not your fault." Raphael sighed. "Tiago, look, I'm fucking forty next month. Forty. And you're so much younger. I know some people think that doesn't matter. Some people even prefer it like that. But I don't. Eleven years is a lot, believe me."

He took Tiago's hands and turned them over in his own. "I mean, just look at our hands. See how different they are. See how perfect your skin is. Look what the sun's done to mine. Just imagine how different our memories are, our dreams. Just how likely is it that I could ever make you happy?" He gazed down, stroking the smooth skin. "Or keep you happy?"

It was a breakthrough. Tiago fought to suppress a grin. He'd been wasting his time with words. Raphael loved art, the physical world. He made decisions with his senses; the tougher the decision, the more he would rely on what he could see, and taste, and touch. All Tiago had to do was give him a little help in that direction.

He took Raphael's hand and kissed it.

Raphael's eyes followed the action, but there was no resistance, only unmeant words. "No Tiago. Don't. Stop."

Tiago held on. "I can't stop." He kissed and bit the fingers; a lover's bites, soft and teasing. "I think your hands are beautiful. I can't wait to see them on my body, pleasing me."

"Jesus, Tiago. No." Raphael made to stand.

Tiago pulled him back down. It was about as difficult as restraining a particularly placid kitten. "I know you want to please me. I can tell." He smiled and began unbuttoning his shirt. "Look Raphael. Look at my body. Touch it. It's yours." He placed Raphael's hand on his left breast. "Caress me. Here. I'm beautiful, aren't I?"

Raphael gazed through his own hand, unseeing. "Jesus, Tiago." He pulled Tiago against him, making them both gasp, saying words that didn't go. *Fuck. No. Really no. No. Look, Tiago. This is a really fucking stupid idea. It's all fucking wrong.* And Tiago said words that did. *No. It's all fucking right.* He put his mouth to Raphael's ear, dropped his voice to a whisper. "Raphael. Fuck the age difference. I don't care. You shouldn't. Just take me to

bed with you. Please me. Command me. Enjoy me. Possess me."
And quieter still. "Fuck me, Raphael. I know you want to. I'm
inexperienced. I'm a virgin. But I'm a quick study."

Raphael drew back and looked him over. "A virgin?"

"But a quick study."

"A quick study." Raphael was out of words, his face a parody
of lust; dark eyes like a merman, hard, carved and soulless, his
mouth half open, skin pale, blood surging elsewhere.

Tiago smiled. The crew were in the engine room, there was
no one left on the bridge, and he was going to take this ship. He
tipped his head back, accepted the lips locking on to his offered
neck, and murmured into Raphael's hair the line he had practised
alone in bed for years. "Take me Raphael. Make me yours. And
fucking do it now before I change my mind."

...

Amelia's froggy goggled face popped above the rippling surface
with a snock. She climbed the rusty ladder, ditched her mask
and flippers, took a notebook and a pen from the breast of her
neoprene suit and sat down on the quayside. After a few moments
she directed her head torch onto the squared page and started
chewing the end of her warm pencil with a scheming expression
that added character to an otherwise blandly pretty English face.

Two minutes later she popped a boiled sweet in her mouth
and swatted away a midge. She was annoyed, but the situation
was fixable. The total cost of her *Twins* project was still too low,
but she could inflate it; high design charges, radon testing, an
environmental audit. She wrote 'Tittlebats survey. Bat licence.'

Better. And as for *Triploid* she could get a second hand centrifuge, and thieve quite a lot of kit from work. She had an old thermos flask somewhere; she'd take coffee into work and bring liquid nitrogen home.

Amelia was good with figures, and after a while the two totals agreed. She smiled at the congratulatory honk of an insomniac coot and made one final check that she'd listed everything she needed. Some things would be harder to come by than others.

...

Tiago lay back on the sofa feeling splendid and modern. He'd been stripped of his jacket and his shirt, and now he was listening to Raphael blunt the sharp edge of lust with self-mockery. *You know, I never make love to a man who's wearing a watch. Too scared I might catch him looking at it.* Raphael's lips were as soft as his hands were gentle and unhurried. This was a solid gold seduction, purposeful but tender, the act of someone who knew how a man's body worked and how to please it. *Is it good?*

"Fuck yes." Tiago purred and moaned, trying to obey Raphael's commands, to *be patient*, that it was *better when you waited*, that there was *no rush*, that he would *show him how love should be,* but it was all happening too quickly. Raphael's touch was uncoiling him, a pulsing neon *Anax Imperator*, emerging from a drab exoskeleton, unfurling, and stiffening, and hardening, getting ready for flight.

Uncoiling, emerging, unfurling, stiffening, hardening; Tiago shifted his hips. He'd chosen the wrong suit to get seduced in. And he couldn't wait much longer. "Raphael. Please. I want you to. Oh God." He fumbled at his belt. "Oh Jesus. Fucking Gucci accessories. Three hundred fucking euros and the buckle doesn't fucking work."

"Let me." Raphael shelled him. "Oh baby. Oh my beautiful sable darling." He kissed and licked and sucked, and Tiago watched and gasped; no dragonfly, but a saint, feeling the ichor coming, the sure and certain ecstasy, transmutation, the martyr's rapture, apotheosis. Gold would stream from his eyes, his mouth…other places.

"Oh Raphael. I've wanted you for so long." He pulled at Raphael's hair. "Say you love me."

But he just got a smile and more instructions. "Don't push it, don't try. Just let your love come to me. I'll take care of you, I promise. I'll show you eternity."

And Raphael went back to licking and lapping.

And Tiago watched him, and thought about ice cream, and tried to hold back.

•••

And Amelia smiled and wrote:

- *Cell centrifuge thermo megafuge 11 R. Bucket rotor for 50ml and 15 ml tubes*
✓ *Human sperm (x 2)*

And the English clock whirred and chimed the half hour.

•••

Raphael moved away. "Jesus. This is fucking crazy. Anyone could come in." He wiped his mouth. "You are a very dirty boy. And I am very turned on. But this is not the place."

Tiago sighed and rubbed his eyes. It stung. But he was still ahead, and he could wait. "Okay, so take me home. Teach me how to come. Make me howl like a vixen."

CHAPTER 4

DIGITAL PROCESSING

They slipped through the stale backstreets, avoiding the party guests milling on Faubourg St Honore.

Tiago looked along the road. "You live on Rue Vivienne, don't you? We could go there if you'd prefer not to drive." Fuck; that sounded rather too desperate.

But Raphael was unperturbed. "I like driving. And you've had a long day. You need to be home. Burbs for you, isn't it?"

"St Germain-en-Laye."

Raphael's car crouched like a coral cat under the sodium streetlight. "Get in."

They slammed the car doors shut, and the engine roared like an MGM opening, too loud this late. The CD kicked in, and soon Tiago was leaning back, lulled by the music, the purring engine, the intimacy of their voices. Maybe Raphael was planning to pull over. Maybe they would make love in the car. That would be hot. He closed his eyes and talked about the singer; he'd seen him in Lisbon, singing Dido's Lament, as an opening number. It had been awesome.

"Awesome." Raphael lit a cigarette. "I met him last year actually. At a party, a charity thing."

"No way. What was he like?"

"Oh you know. Awesome." Raphael opened the window, blew smoke out. "Charming, modest, intelligent, unspoilt. Bookish, actually. Beautiful of course." He smiled across. "But nothing compared to you."

Tiago was silenced. He looked out of the window at unlit shop fronts, shutters coming down, boys putting crates of empty bottles out, cats sniffing at gutters. They were ordinary sights, prosaic on this night of realised dreams and answered prayers; this Night of the Acrostic. He closed his eyes. "That line…'He brought me to the banqueting house, and his banner over me was love'…" He turned his head and looked across at Raphael. "I understand that now. The banquet and the banner."

"The banner." Raphael was quiet for a few moments. "Good. I'm glad it feels good."

Tiago kept quiet after that, scared the spell would break; but Raphael drove with little regard for traffic lights and none for the speed limit, and in under fifteen minutes they had reached the suburban, tree-lined cul-de-sac where Tiago lived. A girl was walking a dachshund down the middle of the empty road. She turned back and looked at the car. The dachshund looked up at her and tugged her towards the pavement.

Tiago watched the dog's scuttling legs, felt their rhythm, got nervous. "Funny little dogs aren't they?" He shut himself up for fear another *awesome* might leak out.

But Raphael was miles away. "Dachshunds? Oh yes. Yes they are."

Tiago pointed to an ash tree. "You can leave it here overnight."

Raphael pulled over, switched off the ignition. "Right."

Tiago took his seatbelt off. "Okay?"

"Yes."

Nothing happened. Nobody moved.

"What is it?"

"Tiago. Baby." Raphael tapped his fingers on the steering wheel. "I can't come in with you. Not tonight. I'm really sorry."

"Right." Tiago covered his mouth with his hands. "I fucking knew it." He looked across at Raphael. "You're going to have to explain. And it's going to have to be pretty fucking good."

"Tiago. Baby." Raphael's voice was soft but not calm. "Now take it easy baby."

Tiago shook his head. This was such a fuck up. "You were fucking loving it. Sweet Jesus. I mean, for fuck's sake. What the fuck is wrong with you?"

"I'm not myself."

"Well then who the fuck are you?" But when Tiago looked across, the weary, hopeless Raphael was back, the one from the office, the one who didn't know his luck. Tiago breathed deep and slow. "Sorry Raphael. I'm so sorry."

"Me too baby."

They held hands and stared through the windscreen. The girl and the dog walked away down the street, turned the corner, disappeared.

Tiago chewed his lip. "So what's wrong with me?"

Raphael shook his head. "Nothing. Not a thing. You're beautiful Tiago. You're astonishing, and beautiful, and I want you so much. But I'm so fucking broken Tiago. I'm so fucking fucked." He stared through the windscreen. "I don't know what happened back there."

Tiago snatched his hands away. "Don't you fucking dare say you regret it!"

"But I'm afraid I do." Raphael tipped his head back, eyes closed. "Of course I fucking do." He was quiet for a while, and then he rubbed his eyes. "Come here."

It was a tender embrace, different to their earlier clutching and pawing, and Tiago was encouraged. Maybe love tonight was a possibility, maybe even in this car, here, now, in this surprisingly noisy neighbourhood, where a little owl was calling in the ash tree, and a small dog was barking and setting off a larger one, and a police car was driving slowly past. He let his hand fall into Raphael's lap. "Oh Jesus, Raphael."

But his hand was gently steered away. "No." Raphael drew away from him. "No baby."

"But you want me so much."

"It's just blood Tiago."

"It must mean something."

Raphael shook his head. "It means absolutely nothing. You can love someone with your whole heart and not get it up for him." He smiled. "But how would you know that?"

Tiago stared out of the windscreen. "I just want you so fucking much."

"I know. But sex like that isn't enough. Not for someone like you."

Tiago looked back at Raphael; it was true, possibly. "Meaning what?"

But Raphael was looking out the window. "Oh, you know. Someone with a romantic nature." He looked back. "Everyone's different, of course. But for some people it has to be love, whether it's the first time or the hundredth. And you are one of those people, and so am I. And when it's love, for people like us, it's wonderful. It's heaven on earth. And when it isn't, it's a fucking waste of time." He shrugged. "Look Tiago. Something's wrong inside me. You need protecting from that."

"I don't care."

"You should care." Raphael frowned. "Don't be so keen to be the more loving one Tiago. It's a dog ticket."

Tiago's heart was teeming with words. *But I am the more loving one Raphael. More loving than you can ever imagine. And one day I will bring you to my banqueting house, and my banner over you will be a love that transforms you, and redeems you, and comforts you, and our days will be filled with sunshine, and our nights with bliss, and one day maybe there will even be...* He stopped himself inches away from *the patter of tiny feet* and took out a business card. "Okay. Have it your way. But call me tomorrow. You need me."

"Thanks." Raphael tilted the card towards the streetlight. "Now, that is a hell of a long name."

"They all are in Portugal. You can call me Tiago Jose."

"I will. Tiago Jose. Perfect for you."

"Keep it. Maybe one day you'll let me astonish you with my love."

Raphael put the card in his breast pocket. "Okay. And maybe one day I will free you from your wearisome virginity."

"One day. Maybe." Tiago nodded and smiled despite the

psalmist that was in his head: *how long, oh lord?* "Maybe. And maybe you'll get rid of that fucking useless old clock. Which, I might add, is fast."

"And I might add it wasn't the only thing in that office tonight that was fast, Tiago Jose."

Tiago hated people who said *touché* so he just shrugged. "Whatever."

"That clock is going in the fucking skip tomorrow. Although I must say it did save you from the clutches of a man who was not in a state of grace." Raphael rubbed his eyes and yawned behind his hands. "I'm sorry. Long day."

"Yes." Tiago leaned over and kissed him light on the lips. "Goodnight Raphael."

Raphael took a longer, slower kiss for himself. "Goodnight Tiago Jose."

Tiago got out of the car and leaned down. "Drive home safely. I don't intend to die a virgin."

...

Tiago walked into his apartment and went through to the kitchen. He heard the car pull away and smiled to himself, imagining what to tell Inês.

My boyfriend drives a Maserati.

Hey, maybe he was superficial and materialistic.

My boyfriend, who will be forty next month, drives a Maserati.

Better.

My boyfriend, who will be forty next month, drives a Maserati and wouldn't fuck me on our first date because he was appalled that I was so easy.

Satisfied that this last version would sound wholly convincing and reflect well on both of them, Tiago poured a glass of milk and went through to the unlit lounge. He switched on a lamp and saw smudged writing on his left hand: *ExPhilMorPosns.* He sighed; if he was finishing ahead, then why was today ending the same way as so many other days had, in dark solitude, with a glass of milk, and an aching for sex?

He sat on the sofa and checked his phone.

Sleep well my beautiful Tiago Jose x R Raphael must have sent it before he'd driven away.

Tiago sprang up from the sofa, pressed *call back* and paced the room.

"Well, hello beautiful."

"Hello Raphael. Where are you?"

"St Cloud. I'm driving beside the water. It's pretty. What are you doing?"

Tiago walked to the mirror above the fireplace. "I'm drinking milk." He pulled the collar of his shirt to one side and peered at his reflection. "Jesus."

"No cookies with your milk?"

"No." Tiago touched his neck. Red marks ran down onto is left breast, curled round it. "I'm looking in a mirror. Are there vampires in your office?"

Raphael laughed softly. "I am sorry darling. Your skin is so beautiful. I couldn't help it."

"You left your calling card." Tiago closed his eyes. Lust was draining him. "Raphael, can you pull over?"

There was a pause.

"All right. One second."

The ticking of the indicator, then sudden quiet. "Okay."

"Raphael?"

"Yes?"

"I need you to help me get to sleep."

"Right."

"Will you do that?"

There was a long pause. "From here?"

"Sure." Whatever.

"Yes, I will baby."

Tiago rubbed his neck and sighed. "It won't be the first time you have."

A soft laugh. "Have you been stealing my soul Tiago?"

"Maybe." Tiago went to the sofa, lay back with eyes closed, and unzipped himself. "Oh god." He was so wet, so close. And Raphael's smoky lips were close to the phone. "Oh sweet Jesus. Oh Raphael." But he needed two hands.

"Wait. I'll put you on speaker…

CHAPTER 5

THIS CONTENT DOESN'T SEEM TO BE WORKING

Forty seconds later Raphael was wondering if this was what passed for normal on a first date these days. He shuffled in his seat. "Baby?"

No answer. Tiago was probably used to getting off like this. This was what young people did.

"Oh. Jesus. Oh Raphael."

Tiago was fine with it. He liked it. He probably did this all the time on Skype.

"Oh Raphael." There was a weird low squeak, and a clunk, and distant swearing, and silence.

"Tiago, baby. Are you okay?"

Nothing.

"Tiago. What happened?"

Tiago's voice was breathless. "I fell Raphael. I slipped off the fucking sofa. It's leather." A sigh. "I fell on my glass of milk. I hurt my hand." It was a teenager's voice, plaintive, indignant.

Raphael couldn't help but laugh. "Oh darling. Are you okay?"

A long sigh, some keypad sounds. "I think so. The phone's all sticky. I think it's fucked."

"Oh sweetheart. Do you want me to come round?"

There was a very long silence.

"What, now?"

"Sure."

"You want to come round, now?" There was a very long sigh. "Oh Raphael. You fucker."

Raphael frowned. "Darling?"

"Oh Raphael. Why can't you just fucking love me?" There was a deep sigh. "Fucking hell Raphael. I'm not a fucking bomb. Jesus. I'm so fucking harmless."

Raphael looked at the dashboard. His washer fluid was low. "You said it was what you wanted."

Tiago's voice was muffled. "No Raphael. It was what you fucking wanted. Everything tonight, all of it, has been what you wanted Raphael."

Raphael frowned. "But Tiago, baby, listen. You asked me to." There were muffled words, weird ones *OhRaphaelIwould havemadeyouafuckingsaint,* and then a loud rip hurt his ears, and a sharp slap made him jump, and the line went dead. It sounded remarkably as if the phone had been thrown, or stamped on. He tried redialling; unobtainable.

Raphael stared at his phone. This was exactly the kind of undignified, ludicrous situation he'd tried so hard to avoid for nearly a year, and it was clearly entirely Tiago's fault; too drunk, too horny, too young, too hot-tempered, too fucking Catholic and fucked-up, a phone chucker, clearly unstable. Raphael shrugged. Fuck it. He wasn't going to beg for forgiveness; he'd had a bellyful of blame, ten years saying sorry. Tiago could go fuck himself.

Raphael started the engine; he would drive his beautiful car home and put this ugly day to bed. Things would soon get better; there was lunch tomorrow with his elegant sister, and then a weekend with Rob, a boozy dinner on Saturday and a long run on Sunday. He could see his way through the next seventy-two hours, and these days that meant that life was okay.

He lit a cigarette and was accelerating in celebration when a tiny cat sprang from the shadows and ran into the road. Raphael steered sharply away and the car lurched into a squealing spin. A lesser driver in a cheaper car would have lost control, but Raphael steered grinning into the skid and, a few seconds later, pulled the car up kerbside with a beaming smile. "Textbook."

He thought for a moment, then got out and checked round the car. There was nothing stuck to it; no kitten, no bits of kitten. So maybe cosmic karma was on his side at last. But on the other hand, the tyre tracks on the road were longer than he'd expected. Maybe he shouldn't get back in the car just yet.

...

Amelia smiled. The string of sound effects was just like the first album she'd bought as a kid; the screech of tyres, the slam of a car door, footsteps. She stretched her legs out straight and pointed her toes, wondering how long it would take for the striding driver of the powerful car to reach her.

...

Raphael didn't walk far on his own these days if he could avoid it; a sentimentalist, he found his solitary footfall starkly tragic after the cheerful four-footed muddle of a couple. He walked the few paces to the riverside wall and peered over it at a small mooring; cheap, neglected boats, and a narrow beach scattered with orange and blue nylon rope and plastic bottles. The oily surface of the river was licking blackly at the white hulls, spilling over the wet sand, lapping the slimy bank. Further out, contorted pieces of driftwood bobbed along in sluggish currents. It all smelt rank and foetid. It really was quite fucking depressing.

Raphael put his hands in his pockets. "Oh Tiago. What the fuck was all that about sweetheart? Jesus. You don't want to die a virgin. You fucking will at this rate, you crazy bastard. You nearly killed me off for a start." He kicked the wall. "Still, what do you know about it?" Fuck all, clearly. He looked down at his scuffed toes and wheeled round. "Once upon a time there was an angel from the South. A beautiful angel, who called himself Tiago." He took out the business card, looked at the Mandarin characters, found them pleasing, aesthetically. "And Raphael had long desired the angel in his heart of hearts. The dirty bastard." Was he though? He'd only wanted sex when it had been thrown at him. He stared up at the stars. "And lo, one night the angel came to Raphael, and offered him love that was boundless, devoted and pure. And the angel was sad, and was more beautiful still. As often happens."

Raphael sighed. He always ticked the box marked "atheist," or wrote it in if it wasn't there, embellishing it with a large illuminated "A" and a flourish of Rococo swirls. But everyone has a god that makes life meaningful, and Raphael's god was beauty. Deplorably low on imagination for an artist, he had to worship through his senses; and tonight's new deity was Tiago's taste. Raphael licked his lips, and arousal rose through him again; but then, to his surprise, came a sudden, lurching sense of uncertainty. Doubt pricked through his lust. Maybe this mess was his fault. Maybe he should have been stronger. Maybe it would have been better to have comforted Tiago, calmed him, made him a nice cup of tea; well, maybe not the tea. But still, after days, or weeks of the usual things, sharing music and art and poetry, and letting love grow, there could have been love, the way it should be, on a crystal afternoon, drenched in sunshine. Tiago, full of joy and gratitude, would have slept in his arms afterwards, spent and sated, peaceful between white sheets.

Raphael caught his breath, suddenly shocked at the sense of having fucked up a beautiful future. A blissful private life, Tiago's soft voice offering coffee or wine or home-cooked food, or a massage after a long day, his dry, clever conversation over dinner mutating into the passionate words of a yielding lover at bed time; and in public, pride. They'd make a handsome couple, gliding with calm splendour into noisy parties, two elegant swans among squabbling ducks, going everywhere together and nowhere alone, people coupling their names *Were RaphaelandTiago there?* And printers joining them on cheques, and invitations, and in concert programmes: *Gold Patrons: O Snr Tiago da Silva and M. Raphael Davide.*

But that wasn't going to happen now. Tiago had been a caricature *Please me. Command me. Enjoy me. Possess me.* For fuck's sake. Raphael shook his head. He should have known better, but first lust had got him, and then something deeper had turned him cold. It would have taken a split second to say *No Tiago, put the phone down, I'll come over,* and then it would have taken him ten minutes, less, to drive back, to have held Tiago, and been loving, and saved them both that farcical, digital climax. He was so fucked. Tiago had given him his heart on a plate. And in return he'd given him just enough love to come on his own in a darkened room. "What a fucking catch."

Raphael looked down into the oily water, a reverse Narcissus, hating what he saw, longing to see someone else; maybe the eighteen year old who'd known everything, addled with boundless teenage lust, lying in a fug of sex and cigarette smoke in the dark student room, his head on Tomas Paul's marble breast, watching long harpist's fingers trace his sharp shoulder. *Just enough flesh to make your bones beautiful, Raphael.* Tomas Paul had called him a dark angel, told him that making love at night kept the wolves at bay, and doing it in the morning greeted the sun. It was crap, but it was Raphael's first post-coital crap, and he'd sucked it up. And the next day in Vienna, Tomas Paul had taken him to the gallery and shown him the girl.

"See this girl Raphael? Her gilded rapture, the way she curls up and clutches the air? That's what you do." Looking askance at the picture, then back at him. "Though perhaps you're more beautiful than her. Objectively."

Those first few days had been enough to secure Raphael's devotion to their long-distance relationship for more than a decade. Moderately sociopathic and not highly-sexed, he would have got through the many nights apart psychologically unscarred had he not been too proud for honest porn, and over-indulged in erotic half dreams of Michaelangelo's Adam that had left him feeling bizarrely ashamed and unable to step inside the Sistine Chapel without blushing. But Tomas Paul was different. After three years he had wanted freedom, and women, yet he'd still wanted Raphael to be faithful, so he'd made a proposal. In return for fidelity, Raphael would get the keys to the Gosele family's shabby apartment in Rue Vivienne, and be paid to redesign the place, and manage the fixing up at a generous enough rate of pay to help him get started as an artist. Too deeply in love to negotiate, too weak to resist a rent-free downtown address, Raphael had said yes. Within a year he'd turned the musty dump into an airy urban space, mucking in with the workmen who put in the new central heating, plumbing, wiring, sanding the floors, repainting the ceilings and woodwork brilliant white, stripping off the depressing brown wallpaper, and giving the walls a cheerful palate of natural greens. It was a good project, and he was proud of his work; but the oak floors were hard, and the ceilings were high, and the wallpaper was filthy, and on lonely evenings Raphael would sometimes lie back in the bath, wondering if his project were a labour of love, or the act of a deluded obsessive. But if Raphael was a bower bird, he was a successful one; Tomas Paul was soon arriving from Heidelberg every Friday and staying until Monday. And when he'd bought the gallery in '96, and got Raphael a well-paid job there, he'd insisted Raphael stay on in the apartment; it was ideal to have someone so close to the new shop. The only change came when Tomas Paul got a job at Turing; because then of course Raphael's allowance had to be doubled to cover the cost of visits to London, visits that never happened.

Raphael looked at his nails. It wasn't helpful to be ashamed of what you were, but it was sometimes useful to be ashamed of things you did, because occasionally you let yourself down. There'd been no shame in taking Tomas Paul's money to do up the flat and run the gallery. It had been business. But allowing himself to be retained like a minion was arguably something else. Raphael was pretty buttoned-up by modern standards. For him, secrecy was an appropriate measure of shame, and whereas he knew for a fact that he'd told a handful of people about the first two arrangements, he'd never told a soul about the last one, nor that when he'd reneged on his side of the deal after nine years, Tomas Paul had sold him the apartment at the very attractive price of one French franc.

Raphael stared at the dark surface of the water; tiny waves were spreading his gloomy reflection to nothingness. He'd spent nine years waiting for Tomas Paul to make up his mind. And Tiago had apparently waited six years for him. Maybe they should get together after all, take one another out of the system, make the world safer for more normal people. People like Martin who had picked him up in a silent, fusty Oxford library on a wet afternoon with a dazzling smile and a message on a post-it in terrible handwriting *You are a beautiful man*. Raphael had shaken his head, written back. *I'm sorry. I'm already seeing someone*. Martin had shrugged. *Vita brevis est, call me on this number*. Raphael had thrown the note away, but Martin had got the gallery address from the librarian, and turned up in Paris two weeks later with a rucksack, nowhere to stay, and poetry on his lips. Raphael had been a pushover.

He'd been nervous that afternoon, but apparently he'd done

all right; at least so Martin had said last year at the Graduation Ball. It was gratifying to hear, of course. *What a fucking afternoon. Like fucking Ovid with Corinna, you know? Jove send me more. Oh yes.* Though maybe it would have been better heard in private. *You know what Patricia? He was so fucking hot. Raphael is the best fuck I ever had.* And said by someone sober. *'Strue. Not a word of a lie.* Martin had made figures of eight in the air with his wine glass, stirred a big pot with it. *He's a fucking stud. Jesus, I'll never forget that first time. We only got as far as the stairs. 'Strue. I was howling like a fucking vixen. He really taught me how to come. Oh hi baby. Is it time to go already?*

Raphael nodded. Ah, yes. Tiago's words had been tin foil on amalgam, a bad nut on the tongue; sudden, revolting, sobering. But Martin was a poet and he didn't waste a word. Especially in bed, afterwards. *Jesus fucking Christ. You know why I took you as my lover, don't you Raphael?* Taken, like an apple from a bowl, or a book from a shelf. A book, actually. You could put a book back. *You know why I stay with you don't you Raphael? Because you're teaching me how to come, that's why. And I'm getting better every time, aren't I?*

Raphael closed his eyes. The past was clawing at him; Friday and Saturday evenings at their place in Burgundy, The Retreat, the place they rebuilt together, the life that had become his cornerstone, his comfort. He'd read, and Martin would lie on the sofa, and they'd drink good wine, listen to music. Raphael liked Chopin but Martin's parents were folkies, so folk it often was.

Oh, but I'll cut off my yellow hair, and I'll go along with you.

I'll dress myself in uniform and I'll see Egypt too.
I'll march beneath your banner while fortune it do smile
And we'll comfort one another on the banks of the Nile

Banner. Raphael bit his lip, angry with a past that had turned his present into a minefield but unable to leave it. It was eleven o'clock and Martin was flinging the scripts aside. *Fuck that for a game of soldiers. Fuck them all. Referees and peer reviewers. Useless talentless tossers. Worse than fucking students. Why do I fucking bother.* Getting off the sofa, filling their glasses, going to the piano, picking out an accompaniment with long inky fingers, singing softly. Martin was an English tenor. His voice turned into speech without breaking step.

"This is rather lovely actually, simple and charming. We sang it at school." Putting his glasses on top of his head, the heavy black frames pushing back the thick fair hair. Squinting at the score cutely. "I think I may have sung a solo in this actually. Just after my voice broke." And singing again, and playing, and saying something quirky over the chords. "Do you think she would though? Forsake her Cyprian Grove, for England?"

"Who darling?"

"Er, Venus. Yes, Venus, on this occasion."

"Maybe."

"I would. But I'm not sure she would."

"I would if you were there Marty."

Would you Raphael? Stretching, coy, sexy, the girl in the Hogarth. *Would you, really though?* Martin coming across to stand behind Raphael's chair, stealing his hands down into Raphael's shirt, kissing his hair. *I think you would too.* Kissing his neck now. *I'm tired now. Are you coming to bed?*

Yes baby. I'll be up in a few minutes.

Raphael ached to say the words again, to feel the sweet certainty of being wanted so much, to hear Martin going up to bed while he went round downstairs, smiling to himself, putting out the lights, locking the front door, before going upstairs and finding Martin sitting on the bed half dressed, half-draped. Always there'd be just five words.

RAPHAEL: Hello you.

MARTIN: Well. Hello you.

And then there were the mornings after.

Oh darling. You made coffee. Aren't you an angel? I slept so well. I love you so.

Sex smoothed their arguments, especially the ones started by Martin, which was all of them. It wasn't his fault, he came from a long line of cheerful bickerers. John and Fenella turned their whole house into a stage for their interminable squabbles, their grievances venting from separate rooms like the sporadic buzzing of dying flies on window sills.

Why can't your mother leave things alone Martin?

I'll swing for your father Marty, I really will.

But Raphael considered himself above quarrelling with a lover. When the rows began he found it more dignified to let Martin's spat words drop like sparks into the space between them while he stared at the ground like he had at school – *The answer is not on your shoes, Davide.*

Eventually Martin would run out of words and reach a point

at which he would let himself be embraced, something that in recent years had become a rough process, leaving Martin sighing afterwards, complaining but smiling with it. *You quell me with sex, you bad man. You dominate me. You break my spirit.*

No baby, no. I make love to you to comfort you, to calm you. I adore you.

But adoration hadn't been enough, and in the end the bed in the flat was empty, The Retreat was full of ghosts, and all that had remained one crisp, autumn morning was a grim battleground; grey sky, frosted grass, white ash in aboriginal patterns on charred wood, pale orange flames crackling and spitting. Raphael had braved it out with the vintage single malt they'd been keeping for their tenth anniversary and the music they'd heard on their fifth – *Troppo e insoffribile fiero martir* – but the varnished wood, photographs and drawings raised acrid smoke that had stung his eyes, so he'd walked away from the fire and let Rob finish it all off.

Raphael looked down at the broken pavement. Though bitterness and menace had gone, something was still bad deep inside him. Love needed trust, and trust was dead. It was hardly surprising that Cupid was giving him a wide berth, taking away his touch, letting lust and farce take over. He stalked moodily along the waterside path, wanting to get away from himself. "Evil, twisted, squandering, predatory, bitter fucking bastard."

A wave slapped the dark wall ahead. Raphael lifted his head to avoid the bad air and saw a new annoyance; a lamppost that didn't match the others, too short and curvaceous for the proportions of the path. It irritated him far more than any other aspect of the night so far and he took out his phone, glad for only the second time in his life that the fucking things took photographs. "Unforgiveable. Inexcusable. Unbelievable."

The lamppost took it personally.

"Hey. Take a chill pill, Mister Stressy."

Raphael dropped his phone, but the shock was only momentary; lampposts didn't talk, no matter how weird the evening had become. Only people talked, and this was a person, an inverted girl in a wetsuit, an English girl apparently, given that she was saying *gosh, sorry, she hadn't meant to startle him.* He knelt and groped for the phone, his eyes locked on the girl while she brought her legs slowly down, and stood up straight, and looked back and down at him, hands on hips like Miss Forces Sweetheart July 1944.

"Get up angel. You look like a Pekinese."

CHAPTER 6

COMING TO HIS SENSES

Showered and dressed in a new white shirt and old jeans, Tiago was ready to reclaim the evening. Sulking without an audience was ridiculous when he could be doing something to prove he had invested the last six years in more gainful activity than pursuing a man who couldn't love him. There were four possible options. He could cook something marvellous – he did, in fact make excellent *pasteis de nata* – but he wasn't hungry. He could do some algebra – but no, his brain was addled, and that would mean the misery of getting things wrong and crossing them out. If he went running he could probably get a personal best – but his legs were still a bit wobbly.

It would have to be music.

...

Raphael sighed. Those ghosts were fucking everywhere tonight. "Philip Marlowe."

"Very good." The girl sprang lightly off the wall, and rubbed her hands like a gymnast. "Is The Big Sleep a favourite film of yours?"

Raphael stood up. "Not of mine. Of my. Ex."

The girl looked up at him. "Ah yes. The x. The unknown. The

known unknown." She put her hands behind her back, a little Degas dancer, poised to pirouette, or strike.

Striking seemed more likely. Raphael decided to reassure her. "I'm not a nutter."

The girl peered at him, and bit her lip. "Mmm."

"I'm just on my way home." Raphael squinted, trying to see her better. "I've been working late."

The girl frowned. "Obviously."

"I'm Raphael." He held out his hand, palm up, peaceful.

The girl looked at it the way a cat would.

"Raphael Davide?" He tried the upwards intonation he had heard younger people use.

The girl stood back, scanning his face and body up and down. "Oh my god. You are." She looked away and mumbled; it sounded rather like *Fuck a duck, you actually fucking are.*
Singular girl, but still flighty. He needed to appear completely and utterly innocuous. "I'm an art dealer." Good. "Here, in Paris." More maybe. "Mainly Renaissance." That should do it.

The girl turned, and beamed, and took his hand and pumped it, unleashing an auctioneer's battery of words. "I know your name. I met your sister, Clara Davide. I met her, after a seminar she gave last week. Bayesian Statistics for geneticists. That's what I am. A geneticist. Not a Bayesian statistician. I work for Pomona? We make apples? Well, we design apples. I design apples, perfect ones? You know, Frankenstein food?" She pulled back her rubber hood, shook her hair out. "I'm Frankenstein."

Raphael caught his breath. He collected beauty and this girl had plenty; the pale variety, reed-thin, long straight hair the soft white of moonlight on water. She was exquisite, quite beautiful, a Naiad, elfin and lissome. And as Rob would say, she couldn't half rabbit.

"I'm Amelia, actually. Amelia Postthridge. Dr Amelia Postthridge. I'm English. From Kitminster? In Devon? I'm doing a postdoctoral project at the University. They call it technology transfer? Putting industrial scientists in University labs. It's hugely enriching for all of us, naturally."

Raphael caught the irony, smiled. "Dr Amelia Postle Stridge?"

"Near enough." Amelia tossed her hair with a practised move and gave him her hand again, palm tilted down; a flipper. "Amelia Postthridge. Forget the Dr." She looked down at her perfect neoprene form. "I'm afraid I don't have a card on me."

Raphael looked at the river, the pale feet. "And were you, er…?"

"Was I er what? Was I standing on my head?"

"Yes."

"Yes I was standing on my head." She bit her lip, nodded towards the sea wall. "I find it easier to think like that. Silly, I know."

"Impersonating street furniture?"

"Mmm. Eccentric, certainly. But who wants to be normal?"

"Indeed."

They looked at each other. The water slapped and clapped and rolled objects against the wall. Unseen birds squabbled and settled. Amelia nose-pointed towards the water. "Noisy little bleeders out there. Coots. Coot, I should say. *Fulica atra.*

Scrapping with a cormorant. *Phalacrocorax carbo.* I've got one at home actually. A cormorant. I call him Leander."

Raphael nodded. The girl wasn't nervous now; she was just letting her mouth talk while she thought about something else. Clara did it too. He smiled and took in the regular English features, rather wan in this light, but still luminous; a Giotto Virgin with attitude. *What me? Pregnant? Up the duff? You're pulling my leg.* "A cormorant?"

"Yes. Have you ever tried it?"

"Have I ever tried cormorant?"

"No." Amelia laughed. "Have you ever tried standing on your head?"

"Oh. No, I can't say I have."

"You should."

Raphael coughed. Fair enough. "I stopped because I nearly hit a kitten back there." He pointed back down the road. "Tiny thing. It just ran into the road."

Amelia nodded. "A kitten." There was something funny about her voice, a metallic clacking.

"Yes, I stalled my fucking Maserati. My car." Raphael ran a hand through his hair. "Sorry for saying that, for swearing. I'm still a bit shaken up." He played with the car key in his pocket, found it reassuring.

"What is it, a Grancabrio? Good brakes, I imagine, on a car like that."

Raphael was taken aback. "Excellent."

"What is it, four hundred BHP?"

And again. "Four fifty."

"Goes like stink I bet." Amelia rubbed her chin. Her lips parted a little and Raphael glimpsed a metal stud in her tongue. Clara used to have a gold stud in her eyebrow. Actually, nearly everyone used to have a gold stud somewhere, back in the nineties. Even he had an earring, but Tomas Paul hadn't liked it, so it had gone. He rubbed his ear and put Tomas Paul to one side for now. "You know Clara?"

Amelia shrugged. "Not really, but I'd like to. She's an Athena lecturer. I suppose she's a bit of a heroine of mine. But I'm not a mathematician. I'm a scientist." It was the kind of pointless distinction Tomas Paul used to make; these people were scientists, these people were not. "I stack up genes and shoot them into germplasm. Yeehaw!" She peered at him. "I mean, I use science to make better apples. And I like to rediscover old varieties, lovely things that haven't survived – not because they were bad, but because we've lost our sense of taste." She smiled at him. "And you love Renaissance art. So maybe I'm a bit like you."

"Maybe you are." Raphael thought about his sense of taste and wondered what Tiago was doing. Maybe he should write him a letter? Yes; he would go home, and write a letter, a really beautiful one, on expensive Japanese calligraphy paper, in black ink, with a graphic pen. He would explain himself in romantic terms, express his love, quote Baudelaire maybe, or Verlaine, ask Tiago to be patient.

"Genetics are great. So much faster than breeding. It's like the difference between walking and air travel. The best way to think about it…" Amelia paused and frowned, "…is that genes are like machine code."

"Right." Raphael knew from the way Amelia was constructing her sentences that it wasn't the kind of thing he needed to hear. It was A Science Thing, explained in the way Clara and Tomas Paul tried to explain Science Things to him; the first sentence linking the Science Thing to something simple he might already understand, the second the Science Thing itself, the third a further more confusing explanation of the Science Thing itself, the fourth – presumably triggered by the vacancy of his expression – likening the Science Thing to something still more absurdly simple he might already understand. The occasional words got through; *triploid apples, multiple pollinators, gene pairs, nucleic acids, editing* – but he wasn't processing them. He was thinking about how the black ink would look on the thick paper, or in an art card, one of the Klimt ones he had in the drawer, the one of Danae maybe, and how he might write Tiago's name with an illuminated T; but should it be "My Dear" or "My Darling", or just "Tiago"?

His heart sank. It was pointless thinking about a letter he didn't even know how to begin.

Amelia had dried up, her head on one side. "Do you need to be somewhere else?"

"I don't know." He looked at her. "But I shouldn't leave you here on your own."

"I'm fine. I come here lots at night." Amelia crossed her arms. "Look, I heard you talking you know. You can tell me it's none of my business but you sounded pretty wound up. You were a bit ranty."

Raphael nodded, wondering how much she had heard. "Yes, I

was a bit."

They stood in silence for a while, looking away from each other.

"You shouldn't really get back in the car till your head's straight. You could hurt somebody."

Raphael winced; it was a bit late for that.

•••

Tiago worked through a Nocturne with fingers as precise as the brass tines of a music box drum. At the end he sat back and rubbed his chin; not bad. At least his motor system was working okay.

He took the music book off the stand and flicked through the pages, looking for something more demanding, wanting the distraction. After a moment's indecision he selected opus twenty seven, cracked his knuckles like a cartoon cat in a tuxedo, and started the deep arpeggios in the base faster than he should have.

•••

Raphael and Amelia ambled wordlessly along the towpath, waves lapping to their right.

After about fifty metres Raphael folded his arms. "So then, Amelia, what have you come here to think about in your strange inverted way?"

"Me first?"

"It was your idea."

"True." She looked down at her bare feet, side-stepped some broken glass. "It's not novel."

"So I'm guessing boys, or girls."

"Boys."

"And you must be able to take your pick, so I'm guessing you must have someone."

"Two someones actually."

Raphael tried to see her face, but it was in shadow. "Two?"

"It's not like it sounds. They know about each other. But I can't choose." She stopped and looked out across the water, wrinkling up her nose. "Crispin's smart, and he rows and runs for the University, and he's a lot of fun. But the last time we made love it was the most dispiriting four and a half minutes of my life."

Raphael stopped, turned, frowned at her. "Four and a half minutes?" What could you do in four and a half minutes? It had taken him five minutes to get Tiago's shirt off.

"He had the football on. I could see the clock on the TV screen. Spurs went into extra time."

"And Crispin didn't?"

"No. He didn't." Amelia rubbed her nose. "And then there's Jon. He has beautiful strawberry blonde hair, and he's sweet and great in bed. But he drinks." She shrugged. "I don't know what to do. I want to be with someone for a long time. But it has to be the right someone. And even then it might not work out."

Raphael turned away. "Indeed."

"Oh right. Sorry. " Amelia started walking again. "It was perfect, was it?"

Raphael stopped again. "What was perfect?"

Amelia turned and shrugged. "Your life." She crossed her arms. "You're a good looking man in an expensive suit wandering around on his own on a towpath at two in the morning. It's not normal, is it? And it's not money, or work. You could be doing something about them. It must be love. Only love could make you come somewhere like this in the middle of the night. And if you had someone, you'd be with them. And you must have had someone, at some point, because you're a knockout, aren't you? And it must have been perfect, or you'd have got over it. And you haven't yet, have you?" She rubbed her muzzle and her chin, and frowned deeply, leaving a line. "Stands to reason."

Raphael stared, too angry to speak. It was a brutal, Clara-style deduction, the kind of thing that made them fight and left Rob to pick up the pieces. *She can't help it Raph. She's trying to help.* The thought of Rob calmed him down. "Yes, well, actually, it was perfect. I mean, he was perfect, in some ways." The morning-after taste of Martin's lips, coffee and sex, his own taste on his lover's lips, the words that thanked him for their night together. *Thanks baby. Aren't you an angel? I slept so well. I love you so.*

The fatal addendum on the final morning.

I'll miss you this week. Pause. *What time's your flight?*

The old acid flowed into Raphael's gut. He spat on the path. "Sorry."

"It's okay." Amelia shook her head. "Look. I'm sorry if I was rather direct there. I'm an empiricist. We can get a bit factual."

"It's okay." Raphael wiped his mouth. "Jesus. How long can you be on the rebound?"

"Depends. How hard you hit the wall. How fast you're going."

There were sudden voices, mumbled swearwords, laughter,

shuffling footsteps. Raphael picked up a discarded beer bottle, broke its neck on the wall, checked the jagged edge. "Stay here in the shadow Amelia. I'll handle this."

Amelia melted away and Raphael walked down the path, the bottle behind his back. After a few seconds three lanky alien shadows appeared, followed by three older teenagers, students maybe, swaggering and unsteady. "Hey man." The first boy offered Raphael a joint. "Beautiful night, man. Beautiful. PSG won. You want some of this?"

Raphael smiled and shook his head. "Not tonight thanks."

"You're a beautiful guy, you know? You're like an angel." The boy put his arms round Raphael, breathed beer and skunk fumes into his face. "I love you man. Jesus. You smell good."

"I love you too. Now go home son." Raphael turned the boy gently away, watched him walk on. "Kids." He threw the bottle into the hedge. "You can come out now Amelia."

Amelia emerged from the darkness with crossed arms. "You're a pretty scary guy."

Raphael ignored her. "What were you saying?"

"The rebound thing. Sorry."

Raphael waited for the acid to rise, but the adrenaline had killed it. "Oh, that." He scratched his stubble. She wanted him to talk, and he didn't want to talk. It was like being with Clara. He reached up into the branches above him, pulled two heads of lilac off, handed one to Amelia. "Well, who gives a fuck? I just got cheated on. It happens every day." He nodded towards the houses over the road. "It's probably happening in there right now, to some poor bastard working a night shift."

"Thank you. *Syringa vulgaris*. Always sounds rather medical to me." Amelia inspected the flower head. "Why don't you just find somebody else? Fish, sea, you know? You're hardly a gargoyle. And you drive a Maserati." Amelia looked up at him. "So you must have a few bob."

A few bob. Raphael shrugged. "Maybe." Actually he'd salted away over two million euros of Tomas Paul's money over the years, in property, art and fast cars. Of course, he'd squandered the rest. He was only human.

"Is there someone?"

Raphael shook his head. "Not exactly." He sighed, remembering Tiago's words, Tiago's lips.

"But there could be?"

Raphael shrugged.

"And he's perfect, isn't he?"

"Why do you say that?"

"The look on your face." Amelia gestured to a bench about twenty feet ahead. "Let's sit down."

She set off into the shadow and Raphael sighed. He didn't want to sit down. He wanted to go home and write his beautiful letter. But he didn't know what to put in it. And he was so wound up he'd nearly glassed three harmless boys. What did he have to lose? "Sure. Why not?" He followed Amelia over to the bench and sat beside her.

Amelia held the flower head up close to her eyes. "Right. No one's listening except me and these beetles. Tell me. You can always shoot me afterwards, fling me in the river."

Raphael looked at her for half a minute. "I could couldn't

I?" What the hell. He tipped his head back and closed his eyes, preparing for the slump into the dark place he'd tried so hard to avoid.

"It was an afternoon." The rucksack in the hallway was Martin's, the iPod on the table wasn't, the sounds from upstairs were Martin's voice, saying the things that Martin said, the dirty, beguiling words he gave him when they made love. "I found him at home." Raphael put his hands over his face, pressed his eyes in; he was walking quietly up the stairs, an intruder in his own apartment, open the bedroom door and seeing the boy again. "With one of his researchers." The boy's flawless body, tanned against the white sheets, nose to tail with Martin like insects mating on the wing. "From Kansas, somewhere like that." Somewhere they had tornados. Raphael held his stomach. The pain was back, his guts being scooped out with a cutlass, not a scimitar. "I took a picture of them with my phone." The phone he'd later burned; but it hadn't completely burned, so he'd smashed it up with a mallet, because he was an idiot. It was hilarious, though oddly Rob hadn't laughed once.

He heard a voice, soft and silvery. *Wow. They were so busted.* But he ignored it. He was staring ahead, remembering in wonder how he'd driven to Patricia's office without crashing, like a farmer carrying his severed arm ten miles to the nearest doctor. Patricia's office was a big glass fish tank and he'd slumped forward in the slopey chair like a toppled plastic diver. "I went to see his boss. I showed her the picture." She had been so calm; maybe it happened every day. Academic Moral Turpitude, Emergency Drill 1.

There was a scratching sound; something cheap and plastic scraping the rough tarmac. Raphael looked down. A split fast food drinks cup was making its way along the path towards them.

Amelia stood up. "That." She pointed. "Is a fucking rat." She walked over to the cup and bent down to watch. "Horrid thing. Must have come out of the river." She looked back at Raphael and raised her right foot over the shaking cup. "Shall I kill it? I should do, really. They're revolting, doubly incontinent, vectors for all kinds of filth."

The cup stopped moving. There was a quiet *squeep*.

Raphael looked up. "Is it really necessary?"

"I suppose not." Amelia stood back. A dark, fat pink-tailed shape shot out of the cup and scuttled away. "So, Ratty lives to fight another day." She walked back to the bench and sat down again. "Go on. What did she do? Did she fire him? She should have. I would have. I would have kicked his sorry arse out. Creep."

Raphael nodded. It figured, this squalid scene; the trash, the rat, the rank air, the smell of death and decay and the end of things. He'd been avoiding it for months, but this was where this story belonged. And this would be where he could leave it, if he were brave enough. He took a deep breath. "She said she was sorry. And then I knew it was true. Because she wouldn't have been sorry if it wasn't." He felt it again, Patricia's pity, her touch on his shoulder that had scruffed him limp. He leaned forward with his face in his hands, trying to cry; trying so hard he thought his eyes would bleed, but nothing came. He heard his name said but ignored it, staying hunched over, hearing waves break quietly against the wall.

...

Tiago listened to the final notes die away. He'd played with taste and discipline; but towards the end he'd zoned out, and the score in front of his eyes had become black ants dancing on a page, the image in his front brain an old dream; standing outside the Salle Pleyel with Raphael, late on a warm summer night. *Home? Or a drink first?* And grinning at Raphael, making him wait. *Oh, I think a drink first, don't you?* And Raphael sighing, and putting an arm around him. *I was rather afraid you'd say that.* And going for that drink, and being splendid and glamorous in front of the dull, envious multitude.

He scratched wax off Middle C and wondered what to do next. He had a very forgiving nature, but he wasn't prepared to be a doormat. He got up, walked across to the window and stared into the dark garden. It wouldn't look too good if he were still up and dressed when Raphael came round to apologise.

...

Raphael heard an unzipping noise.

"Here. This will make you feel better."

Oh please, not again. He sat up. "Amelia. You're very charming, but..." He opened his eyes.

Amelia was fishing around in the front of her wetsuit. "They're a bit warm and sweaty."

Doubtless. "Amelia, I'm very flattered, but really."

Amelia took out two boiled sweets and held them up to the light. "Sharp or sweet?"

Raphael breathed out. "Sharp please." He put it in his mouth and tasted warm, salty apples.

"What happened? Did she fire him?" Amelia stared ahead, sucking noisily.

"Sort of. But not for my sake." Raphael leaned back, crossed his arms. "She explained that would be revenge. And revenge would diminish me. That if I couldn't forgive him, it meant I'd never loved him. And she was right." He found himself smiling. "Then again she is a Professor of Moral Philosophy so this is pretty basic stuff for her. It's elegant really. Diagnostic."

"Real love can bear anything."

"Yes. Even its own demise." Yes. Even that.

"So you forgave him." Amelia was still looking ahead, looking away.

"Well I had to, didn't I, if I'd loved him." Raphael moved the boiled sweet round on his tongue. It had been a strange form of forgiveness – throwing Martin out, changing the locks, freezing the accounts, burning his stuff, their stuff, their photographs, their bed – and after a while he'd realised that he hadn't rallied because he was strong, but because he was stunned, that shock had inoculated him against all but the most superficial of emotions, leaving him to thrive for months on a cheerless cocktail of disdain, indignation, and contempt. He swallowed hard, making the syrup push down the bile rising in his throat. "But it didn't really work."

"It's hard, forgiveness."

"Yes. Revenge is far more satisfying."

•••

Tiago sat on his white bed, in his white bedroom, glumly inspecting a gold cross on a chain in the palm of his hand. He'd planned to get into bed and make an attempt to get to sleep, but at the last moment he'd reached into the bedside cabinet to look at the leaving presents Rogerio and Inês had given him at the airport in Lisbon on Monday. The cross was from Rogerio, solid gold, identical to the one he wore himself, and probably blessed with holy water and wafted with incense as his own had been (Rogerio having rather a predilection for such weak and foolish things).

Tiago smiled and put the chain around his neck, the first time he'd done such a thing for six years, wondering if the cross would bring him better luck than the gold lob now sitting on Raphael's desk, and knowing for certain he was certainly going to need some luck if Inês's gift was not to be wasted.

Tiago loved Inês. They'd been raised as little brother and big sister since his own parents had died in his infancy, and he could forgive her anything; but sometimes she really went too far. At least she'd warned him not to open his leaving present on the plane. Even from the rarefied atmosphere of seat 1B it would have been hard not to die of shame unwrapping a box of one hundred large condoms ribbed for heightened pleasure. Still, Inês was a doctor, and it was the thought that counted, and thanks to the wonders of modern packaging the sell by date was several years into the future. Tiago sighed; he had never had cause to use a condom in his life, and it rather seemed that wasn't about to change any time soon, but he liked to be prepared for all eventualities, so he unwrapped the cellophane, opened the box, took out the instruction leaflet and read it the way a bored child reads the information on a packet of cornflakes.

...

Amelia got up and checked her watch. "Are you meant to be somewhere else?"

"Not really." Raphael looked up. She had good lines and might make a good life model, but Tiago would make a better one. In objective terms they were probably about even, but Tiago was probably better at keeping still for long periods of time. And maybe drawing Tiago from life was still on the cards. He moved the sweet with his tongue, thinking about how best to capture Tiago's slender torso and thighs in black ink on thick white paper.

Amelia went up on her points. "So if you didn't forgive him, what happened?"

"Oh, I got pretty down for a while." Raphael sniffed. Melpomene was the sniper of the Muses, and she'd pulled the trigger on him one morning in the cafe in Dusseldorf Hauptbahnhof. Her bullet had been his bonfire aria; he'd looked into the mirrored glass behind the counter and seen a thin, elegant guy, a lonely striver, ridiculous among smiling couples. For five sleepless nights he'd relived long-forgotten adolescent fears – not that he'd never have anyone to hold, more that he'd never have anyone worth holding – until the night he'd locked the door against the pounding rain, and poured the drink, and typed the first search string he had ever written into the unwanted laptop from Clara.

Quick dignified painless death.

He stared ahead. "Yes. Pretty down." He'd put the music on, popped thirty-two pills out of the blister pack, taken the final look out of the window, and seen a bedraggled Clara in the street below. And changed his mind. "But you get over stuff."

A police car went past. They both turned to look at it.

Amelia stayed turned away. "Rapprochement?"

"Yes. Last month. The equinox, actually." The dinner in a gastro pub near Henley, and the walk in the wood where years ago they'd breathed hard among peppery bluebells. He'd been weak and drunk and sentimental, and Martin had coaxed him down onto the forest floor and talked him into giving head, breathing a soundtrack of promises *Oh Raphael, I swear I've learnt my lesson, I swear things will be different darling. Do that thing with your tongue again.* He'd let Martin finish, held him as he came, laid him back and let him vent the drivel from his system. *That was wonderful baby. I've missed you so. Oh look at the celandine. It smells so sweet.*

But all Raphael could smell was the bawdy scent of wild garlic.

I've missed you too Marty. But, you know, I think I'm done with all this. I think it's better if we don't see each other again.

The slap had left a mark, but it had been worth it. Raphael grinned. "It was good."

"You said goodbye."

"Yes."

"You laid your love to rest."

"We did. We buried it, in a bluebell wood, in a shallow grave."

"All love is buried in a shallow grave." Amelia turned towards him. "But growing apart is not inevitable. You might grow together. People do. With this new guy, the perfect one?"

Raphael crossed his arms. "You're right of course."

Amelia looked at him for a moment. "So what's wrong with him?"

"Nothing really." That was the problem. "That's the problem. That and he appears to be crazy about me. He even remembers the first night we met. It was at a party, in a gallery. February 17th, 2006, apparently. And it was snowing." Raphael frowned, surprised how well he remembered that night; seeing Tiago from upstairs, having to go over to him, to see those grey eyes closer up. He took out his phone, half aware he might want to make a call, not sure what to say.

Amelia stood up. "The thing is." She turned away. "Life is only meaningful when you know where you're heading." She turned back. "Like me. I love my job, don't get me wrong. But I have this project, this temple to Diana and Apollo. It's eighteenth century, at an old place my family owns. I want to restore it, the temple. It's in an orchard."

Raphael frowned. An orchard? He had an orchard. Hell, he'd planted an orchard, at the Retreat, a few years ago. It had become a headache once Martin had gone, a pain to look after – and it was still a pain now, on the market, not selling. He'd had enough of orchards. But he'd always liked Apollo. "Diana and Apollo?"

"Yes." Amelia smiled. "I know. It sounds mad, but it's a charity thing." She looked away. "Actually it's for children, to help them learn to play, love and appreciate music. To find themselves, their identity, through music." She scratched an eyebrow. "But I need money. I need patrons. Not a huge amount, actually." She smiled. "Maybe you might know the kind of people who would be interested?"

"I might."

There was a sudden shrill ringing. Raphael looked up. The kitten was scampering towards them. It arched its back and rubbed itself on his shoelaces.

Amelia smiled. "Is this the one? Good job you didn't squash him. He belongs to someone." She picked the kitten up by its scruff, looked at its name tag. "Iago. Someone likes Shakespeare. Or Verdi, maybe. It means James in Portuguese, doesn't it?"

Raphael put his phone away. Tiago had smashed his phone. But that was good. It meant he had to drive round. And fuck the letter. He knew what he needed to say, and it couldn't be written down. "It's Spanish for James. It means the Usurper, the one that turns you upside down." He smiled and shook his head, tilted his watch towards the streetlight. It was two. He could be at the flat in ten minutes if he broke the law. The police would understand. It was an emergency. *It's love Officer. I have to get on with the rest of my life.* They might even give him an escort. It was Paris, after all.

"It sounds like a sigh." Amelia was stroking the kitten's chin, looking at its name tag. "Actually it's my neighbour's name." Amelia started talking in short bursts, like a machine gun. "Uh-huh. He's a banker, works at Credit Dijonnais. Nice lad, tall, very slim. Very shy, blushes a lot. Just back from Lisbon. One of those long Portuguese faces, you know, a bit horsey? Tiago da Silva, I think. Tiago DuBois. Tiago of the Woods."

Raphael swallowed hard. "Tiago da Silva." He could be there in ten minutes.

"Yes." Amelia rattled on, teeth bared like a terrier; she'd met Tiago on Tuesday night, putting packing boxes into the recycling. They'd drunk coffee, red wine, and Vodka Red Bull, and swapped spare keys and emails. He had a beautiful piano, a Pleyel, and a Spanish guitar, and lots of pictures, mainly Renaissance, millions of books. He was a sweetheart, who'd sneaked owl boxes and bird feeders into the trees in the communal gardens. He'd told her about his hero grandfather, killed by Salazar's henchmen, and about his parents, and that he'd left Lisbon for Paris, not for work, but for love. That was it; he'd come back for love, some guy he'd loved for years. Six years. Like something from the Bible.

There was a sudden, startling silence.

"Are you okay?"

Raphael wasn't entirely sure. He knew his mouth was open, because a moth had flown into it. "I'm fine." He scraped his tongue with his thumb, got the bits off, flicked them away.

She stared at him, beamed. "Is it the same chap?"

"Yes. I think so."

Amelia frowned. "Is he expecting you, Tiago? I only ask because it's awfully late."

Raphael rubbed his eyes. "I don't know. We argued."

"Your fault?"

"Possibly." Raphael checked his watch; certainly.

Amelia folded her arms. "You're the hardest guy to get anything out of." She tapped a bare foot. "You don't even move your ears."

"I'm sorry?"

"You don't say much."

"No."

They looked past one another for a while, and then Raphael asked Amelia if she wanted a lift home, and she said no thanks, she didn't want to stink the car out.

...

Tiago was looking in the bathroom mirror. He had a thinner neck than Rogerio, so the gold chain placed the crucifix between his breasts and level with the comet tail of lovebites Raphael had made. He twisted the cross in his fingers, indulging in lazy metaphysical thoughts; maybe Jesus would heal the wounds Raphael had left, maybe that was profound somehow, maybe he should get the first plane to Lisbon tomorrow morning and never come back.

It was a loser's train of thought, unworthy of its thinker, and luckily it was soon interrupted by a grumbling V8 engine and the rasp of a carelessly set handbrake. Tiago ran into the bedroom, peered out the window, swore, ran halfway down the stairs, turned, ran back up again, stuffed the box of condoms back into the bedside cabinet, and scuttled back down to the front door.

CHAPTER 7

CABIN CREW:
DOORS TO MANUAL PLEASE,
AND CROSS CHECK

Three hours later a cloudy dawn was breaking over Paris. It was grey and dismal, a good day for ducks, who like it wet, and for lovers, who don't care what the weather does.

It was a good day for Raphael. He'd woken to find Tiago asleep beside him in careless perfection; his hair falling across his face, his eyelashes like spider legs, his neck ringed with gold, his hands on the pillow in front of his nose.

Raphael touched the fingers and Tiago clenched his fists. "Dragonfly."

"Sorry?"

"Sleeping is Tiago."

"Sorry baby. You sleep." Raphael sat up and looked out at the approaching storm, sensing a new start, a new story to be told down the years. *Remember that storm on our first morning together?* Soon lightning was forking down in spooky silent tap roots, uplighting the cloud base with the mute flashes of giant searchlights. Raphael counted the thunder claps and smiled; the hard rain was strafing the trees like volleys of tiny arrows, and slapping the window and the wooden balcony, and plopping from the gutter above the glass doors onto the sheepskin rug below.

Raphael sighed; he wanted to stay beside Tiago's warm body, but the leak on the window seal was driving him nuts. He got up, went over to the window, ran his finger inside the frame to re-fit the seal, and slid the door closed, making the room suddenly quiet. It was a good bit of naked DIY, but his reflection in the window shocked him; the night had taken its toll on his face, and though grainy and chiselled was a good look for a model in an aftershave commercial, it wasn't very appealing in real life. A glancing blow of doubt jolted him, a doubt that Tiago's desire wouldn't survive daylight; but then he remembered what that desire had survived so far, and shook the doubt off as unworthy of so constant a heart.

And so constant a heart deserved coffee in bed.

Raphael put his trousers on, took one last longing look at Tiago, and went downstairs to the kitchen. He smiled at the realisation that this would be the first time he'd ever awoken in a new lover's house, wondering if Tiago might find that rather odd, and deciding there wasn't much he could do about that. He found fresh coffee in a sealed jar and whistled softly while he spooned it into an antiquated percolator, but the fridge silenced him; it contained milk, yoghurt, cheese, fish, even shellfish, and fresh fruit and vegetables, and not just potatoes, but weird ones, like broccoli and celery. It was quite unlike any fridge he'd ever owned. He had stumbled across a homemaker.

He started the coffee and milk off on the stove and scanned a cork notice board on the wall; three palm crosses, a card for a salon, two one hundred dollar bills, a postcard from Rio, and a photograph of a soldier, with a girl and a little boy, all smiling. The boy was waving a Portuguese flag and looking almost as cute as Tiago.

Raphael pulled at the postcard to look at the back.

Deus e justo. Deus e amavel.
Abracos, Rogerio xxx.

"Hmm." Raphael snarled. Still, it might be old. He twisted the card.

avril 2012.

The drawing pin popped out and the card fell edgewise onto the cooker with a clang.

"Fuck. Double fuck." Raphael smoothed the card flat, scrabbled for the pin, pinned the postcard back and forced himself out of the kitchen and into the lounge. He'd seen a rather beautiful Pleyel piano the night before. That would keep him out of trouble.

The score on the stand was a Chopin nocturne, horrifically difficult and lightly marked in pencil. Raphael studied it and sighed; another lover who was a better musician than he was, and yet more evidence that muddling through, although preferable to the extreme inconvenience of having to find a pencil, might not be the best way to improve. He abandoned the piano, went across to the sofa, and found his car key on a coffee table next to the waxy remains of three candles. Raphael smiled; he'd intended to take things slowly and tenderly, but Tiago had quickly declared himself *utterly fed up with fucking sofas* and taken him up to bed, the candles forgotten.

Murmuring a quiet *thank you* to a god he didn't believe in, Raphael wandered over to a large, ceiling-high set of bookshelves. At head height there was an old Olivetti typewriter and the young expat family shrine of large, iconic photographs, the first in black and white, a serious, handsome man in dark-framed glasses; unmistakably stern Grandpapa, the revered ancestor. The next was gold-framed, a young bride and groom, longed haired and beautiful, very seventies. But the third picture took Raphael's breath away; a tanned and smiling teenage Tiago, reed-thin, in dusty riding boots, jodhpurs and polo shirt, leading a massive chestnut horse over white sand dunes, with tall pines, eucalyptus, and an azure sky in the background.

Raphael touched the boy's face through the glass. At least he knew now it was love; in the last three hours Tiago's gentle reasoning and other less cerebral talents had defeated all doubt of that. So what if he was on the rebound; wasn't everyone on the rebound? So what if there were ten years between them? Lots of people made that work. And Tiago knew couples who'd been born on the same day and were miserable together. The fact was, Tiago had said, that they were perfect for one another. Love, sex and intimacy were a natural addition to their loving friendship. They would be happy in one another's arms as long as they lived.

It had made perfect sense at 2.30am and Raphael felt no inclination to let it unravel now. He took the picture in his arms and held the cold glass tight against his skin while he scanned the teeming bookshelves. Hundreds of books, maybe a thousand, on everything from catholic theology to astrophysics, politics to volumes of poetry. There were two rows of books on birds; bird atlases, guides to the birds of Europe, Asia, the Americas, books about bird migration and the lives of birds, even the history of the discovery and naming of birds. Raphael frowned; he knew bugger all about birds, but they were clearly Tiago's big thing, so he would make an effort. He slid the largest book off the shelf. It was an illustrated atlas of Portuguese birds, the cover showing a pastel drawing of a handsome, long-tailed, black-capped bird with Prussian blue wings and pink breast. Raphael found the name of the cover bird – a magpie – and put the book back before moving to the glass doors that gave onto the garden.

Day was breaking in the gaps between the storm clouds, and Raphael welcomed it with a nod; the past was purged and dawn was rushing towards him, a smiling, flaxen-haired, Mucha virgin, her arms laden, for some reason, with lilacs. A surge of joy left him reeling, his head filled with one of Rob's absurd pump-up, pre-running mantras of banal optimism. *There is time, there is time, there is time, there is time, there is time, there is time, there is time.*

He closed his eyes, wanting the future to start, savouring the new and sweet conviction that he wasn't destined to be lonely for the rest of his life. Somebody wanted the love he had to give. Someone worthwhile and good understood him, and wanted to be held by him, and called an angel, and told he was more beautiful than the night. And that somebody wasn't just anybody, but a beautiful, forgiving young man of integrity.

And Raphael was going to bring him coffee.

There was a loud hiss.

"Fuck." He ran through and took the milk off the heat. "Right." He put the picture down and glanced at the boy. "Where do you keep things my beautiful darling?" He looked in cupboards, selected blue and white cups and saucers, placed them on a red tray. "Are you a coffee cup? You look like a coffee cup. You'll do." The first breakfast was important.

In the bedroom, Tiago was still out for the count. Raphael placed the tray on the bedside cupboard and sat on the bed, drinking in the perfection of Tiago's sleeping form; a Canova, no less, as perfect as an alabaster knight. Raphael swallowed hard; he would reward this angel, his restorer. He would throw a force field around him, protect him from all the suffering and menace in the world, forever. And he would wake him with Monteverdi, '*O mia vita, O mio tesoro*'.

Tiago murmured into the pillow. "Kittens in bread are fucking awesome." He turned his head, opened his eyes and smiled. "Oh, hello."

Raphael smiled back. "Hello you. I made coffee. I hope I used the right things."

"It smells great." Tiago sat up and turned the cross, putting Jesus at the front, facing forward, the guardian of the gate.

But Raphael knew the magic word, so he smiled. "That's beautiful."

"Thanks. I wear it in bed. To keep the vampires away."

Raphael traced the love bites on Tiago's neck. "It doesn't work."

"Apparently not." Tiago stretched. "So what have you been up to?"

"Oh, you know. Prowling around, learning about you."

"So I'm busted, am I?"

"Well, I know you eat properly, and you don't like pop music."

Tiago frowned. "I do. But only epic stuff about sex, and guilt and death. Sinister undertones of bondage and crude religious iconography." He smiled. "You know?"

Raphael grinned; it was pretty good for someone still brushing sleep from his eyes. "Indeed. And you play piano better than I do, and you speak a fuck of a lot of languages."

Tiago yawned. "Only seven actually, including Mandarin."

"That's all?"

"There's really no end to my talents."

"And you like birds."

Tiago gave a tight little smile. "Oh, that. Yes, well, that's schoolboy collecting stuff. I used to watch birds when I was a kid, especially during migration. I still feed them. I have feeders out in these gardens." He nodded towards the window. "And I learned all the names. You never forget that kind of shit. That stuff you learn as a kid. It stays."

Raphael was keen to impress. "I've learned one. Blue magpie. *Cyanopica cyanus*. Pega. You marked the page in the bird atlas." He stopped; maybe he'd been snooping too much, poking around inside books. "And I learned that you ride."

"Oh, that photo." Tiago smiled the tight smile again, looked away. "Inês, my cousin, she took it the last summer before college. The sand dunes in the Alentejo, the pine forests. We rode on the beach, in the waves. It's fucking awesome. You ride really hard, and when you fall it's just deep white sand and pine needles."

"Do you fall a lot?"

"I do. All the time. I'm not good enough to ride as fast as I do."

"You're from there? From the south?"

Tiago looked out of the window. "I was born there. I grew up in Lisbon."

"Right." Raphael watched the looking away, knowing he was being distanced for asking too many questions. He should lighten things up. "No riding hat to protect your giant brain."

"Nobody bothers in Portugal. I come from a simple people, close to the ground. Especially when I fall off." Tiago stretched and smiled. "I'm afraid one thing you haven't yet learned is that I am a complete fucking idiot sometimes."

"Yet another thing we have in common." Raphael smiled back, immensely relieved. "But that's an immense horse."

"Yes, O Campeão, eighteen hands. Silly bastard tried to kill me twice. My fault, of course." Tiago spider-walked a hand up Raphael's arm. "You like to ride hard, don't you?"

"Yes."

"Horses?"

"Stallions." They shared a grin, and Raphael lifted the hand and kissed the back of it, the palm, the inside of the wrist. "I like your other photographs. Especially scary grandpa."

Tiago was silent for a few seconds. "Oh right. You mean O Avô João. I guess he was scary. He died in seventy-four, before I was born."

"Seventy-four." Raphael closed his eyes; idiot. "Oh God. Of course. Fuck. I'm so sorry."

Tiago smiled and squeezed his hand. "Hey, don't worry. How were you to know? No one gives a damn about Portuguese history." He rubbed his eyes. "O Avô João is our family hero. He died under torture, electrical torture. I can't imagine that."

"No." Raphael knew his failings, but cowardice wasn't one of them. He knew he would sooner die than let harm come to someone he could defend, and he wanted to say that now, but the right words were slow in coming, and Tiago was telling the story saying that he wanted to be as brave as Avô João, that he wasn't sure what that would mean for him.

Raphael sighed. "Still plenty of fascist fuckers out there baby. More now than ever."

"Yes." Tiago grinned and sat up. "Hey, I know. You could sell them bad art for lots of money. That would be brilliant. You already give beautiful things to good people with no money, like the girl for Ontario. So you could copy them and sell the fakes to rich fascists, bankrupt them. And the rich fuckers could never admit they'd been conned. That would be so sweet. That would be justice."

There comes a time in every relationship when you know you've met your match; you've read the same books, you have the same taste in music, you like the same wallpaper. Had it been the wallpaper thing Raphael would have been able to say something. As it was, he looked at his nails and let Tiago carry on talking.

"And I could fuck up their investment portfolios. Deliberately, I mean. Or I could fake a mine, make them buy worthless land. I've always wanted to do that. It's easy if you understand geophysics."

Raphael looked at the coffee pot. "It's an idea."

"Did you see the photograph in the kitchen?" They were Tiago's elder cousins, João and Inês, and the little boy was Tiaginho, João's son, just five but smart as a whip. "I'm his favourite babysitter. He's coming to Paris in the summer. We're going to eat the Eiffel Tower. It's made of black spaghetti, you see. You can come too, and watch us." Tiago stretched and pulled the quilt up, covering the cross. "And Inês is a doctor. She's bringing her girlfriend to our quinta in the Alentejo in July. We'll go too. It'll be too fucking hot but it's beautiful and we can ride horses and go surfing." He glanced at the tray and sighed. "That coffee smells good. Can we have some?"

"Sure." Raphael picked up a cup. "Are your parents there then?" He turned the cup over: *Ceramica do São Placido*. "Will we meet them too, in the Alentejo?" He put the cup down. "When we go in July?"

But Tiago was staring out the window at rain that wasn't there.

...

Two doors away Amelia turned smiling in her half-sleep, drooling slightly on her pillow. Separating Raphael from his money was going to be as easy as peeling a ripe banana. And it was going to be fun. Raphael was interesting and complex; a tough guy, a bit of a Kingston Black, a vigorous, bitter sharp apple, serious and smokey, with lots of tannin. And Tiago seemed quite adorable. She liked his obsessiveness – it was always nice to find another anorak, someone to play Linnaean name games with – and he was surprisingly gentle, considering what he did for a living.

Amelia wished she hadn't asked him about his parents, but it had been impossible not to, seeing him staring at the photo, dismissing the tragedy *Oh, It wasn't so bad, I was only four. I didn't really understand, you know. I was only little.* The last word more honestly bereft than the others. He was more of a Dabinett; mild and sweet, thinner-skinned.

They would make a good couple, a perfect blend, like the Black Dabinett, with its firm, dark, skin; the crisp, sweet white flesh that pinked at the surface when bitten. And they were rare varieties, an Ashkenazy and an orphan; and both, presumably, the end of lines.

Amelia opened her eyes in the darkness. "Fuck a doodle do."

...

"I thought you said the storm was over." Tiago was still looking to the side like a spooky cat.

Raphael watched him, put the coffee cup down again. "It is."

"You closed the window?" Still looking away.

"While you were sleeping. It was coming in, onto the rug. The seal's failed on the outside. I'll fix it for you. It won't take five minutes."

Tiago nodded slowly, sniffed, scratched his head. "Thanks. What time is it now?"

Raphael looked down. One night of passionate love could do a lot of things, but it couldn't heal the human heart, and it couldn't placate disapproving parents; maybe they'd wanted Tiago to be a priest, or marry Inês, or stay in Portugal, or just be somebody different. But there was no smiling graduation picture in the shrine downstairs; in fact there was no picture of

Tiago with his parents at all; just a dead grandpa and a killer horse.

"It's about five thirty. It'll be dawn soon, a beautiful one too, despite the inauspicious weather." He kissed Tiago's hands lots of times, his heart flooding with pity for his brave, rejected young lover.

"Inauspicious." Tiago turned back, glassy eyed. "It's always raining in this fucking country."

"I know. I apologise on behalf of my fucking country." Raphael smiled and stroked Tiago's neck with the back of his hand; only a brute asked questions at breakfast the morning after. It was a time for loving words that would anneal the lurid physical liberties taken during the night. "It is the most beautiful morning of my life. You are peerless and immaculate, and way out of my league." And if you were lucky, set you up for some more. "I am an incredibly lucky fucker, utterly and helplessly in love with you. Give yourself to me angel. Your Raphael wants you."

He pounced, but although Tiago offered up his neck and closed his eyes, he wasn't that easily honeyed. "Where did you get to last night? You came back tasting of apples."

Raphael sat back, thwarted. He wasn't going to talk about Amelia. He wanted Tiago to think that he'd come to his senses all by himself. He turned to the tray. "The coffee's getting cold. I make really good coffee. It's the full extent of my culinary expertise."

"Did you go for a drive?"

Raphael poured. "I wasn't sure if these were the right cups for coffee."

"They're fine."

"Good. Do you want milk in this?"

"No thanks." Tiago stacked up the pillows, leaned against them, took the cup. "Thanks." He blew on the coffee, sipped it, said *wonderful*, took another sip. "Where did you get to?"

"Where did I get to?" Raphael poured milk into his cup. "I just had a drive, a walk, you know. Thought things over."

Tiago emptied the cup, placed it on the tray. "Where?"

"No more questions." Raphael rolled Tiago onto his back. "Desist, young Torquemada."

Tiago laughed and pointed out that Torquemada was fucking Spanish.

...

Amelia sat at a table in her dressing gown, listening to the play growls and low faux yelps from the next apartment but one. Getting the samples wasn't going to be a problem. She had a spare key and had pursued grubbier assignments. But was it the right thing to do? Was it good science? Or was it just lazy opportunism, like shoplifting? After a few minutes she'd made up her mind. She went to the freezer and took out a small Tupperware box labelled *Triploid*, extracted two frozen sample jars labelled *Crispin* and *Jon*, and chucked them in the bin.

"The Duelling Cavalier is now a musical."

...

Three minutes later Raphael and Tiago were lying back on the pillows. Raphael had become the interrogator. "Tell me about this."

They both stared at the squared paper, the neat letters written across and down.

"I'm a wizard." Tiago put his head on Raphael's shoulder. "I have a romantic nature."

"It's not romantic." Raphael traced the letters. "You wanted me to run you through."

"Mmm." Tiago closed his eyes.

Raphael kissed him. "Poor sleepy puma."

"Puma?"

"Your hair is so dark. Both my other lovers were fair. You're my first puma." Raphael grinned; he loved thinking up pet names. "Actually, no. Pumas are cats, and cats are cruel. You're playful, like a wolf cub. Yes. I shall call you wolf cub. My beautiful wolf cub." He looked across at Tiago's silence. "Do you like that?"

Tiago was looking up at him. "You've only slept with two men?"

Raphael shrugged. "I don't party. And I don't sleep with men I don't love. And I don't fall in love easily. But everyone needs different things."

Tiago was silent. Raphael held him closer to reassure him. "It's not about numbers."

"I know."

"It's about the next time. And that will be in my bed, tonight." Raphael smiled, picturing Saturday morning, waking Tiago in the big brass bed with fresh coffee, and croissants from the bakery over the street. It was a good picture. Life was starting to come together.

Tiago sighed. "I'm guessing your bed is an altar to love."

"You're guessing right. And you'll burn on it baby. You'll blaze like a fucking comet."

...

Amelia worked for an hour and then got back into bed and nuzzled her pillow. It was true what Tomas Paul had said. Great science was all about luck. She would give her acceptance speech in Latin, wearing a well-cut black trouser suit and a white shirt, her hair cut into short chunky layers; and people would incorrectly say she was the first sexy lesbian to win the Nobel prize for Chemistry.

PART TWO

GERMINATION

CHAPTER 8

OBJECTS IN THE MIRROR MAY BE CLOSER THAN THEY APPEAR...

...And weather systems move more slowly than you might think. For an hour or so Raphael's storm snagged on the Paris urban heat island and spiralled aimlessly above St-Germain-en-Laye. But eventually the electrical storm went west, and sounds of birdsong, and rainwater gurgling in drains filled the air of the quiet suburbs. In a smart garden about a mile from Tiago's apartment, water seeping through the mossy liner of a hanging basket dropped onto the dome of a red kettle barbecue with the sound of someone striking a gong with a felt hammer. After five minutes a door opened and a russet spaniel sprang out.

"Quiet Wandy." A fair-haired, solidly-built man came out, moved the barbecue, went to the front of the house, checked a padlock on the garage door, the dog padding round after him. The man went back into the house and the dog scooted around the garden, flushing birds from the wet shrubs.

Upstairs, Clara Nelson checked the alarm clock and thanked fuck it was Friday. The bedroom door opened and closed, and someone undressed, her husband probably, and then the mattress dipped away.

"It's me puss paws."

"I know who it fucking is."

"It's me, your hairy monkey man." Rob kissed her hair and the back of her neck.

"That doggy gone out?"

"Yes. It's throwing it down out there." Rob wrapped his legs around her. "Warm me up."

Clara hissed. "Your feet are fucking freezing. Don't touch me with them." There was a moan, and hands stole onto her breasts. "Jesus Robbie. Your fingers are iced bananas."

"I've got a warm banana." Rob turned her towards him, pressed his cock against her belly. "Don't go away this weekend baby." He slid a hand under the covers. "Please. I've hardly seen you this week."

"I have to go. Early music needs me dah-ling." Clara looked at Rob, weighing the factors; she loved him, he wanted her, and she'd be away on Sunday. And it was only six o'clock. "All right then. But no time wasting."

Rob blew on his hands and pushed his fingers inside her. "Warm and wet."

"Subtle start."

"Foreplay is for continentals my love." Rob tilted her onto her back, parted her thighs and entered her with a pleasing sense of entitlement. "Beautiful Clara. Beautiful baby. Don't go away. Don't abandon me for your weird musos."

"Told you, have to. I'm singing."

"So turn over. I can tickle your tonsils. It will help you sing better."

"In a while." Clara liked making love face to face; she had a vague feeling that it set mankind above other species, and a strong conviction that she liked the feel of Rob's torso on her belly while she tightened her arms around his neck and gripped him with her thighs. But she was a reasonable woman in a successful marriage, so after a while she acquiesced, and turned and looked up and back at him as they rocked slowly together. "By all accounts we should be getting pretty bored with all this by now."

"So they say." Rob kissed her shoulders.

"They say couples should try new things together."

"They do." Rob licked her skin. "You taste of ice cream."

Clara closed her eyes. "There's a class in Wagner appreciation starting at the University."

"No. Fuck that. I hate fucking Wagner."

"Fuchsias? Netsuke? Japanese ceramics?"

"Fuck Japanese ceramics." Rob went deeper into her, his hand on her belly, drawing her gently back towards him. "Could it be something we just don't do that often? Because I get a real kick out of doing things that are illegal in Idaho."

Clara breathed deeply. "Indiana, isn't it?" It was a thought, but anal took longer and she had a busy day ahead. "Actually, there isn't time."

"Aww."

"Let's do it on Sunday night when I get back."

"Okay." Rob twisted round her and licked the skin between

her breasts. "You are so beautiful. You are a salty goddess. My beautiful Clara. My darling." He licked his finger.

But Clara pushed his hand away. "No, don't touch that. I'll do that."

It was good sex, in that it drew them closer. But afterwards, while Rob sang badly in the shower, Clara frowned into her mirror. Not at the sight of her body – thirty-eight years old, slender and athletic, and undeniably still beautiful – but at the sudden twin realisations that discovering her brother locked in his flat and seemingly about to take his own life had been a bit of a shock, and that in the ensuing six months the stress that had followed had somehow changed her body, and specifically she had developed a persistent pain under her left arm. She'd assumed the pain, which dated to the night of Raphael's near miss, was simply her heart flexing in sympathy with Raphael's suffering, and she'd ignored it, but six months was getting beyond a joke.

Clara was strong-minded. It was okay that death would come for her. Death came for all living things, and as a true rationalist she knew that eternal life was a far more terrifying prospect. But it would not be okay to slow down and let death catch her up. She had work to do, and she wasn't ready for her body to switch off her brain. And it also wouldn't be okay to spray her midlife crisis around; it happened to everyone, this coming to terms with the beginning of the end of life. Everyone saw the same warning lamp in the cockpit; you were the pilot and it was your job to deal with it. Burdening the people you loved with this kind of stuff was self-indulgent. What if everyone did it? No one would get anything done.

The water stopped. "Shower's free darling."

"Coming." Clara put her thoughts away, knowing there wasn't time for them now, knowing that the best thing to do was plan her fight back in London with Tomas Paul. She smiled. He would tell her to snap out of it, get a sense of proportion. What else were best friends for?

An hour later Clara was sorting through music scores on the piano. A phone rang in the kitchen. Raphael was probably cancelling lunch. He didn't eat much since he'd split from Martin. But then he couldn't boil a fucking egg.

"Can you get that Robbie?" The dog barked. "And can you feed your fucking dog please?"

"It's yours. His Lordship, on his mobile. Wow." The ringing stopped. "How are you doing mate? Yeah, she's next door looking for some music for this DowSoc thing in London this weekend. Yeah, she is a selfish bitch."

"I bet he didn't say "bitch.""

"He did actually." There was a terrific clanging from the kitchen.

"What is that fucking noise Rob?" Clara shoved Dowland and Monteverdi scores into a battered music case and went through to the kitchen.

Wandy was nosing a metal bowl along the slate floor, Rob hoofing at him ineffectually. "Sorry Raph, that was your sister. Yeah, the Professor manque." Rob took the phone away from his ear. "He says fucking charming."

"Fuck off."

"She says, oh, you heard? Will you stop that Wandy? Fucking dog."

The dog barked, having had enough of the swearing, and Ron came over with the phone. "Sorry Raph, yeah. Oh yeah, and how about 20k on Sunday? Yeah? Yeah, great. You're still coming over tomorrow night? Yeah? Staying? Sorry?" He pulled urgently at Clara's arm and goggled at her. "Sure, of course, yes. Meet you in town tomorrow then? Palais Royal café about five? Sure. Here she is. Cheers."

Clara took the phone from Rob and mouthed at him. "Okay?"

Rob mouthed back. "Great. Wants to bring someone over tomorrow night."

Clara put her hand on the phone. "Really?"

Rob nodded and made his eyes bigger than Wandy's.

...

Tomas Paul Gosele didn't particularly love his children. His role model as a parent was the Capitoline Wolf; he gave his twins suck, and he wouldn't let them perish, but he longed for the day they would become independent, and interesting, and remind him of him. Today he was supervising their breakfast from an armchair in the sitting room, and by craning his long neck he could see that things were going swimmingly; Raffaele was juicing half a grapefruit on Emanuela's nose while she tried to whack him on the elbow with a hot spoon.

Four was a lovely age.

Mel's footfall creaked the staircase. Tomas Paul got up, tidied the breakfast table, and wiped the kids' gooey upturned faces with a newspaper. "Hi honey."

"Hi babe." Mel walked past him, untouching. "They eat?"

"Emanuela's had some grapefruit." Tomas Paul went into the hallway and grabbed his jacket. "I'm at DowSoc tomorrow. Remember?" There was a *Sure* from Mel and a squeal from Raffa. Ema had finally made contact. It was time to go. "Late tonight. Investors. Belgravia. Don't wait up."

He pulled the yellow front door closed behind him and looked up at the cochineal masonry. It had been Mel's idea, a surprise, like the twins; but the twins hadn't turned a two million pound house into a fucking Battenburg cake. Still, it annoyed the Kazakhs next door. Actually everything annoyed the Kazakhs next door; pigeons, free newspapers, pizza moped mudguards scraping the cobbles, people nicking the milk. He'd told Zhanik to take it easy; this wasn't Astana, it was a London mews, gracious living. You had to go with the flow.

He filched a pint of gold top and drank it on his way in to Turing.

...

At five to one Patrice flashed a wide-eyed smile at Clara and led her to a quiet table at the back of the restaurant. She took out her phone.

Hi sexy puss ;-) Find out about this someone of Raph's will you? xxx Call me before you set off tonight lovely puss xxx Miss you Robbie

She put the phone away and sat down. She and Raphael always sat at this table. You could talk about anything at this table; eight years ago they'd talked about Rob.

Not much to tell Bella. He's Martin's brother, a half brother, one month younger; the son of John and one of his students. She died when Rob was born, so John and Fenella adopted him, and brought them up together.

He seems really nice.

So call him. You're a grown woman.

And again, a few months later.

It's up to you Bella. I can't decide for you. If you love him, marry him. Don't complicate things. You're clever. Is he clever? Do you respect him for his mind?

Yes. He's intelligent, and he's sharp.

Are you good together?

Yes we are. Very. And he's kind, and reasonable.

So it's love, rather than the other thing?

Love, of course. I'm like you. I don't do the other thing.

Then marry him Bella. Before some other fucker does.

So she did. But the matrix was unbalanced, she and Martin invariably finding themselves standing side by side like two bored horses, while Rob and Raphael had shared each other's ups and downs like dogs share fleas, constantly finding more ways to bind themselves together, and forming such a strong graft that after Martin had gone, it had been Rob that got Raphael through the winter, with nights in with Bialystock and Withnail, Lebowski and Keyser Soze, and weekends of running, and football, of surfing waves and riding horses.

And of course, the odd drink. On the night of the College Christmas Dinner Clara had come home to find her sitting room thick with cigar smoke and distorted Doobies, her husband and brother, crumpled, tie-less, horribly seedy, swigging from litre bottles of airport single malt, Rob lying on the sofa, Raphael standing, lecturing *Will the dancing Hitlers please wait in the wings? We are only seeing singing Hitlers.* And seeing her. *Hey. Hi Bella, sis. Vintage Jean Muir. Perfect on you.* Getting up, swaying, turning to Rob. *Aren't you a lucky fucker?* Rob, an unlit cigar in his mouth, his eyes fleshy pink slits. *Sboofful.* Raphael coming across, his breath reeking. *How were they all sis?* Holding the empty bottle out to Rob, a toast. *The academicals.* And Rob suddenly frantic. *Hey! Raph! Raph! Let's do this bit together mate.* And both men shouting with closed eyes, Raphael's arms out like Christ, Rob shaking his head from side to side like a bladder on a stick. *Without luurrrr-uuuuurrrrr-uuurrrr – uuurrrvve.* Raphael swigging from the bottle. *Fucker's empty.* Throwing the bottle down, turning round startled at the smash, tripping over *Fuck me* disappearing from view. *Christ. Who put that fucking spaniel there?* Crawling back onto the sofa like Mr Hyde, shaking Rob by the shoulders, crying with laughter. *Robert Nelson you fucker, you fucking cunt.* And Rob yelling *MONTY YOU TERRIBLE CUNT* Raphael shouting *Robert Wayland Cuntface Nelson your fucking cunt of a dog tried to kill me* and Rob, rolling from side to side, giggling, snorting, farting. *Raphael, you frucking drunken druntfaced fucking shitfaced crunt. I fucking love you mate. I fucking love you.*

Clara had rescued the dog and closed the door, and nothing was ever said. Nothing needed to be said. Men needed to let off steam occasionally.

Clara took out her phone and was getting ready to do emails for ten minutes when she glimpsed Raphael walking up outside; dark grey suit, white shirt, moss green scarf, sunglasses. She shook her head. Clubmasters on a cloudy day could not go unmentioned.

Raphael let himself in and walked towards her, purposeful. "Bella."

They kissed and sat down.

"Hello darling, you smell lovely. Having a heatwave, are we?"

Raphael took off his sunglasses. "Very droll."

"Jesus Raphael. You look like a fucking panda." He did, but quite a chirpy one. One that had found an entirely new grove of especially juicy bamboo shoots. She leaned towards him, drawn towards his radiation. "Rob said there was someone."

"Did he now?"

She laid a finger on his lapel, lowering her voice. "Tell me everything."

Raphael looked at the table. "Long night. Wonderful night, actually." He rubbed the bridge of his nose and smiled at her from behind his hand. "I'm so fucked. I mean. I'm so tired. I didn't get much sleep. Sorry."

Clara sat back. "And he's fabulous."

"Yes, he is. Completely." He picked up the menu. "It hasn't really sunk in yet."

Clara nodded, drinking in the sea change. Having looked like shit for months after the split with Martin, Raphael had looked pretty good for the last few weeks. But this was different. The brave-faced brittle high of caffeine and cigarettes had gone. Now there was a perky freshness, a scrubbed aura like a new skin. It was hope. And it was pouring out of him.

Patrice came over and poured champagne, one arm behind his back, like a proper waiter. "Have you chosen, madam, sir?"

Raphael closed the menu. "Oh, fuck it. I don't know. What's good today Patrice?"

"Well sir, the lobster is excellent."

"Excellent. Fancy that sis? Lobster?"

"Always." Clara nodded.

"The risotto is also very good." Patrice leaned over, whispered into Raphael's ear, straightened up, and stared ahead like a sentry.

Raphael closed his eyes. "Whatever you recommend, Patrice."

"Lobster for madam, risotto for sir. Excellent." Patrice took the menus, raised his eyebrows at Clara, and walked smartly away.

Clara leaned forward. "What did he say?"

Raphael shook his head. "Nothing Patrice says is ever worth repeating."

"Go on."

Raphael rubbed his eyes. "Cheeky little fucker suggested I needed to get my strength back." He looked towards the kitchen. "This city is a fucking village. Do people really have nothing better to do than talk abut other people?"

Raphael's dignity was ridiculous. It could only mean one thing; it was serious. Clara grinned. "Us being? Name being?"

Raphael put his glass down quietly. "Tiago." He made the word three legato syllables, tasting each one on his tongue. "He's called Tiago."

"Lovely." Clara could read her brother like a book. Today's page was a poem, *Tiago,* powerful stuff, the title alone an abracadabra with the power to melt Raphael with memory; the taste, the touch, the scent of this perfect new lover. With time it might just be a name again, but right now it was raw and sacred, and Raphael was helpless. He couldn't disconnect the word from what it did to him. He couldn't say "Tiago" and chew gum at the same time.

Or hear it for that matter. For a little sister used to being pushed around it was irresistible.

She smiled and fed the habit. "Tiago?"

"He's called Tiago. He's from Lisbon."

"Beautiful name, Tiago. Very beautiful. And does it suit him? Tiago?"

Raphael sighed and shook his head. "Oh, yes." He smiled. "Yes, Tiago. Tiago Jose. Tiago Jose da Silva." He looked down. "And a whole load of other names I can't remember yet."

Clara touched her brother's arm. "Hey, Raphael. Da Silva, Davide."

"Sorry?"

Clara wrote air words. "Da Silva, Davide. Raphael and Tiago da Silva Davide."

"Sis."

"I'm just saying. It flows. It's elegant."

"Well don't just say. Don't tempt the fucking gods. " Raphael rested his chin in his hand. "Though I admit it does sound good. Da Silva Davide." He smiled, looked younger. "He says he's wanted to be with me for a long time. For years. I had absolutely no idea."

Clara grinned; no shit. Raphael ignored everything until he

couldn't anymore, and was consequently in a continuous state of shock and awe. "Gosh. Did he seduce you darling?"

Raphael looked away, choosing words from across the room. "You know. I think he might have. At first, anyway."

Clara put her chin in her hands. "So what's he like?"

"Well, he's very clever."

Of course he was clever. Raphael could no more love a stupid man than he could love an ugly one, or a racist, or someone who wore baseball hats. Clever was a given. But there were other things that mattered. "What else?"

"Well." Raphael looked at the table. Where to start? Tiago was intelligent, and gentle, and loving, and beautiful, quite flawless, physically perfect, slender, but strong, perfectly proportioned, like the Canova Eros, but without the wings, obviously.

"You're sure about the wings?"

Raphael smiled; maybe he just hadn't seen them yet. And he was subtle, understated, not into fashion, or tattoos, or that kind of thing. "Actually he's rather old fashioned, I suppose. Square. Uncool. A bit geeky."

"Classic."

Raphael smiled and nodded. "Yes. Classic. Good word. He likes chess, and classical music, and poetry, Renaissance paintings. And he's spiritual, a Christian actually, but the good kind, no hang ups. Jesus loves him, and me, and us, together apparently. The whole thing."

Clara pursed her lips. "Oh. Is he going to save you?"

"Don't know. Don't care. But his eyes, my god." Raphael

shook his head and then looked up. "God, I'm sorry sis. Tell me to shut up."

Clara smiled. "It's been too long honey. Too long since you were in love."

"Yes. I was considering giving up and becoming a shallow bastard like everyone else."

"I know." She sipped her champagne. "So where is he now, your paragon?"

Raphael smiled. "My paragon. Well when I last saw my paragon he was asleep." He gazed past her for a while, then coughed and looked down at the table. "He's inexperienced, but he's trusting, incredibly loving."

Clara smiled, not quite sure what "inexperienced" meant, but with a pretty good idea of what "incredibly loving" did. It meant he did what Raphael wanted. "Good."

"He's off work today. He's getting his hair cut. He has beautiful hair. Long, well, like mine."

"You mean too long?"

"Not too long. Collar length, and it's a sort of dark chestnut, very shiny, very soft." He tapped his fingertips on the table. "Sorry. I'll shut up."

"Not on my account." Clara reached across, squeezed his arm again. "So, what does he do?"

"Credit Dijonais, commodities trading. South America."

"Really?" It was a rictus grin but Clara couldn't back out of it. "That's good." That was not good. She'd hoped for someone real this time; a doctor, or a nurse, or maybe a teacher; someone caring and loving, someone who might look after Raphael, put him first. Not some Ritzy stick insect of a banker with a shiny suit and a snowy nose. She stared into her glass. "Successful?"

Raphael shrugged. "I guess so. Actually he's a mathematician. Well, just a Masters. He's twenty-nine. He speaks a million languages." He looked down. "The thing is Clara, he's got money. He's made money. He's wealthy."

"Great. So he's not just after your money, and you're not just after his body."

Raphael covered his face. "Oh don't sis. Please." He peered at her through his fingers. "Don't even joke about it. You have no idea how fucking frightening it is to be thirty-nine and on your own in this city. You question everything, everyone's motives."

Clara felt guilty, but not that guilty. "Darling, don't get so heavy. Maybe it's the other way round. Maybe he's after your body and you're after his money. Don't glare at me like that. What else have you got to go on at this stage?"

Raphael took his hands away. "Nothing."

"Exactly. Don't complicate things. He's beautiful, he's clever, he's gentle. You're a lovely decent man. It's all good." She emptied her glass. "All good."

"Sure." Raphael looked up and smiled. "Sure." His phone buzzed on the table. "Sorry darling." He looked at the screen. "It's him. He wants to know where we are."

"He's missing you." Clara sipped her drink. "That phone is shit by the way."

"I know." Raphael frowned. "I can never remember this address." He sat back from the table and raised his hand gently. "Patrice, what's the address of this place?"

Patrice came across, rested his hand on the back of Raphael's chair, glanced at the screen. "Number twenty-three sir."

Raphael nodded. "Yes of course it is." He looked at Clara. "What is it?"

"Nothing."

Patrice went away and Clara smiled. "He read the message over your shoulder."

"Good for him." Raphael looked at the phone, not taking the hint.

Clara let it go and nodded towards Patrice. "You're still public property."

"Seemingly, though I rather hope my days as "Eligible Bachelor most likely to fuck Patrice silly and then buy him stuff" are numbered."

"Did you ever go for that drink with him?"

"With Patrice? No, thank fuck." Raphael was pressing the keys with deliberation, as if he thought that each character, once selected, could never be deleted. Clara suspected that in fact he did think exactly that. He had certainly shunned email since the day he'd seen a carefully crafted message appear on Rob's laptop in an ugly font with erratic line breaks.

That's not what I fucking wrote. That looks like a fucking monkey wrote it. And he hated texting. At least, he used to.

Clara watched him press the keys. "They call it short message service darling."

An age passed. "I thought he asked you lots, Patrice." She sipped her champagne. "Dozens of times."

Raphael ignored her with the effortless rudeness that makes

every brother sister relationship so endlessly rewarding. "In fact, he asked me twice." He looked up. "So how would you describe this place?"

"I don't know. How about 'an elegant haunt where very upmarket Italian food is served with some elan by flirtatious, persistent and highly-sexed waiters?'"

"Perfect." Raphael typed a quick message and sent it. "Right. I couldn't be bothered typing all that crap so I just wrote "Number twenty-three, Italian place, good food, easy waiters."

Patrice swanned over with their food.

Clara waited for him to go away. "Right tell me more. I want to know everything and I've got to leave at two. How long have you known him?"

Raphael picked up his fork. It had been about six years, but he'd never dreamed that there could be anything, and of course he'd been with Martin. Raphael put his head on one side, holding the unused fork mid air. "I saw him play the guitar a few years ago. He played *Jerez*, at an Embassy party. Borrowed a guitar from one of the musicians, you know. I stood at the back, watching. He was perfect, unreal, someone you might dream of loving, someone that might really break your heart, and you'd almost think it was worth it."

Clara nodded. This was so entirely typical of Raphael; falling in love with perfection, telling himself it could never happen because he belonged to someone else, screening it out. But she liked Albeniz. Tiago might grow on her. Raphael had drifted off so she blew at him.

"Hello."

"Sorry." Raphael put his fork down and shook his head. "I'm sorry Bella. It's still too raw to discuss here." He smiled. "Can we talk about DowSoc?"

They ate lunch and tried to talk about music, but everything kept coming back to Tiago, and Clara was soon an authority on the books, and the birds, and the music, and the perfect knowledge of everything that mattered that made Tiago so spectacularly suited to be her brother's new lover. After ten minutes they got round to talking about the music Clara would sing at DowSoc.

"Perfect for your voice." Raphael poured her some water. "Will Tomas Paul be there?"

"Yes. I Skyped him at Turing on Monday. He looked well. He asked after you."

"I haven't seen him since Salzburg last year. Whitsun. Give him my love, won't you?" He went back to his food. "And to Mel, and the twins of course. "

Clara nodded. Tomas Paul and Raphael had been together for years before Martin had appeared; a long distance thing, but they'd always seemed happy, and they were still friends. Of course, it was a little odd of Tomas Paul to name both his children after his ex; but Raphael was their godfather, and Mel didn't seem to mind. "I will. Can I tell him about your paragon?"

Raphael laughed. "By all means. Tell everybody. Tell the world."

"So I'll tell him you're in love, shall I?"

Raphael nodded. "Yes, do. I am." He grinned. "I didn't think I ever could be again."

"That's good." Clara sighed hard. "I mean, after what

happened last year." She smiled, but a moment too late, and then she made it worse. "You know. When Martin left? You got very tired."

Raphael had stopped eating, and was watching her, so she tried to box it all up again. "And now it's good. You've found someone new, you're in a better place. That's good. Change is good."

Raphael put his fork down. "Where are you going with this Bella?"

Clara looked away. "Nowhere."

"You are. I can tell. You're theorising. You're thinking about shaking things up, aren't you?"

Clara smiled; thank god she was the intuitive one. "Actually, no."

"You bloody are." Raphael took her hands, held them tight. "Look, Bella. You need to hear this. Change isn't good. Change hurts people." He closed his eyes. "My life changed from good to bad, from success to failure, overnight. Hmm, now. Was that change good? Dunno. Let's see. Before, good wine, comfort, home, a faithful partner, I thought, wanting me, I thought." Rising anger turned his voice to a rasp. "After, fuck all. None of the above; just emptiness, empty house, empty bed, faithless partner having fucked off with someone half my age. Change is good. What a fucking stupid thing to say." He dropped her hands. "Even for you."

Clara pushed her chair back, furious. "That is the first fucking time you have ever talked to me about any of this shit." She felt tears coming, forced them back. "And I was so scared. I thought you were losing hope. I thought you would do something terrible to yourself." She covered her face with her hands and shook.

They sat in a bubble of ugly silence for a few seconds. People carried on eating, knives and forks scraping plates. Someone laughed like a horse, *nyah-hah-hah*.

Clara recovered herself and drank from her water glass. "Sorry about that."

She looked up. Raphael was sitting back, looking guilty. "Oh Jesus." He drank down his water glass and shook his head. "I'm so sorry sis. I've never found it easy to talk about it. It hurt so much. I've only just recently been able to get angry about it. " He took her hand. "But I shouldn't be angry with you. I'm sorry."

Clara sniffed and drank more water. "I'm sorry too."

"I know." Raphael looked at her intently, sat up straight, took a deep breath. "Listen Clara. Don't manufacture pain. There's enough of it in the natural world, coming your way, coming our way. Don't be curious about it. Don't look for it, enough of it will find you." He shook his head. "You've got a good man, better than good."

"I know."

Raphael shook his head. "No. You really don't." He took her other hand. "Look. Do you remember before Christmas, when you came back and found us out of our fucking skulls? Did he ever tell you why?"

"No." A little sister pout. "I knew he'd helped you with your weird bonfire, your faux Suttee, burning all those papers and photographs, all that perfectly good furniture, like a diphtheria outbreak. I assumed you were just letting off steam like men do."

"Letting off steam like men do." Raphael sighed. "Yes we were, and yes he did help me. He didn't question me once. And that day he'd been to England to sort things out with Martin, to get him to agree to sign everything, close everything down – joint accounts, investments, the wine, all the property, everything we jointly owned." He rubbed his eyes, looked at her. "And Martin had said he'd sign, and that he'd never speak to him again. Imagine that. His own brother." He looked away. "Rob took my side. It was hard for him, but he did it because it was the right thing to do." He stared at her. "He's decent. Don't do anything to hurt him Bella. Please promise me you won't."

"I won't." Clara sighed. Raphael had no imagination. He could only view other people's experience through the lens of his own life. This was why you had to handle things alone. "I'm sorry. I didn't mean to worry you."

Raphael sighed and touched her arm. "Let's not argue darling." He shook his head. "I know life gets routine sometimes. I'm no good with that either. But for God's sake don't hurt Rob. Some things are irreversible. Only a fucking idiot thinks that an affair saves a marriage."

Clara shook her head; absolutely no imagination. "Look. I have neither the time, nor the inclination, nor the energy for an affair. I've just been tired recently."

"I know. You must take better care of yourself." He took her hand again, squeezed. It was a frequent gesture, that meant *You are my beautiful sister and I will take care of you.*

Clara sipped water, counted to five. "You know you've never spoken about Martin before."

"It's not exactly my favourite subject." Raphael sighed. "Look, let's just eat darling. I'm starving." They ate in silence for a minute, the tension ebbing away, the restaurant filling up and growing noisier around them.

"I'm sorry Raphael. This should be a happy day for you."

Raphael smiled at her. "It is. Nothing can change that." He suddenly brightened. "Oh yes. I was going to say. I met one of your fan club."

"Really?"

"Yes. English girl. Amelia." He looked around. "I need more water. Where's Patrice?"

Clara looked across at Patrice. "Over there. Staring into space as usual." But he wasn't, he was staring at a slim, pale, dark haired young man in the doorway, dressed in jeans, a black hooded top, a military jacket. People looked up from their lunch and stared at him; most then went on eating, a few went on staring. It was, after all, just a boy in a doorway.

···

Tomas Paul disliked his first year statistical thermodynamics tutorial on Friday afternoons, but he was a professional, and so at two o'clock he was calling the kids in and telling them to sit down and mark each other's assignments, and do it quietly for fuck's sake.

He picked up the lute, leaned back in his swivel chair and played Lachrimae. The plane trees outside were bursting into lime green leaf. He scanned the branches for something auspicious; a sparrow hawk, an owl, a Dryad hanging upside down like a trapeze artist.

What the fuck are you doing up there?

She'd turned her head. *I'm thinking. Problem?*

Don't be impertinent. Get dressed and come in here before someone normal sees you.

The girl had tightrope-walked along the bough, climbed through his office window, and pulled on jeans and sweater from her climber's rucksack. He'd made her drink coffee but she'd been perfectly lucid.

I'm Amelia Postthridge. I'm what you might call the inevitable geneticist. You know, wacko dad, junkie mum, three older sisters as thick as fucking mince. Pardon my French.

She was odd so he'd checked her out on the computer.

There's no Amelia Postthridge on the College directory.

She'd sighed and put her cup down.

I'm registered as Thalia Rockingham. Pointing with a dirty fingernail at the name, the line of straight-A module results. *There. That's me. But my grandmother was Elsie Postthridge.*

Really? Tomas Paul knew Postthridge. She was a post-war heroine, a nutritionist who'd prescribed diets that had saved the lives of Belsen survivors, a wizened old lady on a banknote.

Yes really. I took her name. In her honour. Though not the Elsie, obviously. There are limits.

A week later she'd walked past jiggling a jam jar of frogspawn, creepily gleeful. *Lovely jubbly stem cells magister.* She'd hatched the tadpoles and done things to the frogs that would have broken a heron's heart, but over the years Tomas Paul had fallen for Amelia in the harmless academic way, a Pygmalion passion culminating in a Lonely Hearts ad: *Kooky BMI 18 blonde twitcher, twenty-four, likes film noir, early music, cider, dead languages, free swimming, seeks male sociopath with Reverse Polish Notation calculator for sperm. Non-smoker preferred.*

"Lovely jubbly stem cells." He twanged the bass string and looked across at the silent, bemused students. They were getting a lot of entertainment for nine thousand pounds a year.

CHAPTER 9

GET A ROOM, BOYS

Raphael turned round and melted rapidly from the shoulders down, a snowman under a blowtorch. "Oh. It's him. Tiago."

Clara steadied their glasses. "Careful darling." But it was clearly too late for that.

The boy walked over with his hands in his pockets in a kind of Portuguese, shoe-gazey anti-swagger, smiled at Clara, and greeted Raphael with a shy formal grace that suggested he might have preferred to bow. Raphael gazed at Tiago, Tiago kissed Clara three times, Patrice came over and fussed about with chairs and champagne, Tiago smiled at him like sunlight bouncing off a glacier, and Patrice walked away.

"Well." Tiago sipped his champagne. "Easy was something of an understatement." He put his glass down and smiled at Clara. "If I were that good looking I wouldn't try that hard."

Clara smiled back; Tiago wasn't bad looking but she would go easy on the compliments until she knew whether he deserved them. "Indeed."

Tiago leaned towards Raphael, letting his fringe brush Raphael's cheek; a mild invasion of space like one friendly pony nosing another. "It was a different boy at the salon. He was nice." He took out an appointment card. "Adel."

"Persian name." Raphael took the card, turned it over in his fingers, showed the back to Tiago. "He thought you were nice too." He took out a book of matches. "Shall I?"

Tiago shrugged. "By all means."

Clara watched the card burn; Raphael's Rules. *Come here. Sit down. Drink this. That's perfect on you. Nice voice but she looked about as Japanese / Polovtsian / Ethiopian as Donald Fucking Duck.* The lazy hyperbole of the weary aesthete. *Inexcusable, unforgiveable, unbelievable.* And sentences that began with the words *Do you know, I will never understand why* and ended with a wry, disappointed observation on the ugliness of modern life. It was a game that needed two players, and Tiago was clearly up for it, still glowing with the shiny, shag-happy ecstasy of new possession. *Look at me and my big alpha. We command and obey each other. He's impossible, but I can handle it. It's hot.*

Raphael looked across at her. "So Clara's husband is the famous Rob I told you about."

Clara nodded. "Yes. Oh and Raphael, he says definitely twenty kilometres on Sunday darling." She smiled at Tiago. "Do you fancy that?" Doubtless Tiago could think of better things to do on Sunday morning. Going to church, maybe.

Tiago shook his head gently. "I love running, but not twenty kilometres. Not on a Sunday."

Raphael grinned. "I didn't know you ran."

But he did. Of course he did. Tiago ran a sub-thirty ten "on a good day", had "actually" won medals for Portugal in the student games "he was lucky, just happened to hit a run of good form at the right time." He was modest, and brief, and Clara began to warm to him.

Raphael grinned. "That's amazing."

Tiago shook his head. "Not really. Someone has to win. My College friends still call me Bambi. Which is quite annoying."

Raphael frowned. "Not the Portuguese Puma?"

Tiago gave him a shy smile. "No. I wanted to be the Lisbon Lynx but Bambi stuck."

"I'll call you the Lisbon Lynx if you like baby."

Clara sat back. *Baby.* It was good that they were happy, constructing the matrix to wrap new love around, discovering trivial yet fascinating things in common that would nucleate the fascinating new thing that was "them". It was quite charming in a way, like the nuzzling kids on the College lawn. But being an audience of one was pretty awkward, and maybe Tiago wouldn't be quite so thrilled when the real Raphael appeared; austere, stubborn and demanding. But he was away from the table right now, and a body snatcher in a Raphael suit was watching Tiago speak.

"You're PSG I guess?"

"Of course. You Benfica?"

"Hell, no. Sporting. Do you like football Clara?"

It was a chance to vent and Clara took it. "God no. I fucking hate football. Absolutely hate and detest it. Ghastly pointless game, goes on for ages, awful, dreary, utter waste of time."

Raphael nodded. "She hates football."

"Clearly not a huge fan." Tiago grinned. "You're a singer, Raphael said."

Clara waved it away. "Raphael is the star musician. He was in the European Student Orchestra."

"Really?"

Raphael glowered at her and shrugged. "For a few years. I played a little."

Clara lowered her voice. "For three years. Principal cellist."

Tiago beamed. "Really? I didn't know. It's my favourite instrument." He reached for Raphael's arm. "Will you play for me?"

"Of course. Tonight if you like." Raphael coughed. "Or tomorrow."

Clara didn't want to hear about tonight or tomorrow. She picked up her phone and tapped some buttons. "Oh sorry, boys, excuse me." But no apology was necessary. She was no longer there. She stared at the keypad and overheard an amusing anecdote about someone who had slept till ten, and been woken by a florist with a dozen long stemmed ivory roses from someone called "R", who was clearly a very inconsiderate person, but this was okay, because R had a very romantic and impulsive nature. R was also, apparently, rather demanding, but this was also okay, because he was demanding in all the right ways.

Clara typed her indignation into her keypad.

Oh get a fucking room.

...

Tomas Paul was looking at Aishah's answers. He didn't need to. They'd all be perfect. Aishah was, as the other students said, *awesome.* Her dad was the mayor of Kuala Lumpur, or something like that, she was intelligent and hard working, and most importantly she showed an endless capacity for being amused by Tomas Paul's silly pranks.

"Aishah."

"Prof?" A smile of serene beauty, set off by a fuschia pink headscarf. Lovely Aishah. She thought Tomas Paul was great.

"Question 3. You could have used the Zarniwoop transformation to get there." Tomas Paul shrugged. "It would have been quicker."

Aishah looked away for a few seconds, turned back deadpan and agreed it would have been quicker than the Slartibartfast operator. Lovely Aishah. She'd do well. Maybe one day she'd be President of Petronas, or Prime Minister of Malaysia. A Renaissance girl. She even played cello in the College orchestra.

Tomas Paul stared back into the trees. The cello had once been his favourite instrument.

...

Clara got to her feet. "Boys, I'm so sorry but I must get to the airport."

Raphael stood and took her arm. "Oh sis, I'm sorry. Don't go."

Clara shook her head. "It's all right darling. I really must go." She kissed Tiago. "Wonderful to meet you. See you Sunday maybe?"

Tiago nodded. "Thank you. Have a good time in London."

Raphael walked her to the door mumbling apologies, but Clara was feeling big.

"Don't apologise for anything. I was stupid earlier." She kissed his cheek. "He's lovely."

"Lovely." Raphael nodded and looked back. "Yes."

"He's perfect for you. I'm so happy." She kissed him. "Perfect."

"Mmm?" Raphael was oblivious, staring at Tiago as if aliens were about to take him away.

Clara shook her head. "Go back to bed. You're not fit for company."

"No, I know. I'm sorry Bella."

"Don't apologise. I couldn't be happier."

Clara went outside to button up her coat and looked back through the window; Raphael and Tiago sat, Patrice sauntered over with a tray, Raphael introduced him, Tiago gave him his hand to shake, Patrice took it, smiled broadly. They were playing nicely. Clara got into her car, took out her phone, left a long message on Rob's voicemail confirming that Tiago was perfect, and looked at the clock on the dashboard. She had ages; but she would head to the airport and work there. She started the car and her phone rang.

"Hi honey. Sorry I couldn't pick up then. How is he?"

"Brilliant. Absolutely brilliant. Up all night with this new guy, Tiago, commodities trader, Portuguese, at Credit Dijonnais. Beautiful eyes, lovely jacket, gorgeous buttons."

"Sounds deep."

"Oh but he is, he's clever, and lovely. He crashed our lunch, couldn't bear to be away from Raphael. He's rather reserved, but he's absolutely beautiful, and funny and modest."

"You're not sure about him yet then?"

"Fuck off. He's lovely, slim and good looking."

"Like me."

"Slim. And he smells gorgeous."

"Again."

"And he's warm and sweet."

"Like custard."

"Fuck off. I'm excited. Raphael's totally besotted. It's very cute, they're all tactile." She checked her mascara in the rear view mirror. "God, I'm so fucking relieved."

"How old is he?"

"Twenty-nine. He looks a lot younger though, and seems it. And he runs, Tiago. Five and ten k."

"Good. We can use him as a pacesetter."

"I'm just so bloody pleased he's found someone. This last year has been a nightmare."

She drove to the airport and went straight to the airline lounge. A little girl was asleep on a sofa; fair hair, the shade they used to call baby blonde, like that English girl's hair, the new postdoc she'd met last week. Clara had liked her, and admired her cleverness, and her otherness, her modernity, her effortless beauty, jeans, a sweater and green Doc Martens. They'd talked about apples, and probability and risk, and whether you could trace the evolution of RNA and DNA to see how different varieties had evolved, the girl stabbing at the air with a short-nailed forefinger, getting excited about the science of data, and how you could apply it to predict how traceable things were, to recreate their look, their taste.

You see certain apples in Roman art, Etruscan art. And then Renaissance art. So you know what they were eating. The girl had shrugged. *And maybe you could even spot a fake picture. Because the apple variety would be wrong. Too early.*

Clara's laptop booted up sluggishly, overloaded with macros. She stared at the black screen hoping today was the start of a new chapter. She hadn't liked the last one at all; it had begun with a terse Raphael on her doorstep on a summer evening, giving her his phone, turning and going without explanation, the phone ringing seconds later.

Raphael baby, thank God you've answered. Jesus I was worried darling. Look, come home baby. We need to talk. He's no one baby, it's nothing. We had a few drinks after a viva, and it got out of hand.

She'd interrupted, and Martin had laughed at first, and then become "difficult."

Look Martin, why don't you just write him a letter?

Look Clara, why don't you just fuck off, you silly barren bitch. Click.

But maybe this was a new beginning. Raphael had found love and purpose with someone at least half decent. Your luck could change just like that.

The laptop went to sleep but Clara sat up straight. Raphael's resurgence hit her like a sudden slap, one she should have given herself. There was something wrong with her, possibly something serious, and she'd been a fool to do nothing. But now science was going to save her life. She made a quick phone call, cashed in a few academic favours, and by the time her flight was landing in London she was staring into the serene white abyss at the centre of an MRI machine, making a mental note to find out what on earth that weird clanging was.

HAPTER 10

2/0

$\mathcal{A}$t five thirty-seven that evening the showers over Paris had stopped, and the battered plants on the balcony of Raphael's apartment were perking up. At five thirty-eight a late sunbeam bypassed the foliage, found a flaw in a window pane, and painted a spectrum across Tiago's closed eyes.

The blue light woke him. He opened his eyes to look for the Iberian sun, smiled at the more miraculous reality, and reached past a crumpled pillow beside him for the book on the bedside table. It was Baudelaire. A photo dropped out, black and white, two long haired boys, one dark and sullen, one fair and smiling, both smoking, a foreign train in the background, a stickered cello case in front; Potsdam, Berlin, Barcelona, London, Roma, Dubrovnik, *Atomkraft nein danke, CFC Nein danke*, Ban the Bomb, Save the Whale, Save the Ozone layer, the campaign medals of battles won and lost while he was still at school.

It was a picture of well-travelled, fin de siècle, lefty youth; a little piece of ancient history. Tiago put the photo down and leaned complacently back into the immediate past. He'd led Raphael upstairs from the quiet hallway with straight-arms, childlike, laughing at his own tipsy impatience. *This way to the altar.* But the bed had been a high altar, a massive brass bedstead, the hip-height profanity of the mattress offset with white cotton sheets, and a sky blue counterpane, and innocent lambskin rugs on the dark floorboards beside it.

Tiago had approved. *I love it.*

Good. You're the first person to share it. And then Raphael had set him on the bed, and knelt, and rested his forehead on Tiago's hands, making them both quiet together for a while.

This will be our sanctuary Raphael. Our sanctum sanctorum.

Yes. And Raphael had eased him back and poured honeyed words over him. *My Tiago, my Tiago da Silva, my Tiago of the woods, of the forest.* And Tiago had offered up his neck. *My own Raphael, my own Raphael Emmanuel.*

A pause in the kissing. *Ah. How did you know that?*

It's obvious. Actually it was Google. *God is with us. I prayed to him for you, and he brought you to me.*

I prayed for a bike once. Didn't get one. Didn't bother with god after that.

But he's here. Can't you feel his love Raphael, between us, here in this room?

A smile. *Maybe you could show me this famous love.*

And so Tiago did. And afterwards Raphael murmured in disbelief. *Was it enough for you baby? Was it good? It looked like it was good. My god. Sweet Jesus. You are a force of nature, a gift of the gods.*

I should be. Our love comes from heaven. Our love makes saints of us.

Only saints? Surely love makes gods of us? Or do we make god through love? Or do gods make love through us?

God makes love through us Raphael. I am his vessel, and he loves you through me.

You are his vessel. Raphael had smiled, and got up to get his cigarettes, and stalked back to the bed in easy nakedness. *And thus man makes god in his image.* Lighting his cigarette; a rasping strike, a pale flame in the half light.

You see, I agree we take each other to a place of beauty and truth. I just don't feel we need a god to help us do that.

And that's where we differ. But fortunately god loves you just the same.

And so he should. Raphael waving away smoke, smiling at him. *You get some sleep baby.*

Tiago rubbed his eyes and listened to the two parallel Friday evenings around him. Outside was pandemonium; outside, cars were braking and accelerating, voices of many nations were bitching about the shit weather, the lousy economy, the useless government. Whereas inside Raphael's apartment, someone was whistling Chopin; inside the apartment, the romance in which Tiago had cast himself was in its second act. Okay, maybe it was a romcom, but at least it was far more rom than com, a marked improvement on Tiago's limited previous experiences of intimacy. Rogerio was passionate, but he was a catspaw lover, too cautious to please; Florian was playful and inventive, but usually too stoned to get Tiago's name right; and Jason, though assured, physically perfect and mentally alert, was somewhat lacking in finesse. *Jesus Christ Tiago. Back of the fucking net.*

Tiago smiled; he could laugh about it now. His wasted hours with Rogerio, Florian and Jason and his lost years in hotel rooms hadn't ruined his palate. He could still savour true love. And he was confident that Raphael wasn't going to care about the past; because Raphael wasn't going to know about the past. You wouldn't show a new lover your school reports, your *must try harders*. It was perfectly fair to withhold all evidence of the former imperfect you. If questioned, he might reveal more about Rogerio, Florian, maybe even Jason; but not the other stuff. There was a difference between shoddy and shameful.

The door opened and Raphael came in, fresh in jeans and a black sweater. "Hey, hello. I got up for a shower." He came across and sat on the bed. "Did you get any more sleep?"

"Yes." Tiago stroked the skin on Raphael's arm, ran his thumb over the tiny creases, the sun damage, the scars. It was amazing that something so fucked could be so beautiful.

"You were shattered. But you look rested now."

"I am." They sat quietly for a few moments. Tiago picked up the photo. "Who are these beautiful boys?"

"Oh." Raphael smiled and took it. "That's Tomas Paul. Istanbul. Sirkeci station." He turned the picture over. "Nineteen ninety-one. I'd have been nineteen, he was twenty. We ran out of money on the train. We'd spent all our dollars on beer and cigarettes. We were idiots really. But it was good." He put the picture down and took Tiago's hands in his. "Happy idiots."

They sat quietly again, working through their new cadence; talk, silence, touch, silence. The car horns and angry shouts outside were like the sounds of another species.

Raphael smiled. "Would Sir like some tea?"

"Please. Shall I get up?"

"If you like. Though your body in my bed is an immense improvement to this room." He held Tiago close, then got up and went out, snapping his fingers to a private music.

Tiago got up and got dressed. The room was a no-nonsense space, elegant and uncluttered. There was a cast iron fireplace in one corner and an ivory sofa covered in discarded clothes in another, but it was a room of simple outlines, clear surfaces and empty walls – just a few drawings, a mirror, some shelves with books and candles on them. The candles were white-wicked and unused, symbolising longing in a poignant way that a box of one hundred ribbed condoms for heightened pleasure somehow didn't. Tiago smiled; it was only ninety-seven condoms now, and he'd brought ten more with him, just in case.

Raphael came in and placed a tray of tea on the bedside table. "That's my shirt."

"Like it?"

A brief look. "Yes. Perfect on you. White suits you."

"Thanks." Tiago looked away. "No paintings in here."

"No, I suppose there aren't. But did you see the portrait on the landing?" Raphael held out his hand. "Come and see. You might like it."

It a metre square portrait in oils of a delicate young woman. She was wearing a violet gown, and playing a small, decorated guitar, presumably to a golden spaniel that was resting at her feet and gazing up at her in adoration. Behind her a window gave out onto hills, a temple, olive groves, a sea and ships, a cloudy sky. It was well-composed, and pleasing.

"So. Do you like it?"

"Yes. There are so many beautiful things in it."

"Yes." Raphael drew Tiago close. "There are indeed lots of very beautiful things in it. But?"

"But what? It's lovely."

"Lovely." Raphael shook his head. "Look at it. Look closely."

"I don't know. Tell me."

Raphael squeezed him. "Look at it. Don't just let your eyes drift over it. Take it to pieces. You're an analyst, or you used to be. Use your critical faculties. Don't just let it wash over you." He shook his head. "Don't be lazy. Be patient. You've got a good brain Tiago. Apply the fucking thing."

"I'm trying. But I don't know what I'm fucking looking for." Tiago stared at the canvas. "Tell me. And don't fucking patronise me. Don't treat me like a fucking child. I'm your lover now. Not some waiter that you've brought home for a fuck."

He closed his eyes. *Shit.*

Raphael took his arm away and turned away. "Well. Thanks for clearing that up."

"Raphael." Tiago put his hands on Raphael's shoulders. "Raphael I didn't mean it. You know I didn't."

Raphael shook him off. "Just leave it."

"Raphael. Look. I'm sorry." Tiago reached for Raphael's hand but it was moved out of reach.

"I said leave it."

"Raphael, please."

Raphael shook his head and raised his voice. "Will you just fucking leave it?" And sighed. "Tiago."

Tiago breathed again. Despite Raphael's anger, the final quiet addition of his name was colossally encouraging, making the whole expression sound rather less like something you might say to a dog.

"Raphael, please." Tiago looked down at his unwanted hand, felt the misery of being shut out. "I know you're not like that. I'm sorry." He closed his eyes, and five slow seconds passed while a sense of something broken ebbed away, then Raphael was gathering him in.

"I know."

Tiago clung on. "I'm a fucking idiot. I know you're not like that. I'm sorry."

After a while Raphael drew back. "Oh fucking Jesus. Look Tiago. Love fucking hurts. At least, it does if you're letting it move you, if it's worth having. Hearts are open. It's raw. It's easy to hurt, and get hurt."

"I know."

"And I can be a humourless cunt sometimes." Raphael shook his head. "I have absolutely no sense of humour. I can't laugh at myself. I could once, but not any more."

Tiago shook his head, not wanting to believe it, not quite able to find the word *no*.

Raphael took a deep breath. "Look. You are beautiful, Tiago. And being in bed with you is astonishing. But sex is the easy part. Love takes work, and I've worked really hard in the past, made compromises, kept my feelings to myself. It's always made things worse in the long run. And I won't do it again." He shook his head. "I should drive you home right now."

A femtosecond passed. "No."

"Okay." Raphael nodded. "But look. You have to forgive me. I swear I'll do my best to be patient while we get to know one another."

Tiago nodded. He would have preferred a reference to love, but you had to start somewhere.

"But I'm no saint. I'll still fuck it up." Raphael shrugged. "That's it. That's all I have to say."

"Fine." Tiago turned to the picture, eager to leave this mess behind. "Forget it. Let's do this fucking picture thing. Teach me."

"Right." Raphael looked back at the canvas. "So, as you say, the fucking picture is beautiful, and full of beautiful things. But it's full of shit."

"Show me."

"You don't need me to." Raphael looked over at him. "I'll get that tea, and then you can show me how superbly brilliant you are in every way."

Raphael went into the bedroom, and Tiago looked at the floor and took a few deep breaths. Love was about pain. That was how you knew it was love, fuckhead. *Analyse it. You've got a good brain; apply it.* That was good advice. He followed it, and soon he was smiling.

Raphael came back with tea. "Got it?"

"Sure. Sometimes I'm so fucking smart I scare myself."

Raphael put an arm around him. "Good. So scare me."

"It's Clara. A lot younger, of course." Tiago pointed. "And that's a tortoiseshell Verboam Guitar, late seventeenth century, Paris, northern Europe. But the gown's too early."

"Good. The colour of the silk is suspicious, isn't it?"

"Mauve. Too modern. And the pattern reminds me of something." Tiago scanned the picture for a few moments, sipped his tea. "Anyway that Doric temple is wrong. It's too complex. It looks familiar." He pointed to the ships. "Obviously Portuguese Caravels, Cross of Christ on the sails, so Vasco da Gama or Magellan, much too early for the guitar. It's all fucked up."

"Yes. It is all fucked up." Raphael turned to him. "North European artist, girl in an outdated dress of suspicious colour with an odd design on the bodice, English dog, French Baroque guitar, marauding Portuguese ships of the high Renaissance, full of nasty counter-Reformation types in pointy hats." He sipped his tea. "Good."

Tiago grinned. "And that's the fucking Bank of England."

"Yes, indeed, that is the Bank of England, as rebuilt in the early twentieth century, looming weirdly in the background."

Tiago nodded slowly. It was his favourite thing, a clever puzzle, maybe even allegorical, full of hidden messages, executed with skill. And he had a good idea who had painted it. He turned to Raphael. "And I guess the spaniel is hers."

"Indeed, the oddly named Wandsworth." Raphael scratched something off the frame.

"You painted it."

"I did. For her thirtieth birthday. Though I added doggy later. He's only five."

"So why have you got it?"

"So I can look at her, my beautiful sister. I was going to give it to her, but I thought, hell, she can always look in the mirror." Raphael frowned. "I'm meant to be painting one of me for her, for her fortieth in two years' time." He shrugged. "But I don't know if I can do it anymore."

Tiago took his cue. "You must. I insist. I want to see you in a heavy silk frock coat, dark copper, with big, leather, over-the-knee boots. Like a musketeer. Actually, that." He pointed at the girl's dress. "Fermilab. Bubble chamber trace."

"Very good."

"It's perfect. It looks Baroque, but it could only be modern." Tiago looked at Raphael. "It would be great for fakes, wouldn't it?"

Raphael nodded. "Precisely. It would be a faker's stamp of inauthenticity. You could work it into the frames, hide it, and it would only be detectable by microscopy. Tomas Paul has some kit for that."

Tiago smiled. For once Tomas Paul didn't seem to matter that much.

They finished their tea and Raphael talked him through the rest of the picture; the dress was dyed in mauveine, and the trees were eucalyptus. Raphael grinned, raffish and complacent. "I used to like adding to this, though I haven't painted for months. Or drawn, actually." He looked into Tiago's eyes for a while, then looked away, and shook his head, and said he shouldn't ask.

But he didn't have to.

Tiago had fallen in love with two artists, and that gave him a starting point for two theories; did he fall in love with artists because he wasn't finished? And did they fall in love with him because they thought he needed finishing? But this evening he was too tired to think, so he emptied his mind and played the puppet where Raphael had placed him, leaning back on the pillows in jeans and shirt, legs slightly bent up, hands holding the book that Raphael had smilingly given him to look at. *My well-beloved was stripped.*

He looked up. Raphael was making scratchy pen marks on a sketchpad.

"You're a good model, very placid. Can you look down? Please?"

"Sure." Tiago looked down again. "You said these words last night."

"Which ones?"

"You smile contentedly upon my love, as deep and gentle as the sea that rises toward you as toward a cliff." He closed his eyes and re-ran the memory, his first reverse fantasy, one that happened after the event.

"I did say that. I remember exactly when." A wolf's grin. "It was the point of no return."

"It was, rather."

"And I remember your contented smile."

"So do I." Tiago let words flow. "I didn't think it would feel like this."

"Like what? So good one minute and so shit the next?" Raphael's voice was tender, but his tone was unapologetic. "Welcome to the pleasure dome baby."

"I suppose that's the price, isn't it? The price of it being so sweet." Tiago shook his head. "I clearly have no imagination."

Raphael stopped drawing. "I do worry that maybe you're letting love move you too much."

"That's not possible. And I don't want to love or be loved any other way." Who would? "Would you?"

"No, I wouldn't. But I'm tougher than you." Raphael held the page up to the window, hunting for light. "And love makes you very vulnerable. It's not like loving god you know. I'm fucking fallible." He looked towards the window.

"I'm going to have to finish this soon. We're losing the light. But sadly I can't take my eyes off you long enough to draw you." He laughed and looked back at Tiago, still not hurrying, still not drawing.

"So get on with it."

"So get on with it, he says. And he shall be obeyed, because he is Beauty and his word is law." Raphael drew a long sweeping, horizontal line. "Look down, please."

"Yes. Sorry." Tiago looked back at the book. This wasn't as much fun as he'd hoped. Raphael was detaching himself, lost in his task. "I think you should come over here."

Raphael put the sketchpad aside and came over there. "Your wish is my command."

"Sit here." Said softly, not for a spaniel.

Raphael sat, took the book from Tiago's hands, placed it on the bed.

"When I watched you sleeping this morning, I knew for certain your life meant more to me than my own." He put his hands on Tiago's shoulders, and kissed his forehead. "More than my own."

Tiago closed his eyes. There really was no answer to that. But he didn't need to provide one.

"I love you Tiago. Your power over me is absolute. I would do anything to protect you. I am utterly lost for love of you."

They were the kind of words Tiago had longed to hear all his life. He gave in to desire, breathing deep, clasping at Raphael's clothes, fervent, as if time were running out.

"Love has made gods of us Raphael."

"It has. Sweet Christ, I was so lost."

"You're not lost now. You're with me, my angel. I'll protect you."

"Oh yes. I'm found baby."

"You are found. They can call off the search party." Tiago smiled, ecstatic. This was how belonging felt, how it would always feel. He felt his heart racing. *Oh sweet Jesus.* He reached for Raphael's belt, clasped the buckle. "Oh, Raphael, now."

Raphael kissed him. "Oh Tiago. Oh baby."

Tiago smiled, tugging at the buckle, the zip. "Yes my love?"

Raphael sighed. "It's just the fucking light. I need to finish this picture." He made to move away but Tiago gripped his arm.

"Fuck the light. Fuck the picture. Hold me." He pressed his head against Raphael's breast. "Fucking hold me Raphael. Jesus, how can you walk away from this to draw a fucking picture?" Tiago heard himself and panicked. What was wrong with him? He was out of control again. If he didn't get a grip soon Raphael would lock him in the boot, drive him home, and leave him on the doorstep. "I mean, it's just a picture." He tried a half laugh, expecting Raphael to move away from the bed.

But miraculously, Raphael held him tight. "I know baby. I'm sorry. I'm so selfish."

They were quiet for a minute or so, and then there were two sets of high-heeled footsteps outside, well-spoken voices.

That man is as ugly as a hat full of arseholes.

Raphael muttered into Tiago's hair. "Those nuns down the road are getting worse."

Tiago breathed slowly, felt his heart slowing. "I'm really sorry."

"No need." Raphael sighed. "I'm still learning. Learning what you need."

They heard more voices in the street, a siren approaching.

"They're coming to take me away."

"I won't let them." Raphael kissed Tiago's hair. "I won't let them."

The ambulance went past, the tone dropping.

"Did someone hurt you Tiago?"

A shake of the head. "Someone hurts everyone."

Another minute or so.

"Look, baby. I'm sorry. But we're losing the light. And it's a beautiful picture."

"Okay. Finish it then. I mean, please finish it."

Raphael sat back and looked at him for a few moments. "Okay. He went back across the room and studied the drawing. Tiago picked up his book and stared down at the page, knowing he had to get a fucking grip.

Raphael was quiet for a few moments. "So, last night."

"Yes?"

"I believe we were discussing the morality of dealing in fine art?"

Tiago smiled. Raphael was taking them through the cloud, levelling them out. "We were."

"Okay. Let's start easy – fakes." Raphael frowned. "That painting of Clara is not a fake. Correct?"

"Of course not. It's not pretending to be anything."

"But even if it were, it would still be beautiful. Doesn't that make it valuable? If you had two equally beautiful pictures, one a fake and the other not, which would be worth more?"

Easy one. "Unanswerable. You can't have two equally beautiful pictures."

Raphael smiled. "You can't." He put the pen down. "And this is finished. Tiago One."

Tiago turned and sat on the edge of the bed. "Is it any good?"

"Yes." Raphael closed the sketchbook and held it close to his breast. "It's very good."

"Can I see it?"

"Soon. First tell me how beautiful it is."

"Before I see it?"

"Yes."

Tiago shrugged. "It has to be beautiful because it captures our love."

"True. But who else would think that? Beyond us, I mean."

"Anyone who knows what it's like to be in love like this." Tiago looked at his hands. "What it's like to be growing together, giving elements of ourselves up, for love."

"Well put." Raphael came over, sat beside him and gave him the sketchpad. "Here."

Tiago traced the lines of the drawing. It was someone he'd like to be. A beautiful, tranquil, slender boy looking out of the page with the age-old expression of the odalisque *Put that down and make love to me, you big idiot.*

"The artist's lover."

"Indeed. The artist's lover." Raphael kissed Tiago's hair. "You wouldn't keep your eyes on the book so I drew you looking up at me. Vanity on my part, of course."

Tiago shook his head. "But it's too beautiful."

"Not at all. It's precisely how beautiful you are to me. But I'm glad you like it."

Raphael looked up at the wall above the bed. "We'll put you up there." He took the pen out and wrote on the foot of the page. "*Tiago hash1: The Artist's Lover not reading Baudelaire, Rue Vivienne, cold evening, April 13th 2012. RED.*

"Now." He frowned. "Back to the greater morality of dealing in fine art, which is about deciding who should own it, and look at it." He held the sketch at arm's length. "Who should own this fine sketch of a sensual young man too tired to read after twenty hours on the nest with the lucky fucker of an artist, at whom he looks defiantly in the hope that the stupid twat will put down his pen and come to bed?"

"Is that what the catalogue would say?"

"Unfortunately not." Raphael rubbed his chin. "In fact it would probably say that this drawing depicts a young man reflecting on the intensity of new love, and that the artist is believed to have been his lover." He smiled. "And the right owner is?"

"Us. We are the right owners."

"Yes. But we will die, won't we my darling? And then what

happens? Who deserves to possess this? Remember, it's the only recording of our new, and fragile, and imperfect love." Raphael looked at the drawing for a few seconds. "The expression of my adoration of you, and my gratitude."

"Gratitude?"

Raphael shrugged. "For your trust. Your selfless tenderness." He rubbed his eyes and sniffed. "Fuck. Sorry. Long day." He looked back at the picture and wrinkled up his nose.

"So who gets to stick that on the wall and leave it in an empty house all day?"

"Someone good, who deserves it. Someone who understands beauty and love."

"And justice. Indeed. And who doesn't deserve to own it?"

"Someone evil, some horrible wicked bastard."

"So what do they deserve to own? Evil, horrible, wicked bastards?"

"They deserve to own shit."

"But some of them have lots of money."

"Well that's all wrong."

"Yes. But it can be fixed." Raphael looked at his watch. "Now let me take you for dinner and I'll tell you about the business."

CHAPTER 11

THAT'S BEAUTY, THAT'S LOVE, AND THAT'S JUSTICE

Raphael chose an unremarkable restaurant for dinner, and asked for a quiet table away from the other diners. It was just as well. If there'd been background noise Tiago wouldn't have believed his ears.

There were two sides to the business: tracking down lost art works (usually in Eastern Europe) and caching them with the deserving poor, and then making copies and selling them to the unpleasant people on the black market. Raphael was the draughtsman, Clara "provided" on-line provenances, register and catalogue numbers, Rob ran import-export, and Tomas Paul did everything else. He and Raphael had the idea when they were students.

Raphael shrugged. "He invested family money in it at first. Now it's stuff from his rocket fuel spin-out. They make rocket propellants from green chemicals." He scratched his head. "I can never remember what it's called. Something to do with catapults. Bio-ballistica? Bio-ballisticalia?" He took out his wallet. "I've got his card somewhere."

Tiago drained his glass and poured another. He'd seen a lot of tired spin out stuff like this, clichéd names chosen by academic amateurs with no idea about branding. They should lose the *bio*, cut it down, write a smart tag line. *Ballista. Sustainable Launch Solutions.*

"Mmm."

Raphael took out the card and handed it over. "Here."

Tiago took it. "Ballista. Sustainable Propulsion Solutions."

"Ballista, that's it." Raphael went back to Tomas Paul. As an academic and a musician he was always travelling, always finding things – art works, places to hide them, schmucks to sell fakes to.

"Dodgy guys, greedy investors. And he does authentication at Turing – canvases, frames, panels, pigments." Tiago would love him. He was A Lot of Fun.

"Clearly." Tiago gave a smile that captured precisely how much fun Tomas Paul sounded to him; fortunately the restaurant was fashionably crepuscular.

"So." Raphael rapped the table. "You in?"

"Fuck yes." Tiago smiled. "I can find things. Stuff in South America. The ratlines."

"Yes. And you do have a good eye. An excellent eye, actually."

Tiago slammed his glass down, spilled the wine. "I knew she was a fucking Caravaggio."

"Of course she is." Raphael poured more. "Eat. And drink."

"Where did you find her? Who gets the copy?"

"Later. Eat your fucking food."

"I'm trying." Tiago pushed food around the plate. "Who else was involved? Martin?"

"Fuck, no." Raphael sipped his wine and shook his head.

Martin was too chatty, he couldn't have been trusted. They had to be low key. "There's a calling card in the copy. The Fermilab trace, etched on in gold, individual atoms, invisible to the naked eye. It's a fuck you."

"And if the schmuck sells the copy?"

"Why would he? He's not supposed to have it."

"Or someone finds the calling card?"

Raphael shrugged. "Unlikely. Tomas Paul says you'd need a fucking huge electron microscope to do that." He rubbed his chin. "Actually, we haven't done it yet, the faking bit."

"You haven't done it?" Tiago sat back. "Why not?"

Raphael shrugged. "It's difficult, and dangerous. These are not nice people. They might come after us." He poured more wine. "But to answer your earlier question, if someone tries to sell the fake, the original pops up with an on-line provenance, and we all shrug our shoulders and say we've been had."

"I still think they'll come after you."

"Eat your food."

Tiago ate three mouthfuls and sat back. "How do you choose your beneficiaries?"

Raphael smiled. "Oh, I'm sentimental. Anything that helps suffering, frightened people, especially children." He frowned. "My father's parents were killed by Nazis. I suppose that's influenced me."

"It would." Tiago picked his glass up, put it down untouched. "Tell me about him."

Raphael sighed. "I'm sorry you'll never know him. He was a wonderful man." His father had died four years ago, a gentle, liberal man, born in Paris in thirty-two, put on the boat train to London by his parents in thirty-seven; the last time he saw them. Raphael stared into his glass. "But you know about this stuff. With your grandfather's death."

"But my grandfather died an individual death. He has a grave, a photo in his headstone." *Shit.* Tiago looked up, aghast at the implication. "I don't mean to say that your grandparents died without dignity."

"Of course you don't." Raphael lit a cigarette, blew smoke to one side, fanned it away. "I'm sure they died with tremendous dignity. After all, they had saved their son. But my father never talked about it. He got on with his life. That was his act of defiance." He straightened the candle in its holder. "In fifty-three he came back to Paris, went to medical school, and became a doctor, a good one. And in seventy-one he met a beautiful Italian communist, Cecilia." She had only been twenty-three when they'd married, but he had adored her, protected her from the menace of the world. "Not that she needed it." Raphael smiled. "I don't always live up to his example." He looked away and took a deep breath. "In fact, I'm about to fall short of it."

"Because you're going to ask me about my parents?"

"Yes. I'm afraid so." Raphael looked back, soft-eyed. "If that's okay?"

"Sure." Tiago nodded. He was used to being asked this question; it came up surprisingly often, and his answer depended on what he needed from the asker. In this case he needed Raphael to admire him, and love him, and not pity him, or be spooked.

"Well, actually, I'm afraid my parents are dead. Maybe you guessed." He looked at blobs of wax on the tablecloth and recounted the version of his life story in which he was objective and chirpy and over it all. First, the facts; the wagon drivers worked hard during the cork harvest, they drank a lot at lunchtime, his father had swerved to miss the lorry but hit the tree on the bend. Secondly, it could have been worse; they had a full tank, so it was instant, a fireball. They didn't suffer, not like Avô João had suffered. And thirdly, he'd been lucky, too young at four to understand, and raised with João and Inês in a loving household. "I've been lucky, really." There was a fourth part, about what high achievers orphans were; but it hardly seemed the right time to bring Batman, or Frodo, or Harry Potter into the conversation, and after all, he was talking to an orphan's son, so he looked up with a tight smile. "Worse things happen. Much worse."

Raphael's face was pale. "Yes." He reached for Tiago's hand. "But I'm so sorry."

Tiago shrugged. "Thanks. But it was twenty-five years ago. I'm over it." He drained his glass with theatrical finality; he was resilient, and resurgent, and nobody's victim.

...

Amelia closed the door behind her and stepped quietly into the dark hallway. She was pretty sure Tiago was out, and had her story in case he wasn't – *Oh, I heard burglars and I thought you were away* – but she still wanted to do this as quickly as possible.

She made her way upstairs to the bedroom and stood in the

doorway, arrested by a sudden scent of roses. Her eyes made out twelve white blooms in a tall vase by the bed, a small white card perched among them. She went over, picked up the card and turned it in the moonlight; it was excellent news. Raphael was an impulsive sentimentalist and a fan of extravagant, irrational gestures; a perfect patron of the arts. The money was looking good.

She pulled back the snowy duvet and shone a tiny UV torch over the white sheets; spotless. Checked the pillows; ditto. "Okay. This is not a problem." She headed into the en-suite bathroom, fished about in the bin and grinned. "Pay dirt." She took out three small packages, unwrapped the white tissue, and plopped the three wobbly flesh-coloured objects in a small vacuum flask.

...

At four Tiago was looking out at the street, thinking what high achievers orphans were.

"Oh Tiago, oh Jesus no. Not you." Raphael was sitting up, his voice cracked and creepy.

Tiago went across to the bed. "Wake up." He held Raphael, shook him. "Wake up Raphael. You're dreaming."

Raphael stared, confused, clutched at him. "You're broken."

Tiago switched on the bedside lamp. "It's okay Raphael, I'm here. I've got you." He kissed Raphael's hair and held him tight. "It's okay."

Raphael stared through him. "They came for us. They took you from me." He rambled, horrible dream drivel. *They tortured you. They laughed when they gave me your body. You were bruised and broken, like fucking Christ. They cut off your hands.*

And Tiago denied it, quietly, firmly. *No they didn't. Be still Raphael. Stop this. Be calm.* Shushing him, holding him close. *Enough Raphael. Basta.* Rocking him back and forth. *Shush shush shush.*

After a while Raphael drew away a little, but still let himself be held. "Jesus. Sorry."

"*De nada.*" Tiago kissed the frowning brow, stroked the greying hair. "You know, I knew I'd fallen in love with you last night when I saw these white hairs. Your imperfections increased told me it was love. That's good, isn't it?"

"It's fucking excellent. I have lots of grey hair and a limitless supply of imperfections."

They sat quietly in the lamplight.

"I'm going to take care of you Raphael."

"It's not necessary."

"It fucking is."

Raphael looked up, then closed his eyes. "It's just been a long time since anyone tried."

"Tried, or succeeded?"

"Succeeded, I suppose. Yes."

"You big old alpha." Tiago looked down, but Raphael's shoulders had softened, his breathing slowed. It was a strange pleasure, a splendid, unforeseen triumph, getting Raphael to sleep in his arms. He mouthed Mandarin into the smoky hair; there were things he couldn't say, because he wasn't sure of him. He'd been a fucking idiot, but he would bring him comfort, and make him happy. He kissed Raphael's hair and held him in the pre-dawn calm.

A car went past, the broken exhaust a dull rattle. Raphael stirred. "Hey, beautiful." He kissed Tiago's breast, got out of bed and started rifling through the clothes on the sofa. "Where did I put them baby?"

Baby. Who had cradled whom? "Breast pocket, black velvet jacket you wore for dinner."

"You're quickly becoming indispensable." Raphael found a cigarette and lit it by the open window, fanning the smoke to one side, looking out at the silent street. "Jesus. That nightmare. It was so fucking real."

Tiago went over to him, wanting to stay in contact. "You scared me."

"I scared myself." Raphael put an arm round him. "That shit happened right here, in these fucking streets."

Tiago let himself be held for a few moments. The grand unveiling of his plan deserved a little suspense. "But it'll never happen again. They'll never come for us, or the people we love."

"It doesn't take much for the world to turn on its dark side. This country is full of racists, and fascists, and bigots. People for whom Hitler didn't go far enough."

"So? Fuck them. They'll never come for us."

"Because?"

"Because they'll never get out of the blocks." He put his arms around Raphael's neck and spelled it out slowly. You needed money to be an evil bastard these days. Some of Raphael's clients had lots of money. And some of them were evil bastards.

He grinned. "And some of them are also my clients."

"Probably."

"For sure. You said I should have a quest, and now I have one. The fuckers won't know what's hit them." Tiago stretched out his arms like an angel. "Behold. I am Tiago, James, the Usurper, the Son of Thunder."

"Indeed. I am beholding." Raphael kissed him. "It's quite something."

"And you are Raphael, one of the seven holy angels, the Healing Angel."

"If you say so."

Tiago smiled. "And your love, our love, has been my inspiration."

"Beyond all doubt."

"Beyond all doubt." Tiago turned his back, let himself be held. "There's a small district in Cusco province called Santiago. In the mountains." He stopped, stunned. It was going to happen. Christ Economist would exalt the valleys by laying low the mountains.

Raphael held him more tightly. "What on earth are you talking about?"

"You've done good things with the pictures. But bringing down the bad guys like that is risky." He was brilliant, and he could hardly speak for grinning. "I've been thinking it through. The smart thing is to turn them on each other. And I know how."

...

They sat on the bed staring at the figure Raphael had drawn on the sketchpad; a star of David, the six points labelled *Ut, Re, Mi, Fa, So, La,* little sketches of a shotgun, a chemical structure, a feather, two question marks.

Tiago was pleased. It was coming together nicely. He took the pen from Raphael, wrote *Lux Aeterna* at the top left hand corner, drew a hanged man beside *Ut.* "There are six in the family, six on the model. And the names are based on the Hexachord. Sancte Johannes."

Raphael nodded. "The origins of the musical scale. Guido d'Arezzo."

"Guido. Precisely." Tiago pointed to Ut. "John Filgrave. The eldest brother."

Raphael nodded. "He's dying."

"Yes. And he's still a horrible old bigot."

Raphael frowned. "And he still collects Renaissance art."

"Perfect." Tiago smiled. "Could he be your target for the girl?"

"He could be. If we do it."

Tiago nodded and went round the star. Re, the younger brother, the current CEO of the corporation, a callous man who knew nothing about working conditions in the mines and cared less; his wife, the fragrant Mi, who partied with crooks that ran drugs and girls into the mining camps; and the third brother, Fa, head of communications, whose principal role was to pay off officials and hush up fatal accidents.

"For So and La, I don't know yet. They're young." He took the pen back and wrote underneath the star: *Radix malorum est cupiditas.* "Every venture needs a logo."

Raphael nodded. "Okay. So how we do get them to take each other out?"

Tiago yawned and wrote *Ti* at the centre of the star. "I'll tell you tomorrow."

...

Amelia sat on her bed rueing her poor life choices. She'd been putting the tissues back in the bin when it had suddenly struck her that all three samples could well be Ashkenazy sperm. Nights in with old movies and a nice big hairbrush were all very well, but if you wanted to know what normal people did in bed you needed to get out occasionally.

Still, her money was probably safe; a man who spent two hundred euros on roses for someone he hadn't particularly fancied twelve hours earlier was easily manipulated. She would maybe ask Tomas Paul's advice tomorrow; he knew all about getting funding. And she would press on with the Raphael and Tiago hybrid – not because she had set her heart on it, but because she had put her mind to it, and that was a very hard switch to reset.

Amelia chewed a thumbnail and weighed the cost of a change of plan. Getting blood or bone or even hair from Tiago was going to increase the complexity of her project. But she was cunning and inventive, and she knew she could do it. She would focus on the funding and pounce on the good idea when it inevitably emerged.

...

Raphael lay awake wishing he'd had the sense to fall in love with someone stupid.

"Darling?"

"Mmm." Tiago nuzzled closer. "Sleeping is Tiago."

"You don't really want to do it, do you?" He spoke softly, hoping his words would sink in like overnight hypnosis. These Hexacorp guys might be British, but they were still not nice people. They wouldn't write to the Prime Minister, or text Christine Lagarde, or fax a commissioner in Brussels. They would make you disappear, and then reappear, on a beach, in black bags, a piece at a time. "You don't mean it, do you? Darling?"

Tiago made a *mawp* noise, snuffled, wriggled a bit, settled.

Raphael smiled. There was nothing to worry about. Tiago wasn't going to roll out *Lux;* it was showboating, a shimmering lure designed to dazzle and impress him. He sighed, feeling a pang of sadness for Tiago's loss, and a stab of shame for doubting his sanity, and a sudden rush of overwhelming certainty that he knew what was best for both of them. He would build a fortress of love around them, and pull up the drawbridge, and bar the gates, and they would live quietly in devoted and growing affection that would calm the weird fantasies of Tiago's teeming brain. In a few months, if all went well, he'd propose marriage; in a year or so, children. And in a few years time, the contentment and rewards of home and parenthood would put *Lux* where it should be; a clever, unrealisable idea, born of well-intentioned youthful zealotry, stashed safely in the attic under dust sheets like an architect's model of an impossible structure.

He pulled the covers up and let Tiago's quiet contentment lull him to sleep.

CHAPTER 12

VIOL BODIES

Opinion was divided on Professor Sir Tomas Paul Gosele. A regular visitor to the V&A sculpture gallery where he instructed his first year engineers to draw Cupid and Hymen "because any halfwit could draw a straight line", and alleged author of countless withering remarks at student appeals – "Tarquin may well be the nephew of the Duchess of Blank but he wouldn't know Free Energy if it got up and gave him a blow job" – he was also a serious academic, a talented musician, and successful academic entrepreneur. His early death in…

Tomas Paul sat back and looked smugly round the empty carriage. Re-drafting his obituary on the tube was one of his three favourite things, and after last night's investor meeting he needed to work on it. They were going to give him ten million dollars to build a big shiny prove-out facility. It would take about two years to build, and then three months to start up. And one month later he would be toast.

With time running out, it was good to do his second favourite thing this morning, which was going to DowSoc. At seven thirty on a Saturday he'd normally be heading to the Bushy Park Run. Sure, it was a long way to Teddington but it gave him the chance to see his sister, and the field was big enough to give him options; either to run as himself (PB 18:04) or rather faster as Flamineo

Corombona (PB 17:05). For a while he'd considered creating a third Park Run persona, but the Bushy volunteers were a well-read bunch and would probably detect Irma Prunesquallor the minute she registered. And scamming the Park Run didn't prove much, except that an honour system was vulnerable to dishonourable actions. It wasn't worth the candle to Tomas Paul. He knew the three key elements of worthwhile deception. You chose the right targets, you got caught when the time was right, and the time was right when everyone was ready to learn their lesson.

Tomas Paul's phone rang; it was Mel. "BBC called. Today. Chinese satellite? Too late?" Mel talked like a text message. It was Jim and Evan so he said *yes* and got off at Westminster, enjoying the sudden change of plan.

Tomas Paul liked novelty, and loved surprises, and was addicted to acting on impulse in a way that wrong-footed friend and foe alike. At Turing they called him *TP Gosele, The Bouncing Czech,* because they were a bunch of twats. But his parents had been children of the 1941 firestorms, and he'd grown up perfectly relaxed in the face of unutterable chaos, special in so many ways, handsome, and tall, and super smart, ambidextrous, with perfect pitch, and an aptitude for everything they taught him at school and everything they didn't. By the time he was sixteen, seven girls had fallen like leaves at his feet. And he'd been looking for number eight when he found Raphael.

But that had been a long time ago. He'd been at Turing for fifteen years now. Before he got rich and moved to the Mews he too had glided along the slimy subterranean waveguide with the

Eloi, the Turing boys and Tesla girls, like Thalia Rockingham, the kids that were so cool they were uncool before it was cool to be uncool. And he'd done well at Turing, because he knew his shit. It wasn't easy to launch a missile and save the planet at the same time. But he'd hit on the formula in Heidelberg, in the first year of his PhD, and formed his spin out five years ago, investor catnip, bio sourced rocket propellants, ballistics for sustainable warfare, low carbon extermination. With over a hundred patent applications, and license deals with every defence contractor in Europe, Tomas Paul was now very rich indeed.

The beauty of it was, of course, that it wouldn't fucking work.

Raphael said he was saving the world from itself.

At ten past eight Tomas Paul was sitting on a bench watching the wheel and being sweetly sardonic to Evan and the listeners, but there was no cause for panic, so by quarter past he was walking east towards the smelly mudflats downriver. An oily cormorant was perched stiff-legged on a rotten pole, drying out his wings. The bird rotated his big head to watch Tomas Paul pass. Fair enough. He'd probably never seen a man with a lute case before. They were nice birds, cormorants; clever, purposeful. Amelia had a cormorant.

Tomas Paul took out his phone.

How's Leander? N&S.

He reached the Linnaeus Institute at five past ten, placed the lute on the stage, and picked up the agenda; a talk on Bulgarian lute strings in the morning, and a recital by Clara Nelson in the afternoon. Clara would sing Dowland and Monteverdi, her crystal, pure voice floating like helium above the slack, leaden

twanging of her accompanist, po-faced ecclesiastical twat Father
Basil Pecksniff.

"Hello Tomas Paul. How's it hanging?"

"Far out, Karl."

Karl Cogg Lucifer, President of the Dowland Society, was
Tomas Paul's idol; a hundred per cent hepcat, seventy-five years
on the clock but as light on his red Hi Tops as the seventeen year
old that lived in his head. He was from somewhere like Belgium
or Holland or possibly Theydon Bois, and he rocked the retired
academic vibe with a steely quiff, muppet drummer eyebrows and
teeth like the hammers of a pub piano. Today he'd teamed faded
Levis with a stripy jumper in early music shades of mossy green
and bracken brown, probably dyed in fern juice and squirrel pee
by a couple of lesbians in Hoxton. Never mind those counter
tenor glamour pusses; Karl was what early music was all about.
He frowned at Tomas Paul and two caterpillars kissed over his
nose.

"When I heard you on Radio 4 this morning I didn't think
you'd come today. Should we be worried about this satellite
thing?"

"No sweat Karl. This space junk's falling out of the sky all the
time." Tomas Paul patted him on the shoulder and waved the
agenda at him. "Looks like a great day."

"Well." Karl frowned deeper and the caterpillars tried to make
babies. "Actually I need you this afternoon. Clara's accompanist
has let us down rather."

"Who, Father Basil?" Tomas Paul didn't like Father Basil.
Father Basil gave him sick Thought for the Day fantasies: *And*

our speaker today is Father Basil Pecksniff, a jumped up little cunt from Stepney.

But Karl was looking worried. "Yes. I'm afraid he's had an accident."

"Oh dear." Oh dear. Maybe he'd tripped on his chasuble and done a triple lutz down an escalator.

"He came off his bike and got hit by a bendy bus."

"How terrible." How marvellous. That was one for Amelia. Bendy bus bumps Basil. Basil bashed in bendy bus bustup.

Karl shook his head. "So would you mind playing the G lute for us when Clara sings? It's only Dowland, and Monteverdi. You can do it in your sleep."

"I'd be delighted."

Karl smiled. "Marvellous. And look, there's Clara."

Tomas Paul turned. Clara was checking her phone. She was in a black dress, with sheer stockings and shiny high heels; polished, a performer's outfit. No early music mufti for Clara Nelson. She was always stylish, always beautiful, and so like Raphael, down to the dark green eyes and straight, shiny black hair.

Ah.

Tomas Paul closed his eyes a little. 1989, Potsdam. Young Raphael had been star struck. *I'm Raphael Davide, from Paris. I'm the new first cellist. You're Tomas Paul Gosele aren't you? The harpist. I saw you win the competition last year.* Trying to be polite, hard work for a moody, stick thin, spiky virgin, all Cult, Camus and Camels, not quite an angry brigadier but definitely a raincoat brigadier, an awkward squadron leader in the making, surly and snarly except with his hero, feeling the world solely through music, all other channels locked down. They were sharing a room, and Tomas Paul had recognised him straight away; Jacinto.

Clara yawned politely, the back of her hand over her mouth.

And young Raphael did the same, and leaned back against a Stone Roses poster, one long leg crossed over the other, lighting his third cigarette from his second, talking adolescent crap about how only music made him feel alive and real. A bravura performance, like Lauren; *I'm hard to get Steve. All you have to do is ask me.* But Tomas Paul hadn't asked. He'd gone over, and taken the cigarette from Raphael's mouth, and showed him what feeling alive and real was really like. And very soon he'd been saying *Tomas Paul, oh god Tomas Paul. Say my name. Say you love me. Say "I love you Raphael."*

Oh, I do. And he'd meant it. And then he'd told Raphael what love was for and why fidelity mattered, and then they'd done it again ten minutes later, and Raphael had gazed up at him, knowing for the first time why sex was so much better when there was somebody else to do it with. *When we make love it's as if you hold me up and I touch eternity.* Correct. And when Raphael had finally slept that night, Tomas Paul had written his name into every cell in his body: *Tomas Paul hearts Raphael, Potsdam, 2305 CET 10.07.89.* Save. Click.

Raphael had turned out to have a lion's heart; fierce, possessive, defensive. One night Tomas Paul had woken around two to see him pacing the bedroom, smoking so much it had seemed the curtains were on fire. *Come back to bed Raphael.*

I'm sorry. I can't sleep. I'm fucking furious.

I can soothe you. I can help you get to sleep.

I'm too fucking angry for all that. I'm seriously fucked off. I really fucking am. He could get pretty angry. *Did you see this?* Shoving the crumpled newspaper across. *This guy. He's a fucking war criminal. Everyone knows this.*

Yes.

He's bought a fucking Titian. So wrong, that something so beautiful belongs to someone so ugly. He shouldn't be able to own it, touch it. Fuck, he shouldn't even be able to see it. He should be made to look at shit and rotting carcases and more shit for the rest of his life.

And out it had come, the plan born in fury, full of nasty, spiteful twists.

Because Raphael wasn't just clever, he was cunning; cunning enough to stitch Tomas Paul up into three years of fidelity. Every time they'd made love in a new city Tomas Paul had bought the cheesiest tourist sticker he could find, and they'd stuck it on the cello case, and after three years you couldn't see the case anymore, just the tracks left by two kids making Europe their playground. And when the time had come for Tomas Paul to move on, to complete his collection, Raphael hadn't even been jealous or bitter; they'd seen one another for years until the endgame, ten years ago, in the hotel room in Bloomsbury, a sunny haven among the noisy streets, just the labouring engines of passing buses rattling the bottle in the ice bucket, the sound of a bee flying round in escalating panic. Raphael had caught the bee in his hands and put the silly thing out the window. *Off you go silly bee.* He'd watched it fly away, and then he'd lit a cigarette and exhaled smoke into a sunbeam, making it all dirty and beautiful.

You got my letter? He'd found breath and the soap opera words to wrap around it. He'd been in love, and in love with being in love, with living quietly, in love, and with being faithful, doing it all properly. Tomas Paul had played Kapsberger, a toccata, the third, and then he'd told Raphael the big secret – that when the time came, the rockets wouldn't launch, and the bombs wouldn't go off. And Raphael had said *Tomas Paul, you've saved the world from itself,* and they'd laughed, and made love again, and then that had been it.

"Tomas Paul?" Clara was coming over, elegant and stealthy, high heels on the wooden floor marking out her approach in common time; a sexy andante, one, two, three, four, five, six, seven, eight. Raphael had a good walk too, more of an adagio.

"Hello beautiful woman."

They kissed and Tomas Paul took a deep breath. "How are you?"

"Good."

"And how's big brother?"

"Excellent." Clara smiled a lovely crooked smile. "He's over that bastard Martin Nelson at last." She dipped her head. "He's in love with a Portuguese Adonis." Lowered her eyes. "They're at the FMS stage."

"Huh?" Tomas Paul grinned.

She leaned across and whispered. "Fuck Me Silly." Clara always used swearwords precisely, like a duchess would. She looked over at the stage, musing. "He's Tiago something something da Silva. He's very clever, handsome, very charming. Speaks seven languages, or seventy-seven, or perhaps more. Madly in love with my brother for some inexplicable reason. And musical, piano and guitar. "

He sounded awful. "He sounds lovely. Is it serious?"

"I think so. He's staying at ours tonight." Clara nodded. "And Raphael says he's flawless."

It was definitive; flawless was Raphael's word for unassailable perfection. "So yes."

"Yes. And he's quite adorable. He feeds birds. Not sure what on. I rather thought they fed themselves." Clara frowned and rubbed her forehead. "He's from Lisbon. Some kind of hot shot, one of these go-getters, you know? Economist. Credit Dijonnais, I think."

"Lisbon?" Economist? Bells rang in Tomas Paul's head. There'd been times, after Raphael, where he'd sometimes experimented. And one of those times had been in Lisbon, with a slim, dark haired boy, and economist maybe, very drunk, certainly. It seemed rather unlikely; but still, Tiago something something da Silva. He'd have a card somewhere. He'd have a look when he got home.

Clara looked away. "I believe we're doing the Dowland and the Monteverdi together this afternoon. Which will be lovely for everyone." She put a hand to her left side and winced. "Won't it?"

"Are you okay?"

"Nothing. I'll tell you over lunch. Let's listen to Uncle Bulgaria."

They took their seats, but Tomas Paul found it hard to pay attention. It was of course moderately fascinating that during the Renaissance *some contemporary sources suggested that Bulgarian luthiers may have used cat gut when sheep gut was not available,* but it wasn't that fascinating, and Tomas Paul was glad when the lunch break came.

They went to an empty Korean café and sat at white plastic tables. Clara ordered soup and green tea for them both, and told Tomas Paul without drama that she probably had cancer, that it was probably operable, and that he was not to tell Raphael or Rob "until it was all sorted out." She rested her chin on her elegant hands.

"That's it. That's all I'm going to say. Sorry, but I have to tell someone. And I'm not being brave. I just need to get it out."

Tomas Paul nodded; being shaken wouldn't help. And there might be something he could do. "What do you mean by probably?"

"Good question. More than fifty percent. Based on the density of what they saw yesterday, of course." She smiled the way Raphael did when he was keeping something bad to himself, a burning feather under the nose. "But I don't intend to ruin our lunch talking about death."

"Indeed." Nor did Tomas Paul. "Congratulations on the Chair. First female Professor of Bayesian statistics. What are the odds eh?"

"Very droll."

The food arrived and Clara picked up a spoon the way that people who want to talk and not eat do. "Have we really known each other for twenty years?"

"Yes." And it had passed in the blink of an eye, like time in front of a beautiful painting.

Clara traced the pattern on the table top with her index finger. "This is real neg-head downer shit isn't it?"

"Yes. Why can't you tell Rob?"

She shrugged. "I will when I know how bad it is. Not now. Too many unknowns. He'll panic."

"And Raphael?"

"Raphael." Clara shook her head. "He'll shatter like a cheap glass." She picked up the chopsticks and peered at the text on the wrapper. "He sends his love, by the way. To you, and Mel, and the twins."

"Likewise." Tomas Paul frowned. He wanted to talk about Clara, not Raphael. If he knew what had happened, there was always a chance he could fix it. He tried to craft a way back. "You're right of course. Raphael doesn't always cope well."

"You're not fucking kidding. Last October he was fucking terrible." She picked up a glass sugar shaker. "One night he wouldn't open the door to the flat. I knew he was in there. I thought he was going to harm himself. No." She checked herself. "That's bullshit. I knew he was going to kill himself." She tipped up the sugar shaker and studied the crystal horizon. "I was in the street outside. It was pouring. I was looking at that plaque by the door." She smiled. "You're going to think I'm mental."

"Tell me."

She bit her lower lip. "This plaque, they bought it in Turkey I think. It has a beautiful face, calm and expressionless, very soothing to look at. Diana, or Artemis. A huntress. I was touching it, talking to it, almost praying, like a mantra." She grimaced. "I'd probably lose my job if they found out." And put her hands over her face. "I was saying *Take me not him. Take me not him.*" She folded her arms and looked down. "God only knows where that came from. I must have said it a thousand times. I should be locked up."

Tomas Paul nodded. "Yes." A thousand times would be considered enough. They always took your first answer. Clara was done for. A deal was a deal, her life for Raphael's. Tomas Paul knew his sister as well as he knew himself; she was implacable, and she never changed her mind. Look at Poor Little Actaeon, torn to bits for peeping. Clara was going to die, soon. And all he could do was wait, and watch it happen. He leaned across and touched her hand. Yes. No doubt about it. The telomerase was way down, the cells fucking up their reproduction, doing it faster every second, a demented production line. He said what he felt.

"Oh Clara."

Clara looked at him quizzically. "Oh darling, I'm fine." A smile. "Where was I? Oh yes, so Raphael looked down and saw me and let me into the flat. He said I looked like a drowned fucking rat." She laughed.

Tomas Paul swallowed a lump. "Was it a tip inside?"

Clara shook her head. "Worse. It was like a show home. No evidence of human habitation except *Scherza Infida* playing at 150 decibels, a terrible stench of cigarettes and a stack of empty whisky bottles. No food, anywhere." She laughed. "So, we had a chat. Not about what had happened. Just about how thin he was getting, that kind of thing. And the next day I got a terrible cough being out in the rain, and this pain under my arm."

She pushed the soup bowl away. "I'm not going to eat that.

Lovely though it is." She took out a mirror and checked her lipstick. "You think I'm wrong, don't you? Not telling them."

Tomas Paul took her hand. "I think you're the cleverest person I know, and you have your reasons. But you mustn't give up."

Clara gave him a very hard look, but she didn't take her hand away. "I can assure you I have no intention of giving up. I am daughter of fucking science, and it is going to save my fucking life. But I am also a Stoic. I won't dish out pain and I don't want pity. Everyone has problems."

"I know that." Tomas Paul squeezed her hand, but he knew he was helpless, even with all his talents. What story could you tell a dying child? Maybe one that told them they've been lucky. That their life hasn't been wasted. "Did I ever tell you about the council of nineteen forty-five, in Thessaly?"

Clara shook her head. "Is this one of your bits of metaphysical shit?"

Damn right it was. "In nineteen forty-five the gods had called an emergency council in Thessaly." They were in despair. Europe was being destroyed. They started to debate whether humanity in Europe should be erased again, with earthquakes in Anatolia and Italy, and tidal waves hitting Lisbon and Amsterdam, followed by terrible rain and snow, floods in the east, then plague, smallpox and famine to take out the weak. Zeus and Poseidon couldn't wait to get started, and Apollo had designed a new plug and play European human. "There was huge support for the plan. They were convinced that war would never end, that retaliations would carry on for generations, that Europeans would never live in peace."

Clara listened closely. She'd always liked a story. "So why didn't they just do it?"

"They needed unanimity. There was one opposer."

"Athene?"

"No, not her. She was raring to get going. And Mars of course, Ares."

"Who opposed it then?"

"Jesus."

"He was there?"

"Of course he was there."

"Sounds pretty ecumenical."

"It was. But of course, he was the only one with any living followers." Tomas Paul was dying for a cigarette but given the circumstances he didn't bother. "He sat quietly at the back, dropping ludes, listening to all the indignation they were spouting about mankind's ingratitude, and then when it came to the vote he just shook his head and said *Hey man. This is heavy shit, like, a real bummer. We need to give these dudes another chance, you dig?*"

Clara smirked. "Because Jesus was a stoner?"

"Sure. He said they should give them another chance. You know, the New Testament thing; justice, and forgiveness, and second chances. He said it was wrong to wipe the poor fuckers out when they'd been left to themselves for thousands of years. No wonder they'd fucked it all up. But the gods were going to have to change the operating model, to get more hands on. Jesus said *like no fucking way dude* was he coming back to get nailed up again, but some of the others agreed to go undercover, low key, no lightning bolts or miracles, just very low visibility operations, operating as subtle avatars that would embed themselves with humans over time, encourage them, give them hope, and get them back on the right lines, and then handover and exit." Tomas Paul sipped his tea. It was cold now. "Jesus was really confident it would work. He said that when the atrocities of war came to light humankind would be shocked into relative peace for a few decades, and that would give us time to reacquaint them with the beauty and love of human life, and that that would inspire them to create a more just world."

"Give them time."

"Sorry?"

Clara shook her head and sipped her own cold tea. "You said "give us time"."

"Yes. Give them time, of course. Mostly they went along with it, but some were more hasty. Diana was worried about her beasts and her forests, so she came straight down. She had to compromise – even straight after the war it was hard to appear from nowhere, so she had to settle for being a spectre, a figure of dreams and fantasies. That's why there are so many Diana statues. That's where you find her. But the others were more subtle. Some of them even appeared as academics."

"Which would explain a lot." Clara smiled and looked out at the street. "I agree that Europe at peace – even mostly at peace – is a miracle."

"Clara. Look at our family histories. Our having lunch in London today is a miracle."

"Yes."

Tomas Paul nodded. "And your life is full of beauty and love. And your life is inspiring."

Clara nodded back. "Yes. Yes, I suppose it is really."

Eleven blue-backpacked French students of varying degrees of pulchritude came into the restaurant like little terrapins. It was time to go.

Tomas Paul looked over at Clara. He'd said too much, and he'd probably catch it, but he'd done the right thing. And he knew what Clara should sing.

> *Now, now that the sun hath veil'd his light*
> *And bid the world goodnight;*
> *To the soft bed my body I dispose,*
> *But where shall my soul repose?*
> *Dear, dear God, even in Thy arms,*
> *And can there be any so sweet security!*
> *Then to thy rest, O my soul!*
> *And singing, praise the mercy That prolongs thy days.*
> *Hallelujah!*

CHAPTER 13

LOVE FOR SALE

After an afternoon shopping, or rather egging each other on to buy things they didn't need, Raphael and Tiago reached the Café du Palais Royale at five. Raphael chose a table in a quiet corner away from bored dogs and yappy children, and Tiago's phone rang. Inês.

"Take it. Tea?"

"Please. Green."

Raphael watched him walk away. His plans to cosset Tiago weren't quite on track. Tiago might want to be owned, but he didn't intend to be bought, and he'd allowed Raphael to buy him only one present. When the book dealer's invoice came it would be for seven thousand euros, but that wouldn't matter. Tiago wouldn't know it. And Tomas Paul could afford it.

Raphael ordered their drinks and lit his first cigarette of the afternoon. It had been an eventful Saturday; a loving dawn, a lazy breakfast in bed, and then a visit to Tiago's office that had started with a slow kiss in a lift so fast that their lips were still locked when the doors opened. But when Raphael had opened his eyes, he'd halted like a bull in a killing stall. The trading floor was a dump. Stale-aired, filled with crooked banks of scruffy terminals, and rows of stained, mismatched swivel chairs. There was trash on the desks and on the floor; plastic cups, screwed up paper, unfinished food. It looked as if it had been abandoned in a hurry.

Raphael frowned. It was an unloved, grotty midden, the kind of place he had avoided all his life. It was not at all suitable for Tiago. He would have to be rescued from it.

"Jesus. How the fuck can you work here?"

"I told you. They give me lots of money. And I don't work there. I work in here." Tiago led him to a glass wall to one side of the trading floor. "I'll show you."

Raphael looked around. What a dump. "So you trade metals here?"

"I haven't traded metals for years. I develop strategy, build models, scenarios. I told you."

"You must have told me when I wasn't listening."

"Evidently." Tiago opened a matt metal lock in a glass door and let Raphael into a cube of glass, steel and concrete, a goldfish tank about three metres by two. It was less depressing than the trading floor, mainly because it was clean and tidy; there were three slim, symmetrically placed computer screens on a pale wood desk, with two laptops, a phone, and a framed photo of Tiago holding Tiaginho, and Tiaginho holding an ice cream. Against one wall two healthy plants and a Portuguese flag perched on top of a short, shuttered metal cabinet. Tiago talked softly, quietly proud; he'd made this "pod" a condition of coming back, helped the cleaner get it ready on Monday night. He opened chunky white vertical blinds of a kind that Raphael had never liked and broad beams of afternoon light flooded in.

"We had to steam the carpet. There was mouse-shit, squashed

cockroaches. I gave her fifty euros for staying late with me."
He unzipped the bookcase. "And I have space for my books, of
course." The shelves were packed with colourful rows of spines,
some new, most worn. He sat down and reached below the desk.

"Terrible ergonomics here. Nobody gives a fuck." The hard
disk whirred, the screens lit, and dark chromatic techno pulsed
from an unseen speaker.

Raphael breathed a shallow sigh of relief. It wasn't just about
making money: it was about making money with style, with
bookish flair. "This music is way before your time."

"This music is way before everyone's time." Tiago flipped
open a laptop, tapped some keys and sang along with the music.

"Let me take you on a trip. Around the world and back."

Graphs appeared on the three screens above him. "Actually."
He rubbed his eyes, tapped away, and flashed up more graphs,
moving windows around the screens; the stocks owned by
Ut, and the Hexacorp, six month trends on Bovespa, FTSE,
Shanghai; other corporations, good guys, not so good guys, and
"our guys"; prices of copper, iron ore, gold, from the London
Metal Exchange; satellite images of arid, unlovely moonscapes
with giant pockmarks, excavations for huge amoebic swimming
pools.

Tiago paused and placed a finger on an unscarred scrubby
plain. "I'm thinking of this location for *Lux*. For the gold, you
know? The gold that isn't there. It won't be here. But it could
easily be somewhere round here." And finally a geological section,
brightly coloured, shaded and speckled. "Because of the neutrons,
obviously. There'll be an ambiguity. See?"

Raphael nodded; he didn't see but would rather die than admit it. "Right."

Tiago pointed at the screen. "I've always called it *Restauradores*, Restoration."

"Liberation Economics."

Tiago laughed. "Exactly so. The Church of Christ Economist, in fact." He tapped again and cleared the screens. "But now it's *Lux Aeterna*.""

"So where is it? The plan?"

Tiago tapped his head. "Mostly in here. Sometimes I write things at home, and squirrel them away. I work on a typewriter. A 1974 Olivetti. It was my father's." He smiled. "Analogue can be safer than digital these days. And I use a cipher." He tapped his head again. "Which is also in here." He smiled. "And now I'm hungry."

They'd walked slowly back downtown, side by side, Tiago's voice a soft, surreal echo in the deserted, high-sided backstreets, explaining how it might be done. He'd thought about a series of deliberate fuck ups; the rogue actions of a crazy young Portuguese trader, a Lusitanian Leviathan, that wouldn't surprise anyone. But then he'd get the sack, maybe prison, game over. Only *Lux* would do the job properly, a motiveless faking and planting of geodesic data that would set Re and Mi and Fa against one another, victims of their own greed, poetic justice. Raphael kept silent, letting Tiago choose the route, though he knew a better one. He wanted time to reflect on the Carthusian cell, on whether *Lux* was brave or insane, on whether Tiago could be dissuaded from it; but mostly he was dragging his feet to slow down this meander through the backstreets with the cheerful high-hearted young man who had redeemed him from the purgatory of lonely, boring weekends. After a few minutes he stopped to light a cigarette. "Wait."

Tiago stopped and waited, hands in pockets, kicking at the kerb with his navy blue All Stars, a sullen teenager unwilling to admit he needed approval. "So. Do you like the plan?"

Raphael watched. Hell, no; he didn't like the plan at all. It was crazy and dangerous. But he did love the planner, with the messenger bag slung across his body like the sash of an angel; an angel that had fallen to earth, preferring to be a saint, Santiago of the Bourse, of Bovespa, and founding a church to deliver his mission; liberation economics. Raphael smiled.

"Of course I do." He went over to Tiago and straightened the strap on his shoulder. "How long have you been planning it?"

Tiago frowned. "Two years? Yes." He looked up and down the street, kissed the hand on his shoulder, and said that Raphael probably thought he was a bit crazy, didn't he.

And Raphael shrugged and said all geniuses were a bit crazy.

...

Tiago came back to the table and sat down. "Sorry. I had to tell Inês what we'd been buying. She says that when you fall in love, you spend an extra 2000 dollars a month."

"Intriguing. Is that how you know it's love?"

"I don't know but at least it's quantitative."

"So your credit card provider knows you're in love before you do?"

"I suppose so." Tiago grinned at him. "Next, we need to change your phone."

"What's wrong with my phone?"

"It looks like a fucking dog toy."

"It works. Even in the car. And I hate changing my phone. Something always goes wrong."

"It won't. I'll set it up for you." Tiago took out the book. "Hey look. Verlaine had a great signature. Absinthe writing." He laughed. "Hey, can you imagine them shopping on a Saturday afternoon? Or more likely shoplifting. In Aldi, squeezing peaches, and Arthur hiding bottles of brandy under a filthy overcoat, and swearing at the security guards with great hauteur and in the most extreme foul language."

Raphael nodded. "Yes, and doing it with a certain style, but then Paul being so wound up."

"Yes, and telling him to take that straight back where it came from."

"And Arthur saying *Oh fuck you Paul, you're no fun anymore.*" Raphael shook his head. "But it wasn't love. They were just out to shock. They were just horny, bibulous poets looking for notoriety, novelty."

Tiago was indignant. "No. It was real love, real devotion."

"Maybe." Raphael lit a cigarette. He would let this go. He'd believed the same thing once, but he didn't need role models anymore, especially tragic ones. "Like your devotion to god?"

"Yes, I suppose so, in the sense that devotion means making someone's happiness your life's study, your life's work. Else why bother?"

"So can a lover be a substitute for god?"

Tiago shrugged. "If he's perfect enough."

"There it is. Perfection. That's it. You crave it. That's why you love maths." Raphael put his matches away. "It literally adds up."

Tiago grinned. "Yes, okay, I'm a cliché. I love maths. I love the serenity of it, the fact that numbers behave themselves, in series and progressions, and matrices, and algorithms. I love the way you can unravel an equation line by line. When I have a fucking awful day at work I go home and take out some squared paper and a College textbook, and within a few minutes I'm looking at a page of my own writing, an algebraic reduction or a partial differential equation, and I feel a whole lot better about the fucked up world I have to live in."

"You do algebra for fun?"

"No, not for fun. I do it for pleasure, like playing the piano, or the guitar. Why not? You play music, you sketch. It all delights your brain. It takes it out of itself, to a higher plane."

"A higher plane." Raphael gazed at him, then looked at a girl in the square, thought she should have her hair cut short. He looked back at Tiago and saw perfection. "I don't mean to be critical. Your brain amazes me."

"And I don't mean to be defensive. But I was one of those guys people made fun of at College. The geeks, and the kids with the wrong shoes, and the virgins." Tiago looked at the girl Raphael had been watching. "She's pretty. But she should have her hair cut really short."

Raphael smiled. "But you were one of the beautiful virgins."

"Well yes, technically. At least I was until Friday morning. When a bad man caught me."

They shared a long look. The waiter came with their drinks and glided away.

"My point is that no one makes fun of the beautiful virgins. They are powerful."

"Maybe. I imagine you were one of the cool, cruel kids, weren't you?"

"Maybe. But you weren't scared of them. You despise anyone who doesn't agree with you."

"We all did. All the pre-seminarians."

"And derision made you stronger?"

"Of course. We fed on it. Jesus worked all his life to be spat on by trashy people. We got it at eighteen."

Raphael thought about the defiant beautiful boy with the dangerous horse. He imagined Tiago could take quite a bit of derision; take it and fire it back. That was what *Lux* was, in a way, a pre-emptive strike on the bad guys.

"It strengthened your faith, I suppose. Either that or you'd give up."

"I suppose so. I've always believed in Jesus's divinity, and in heaven. But a lot of the other stuff is just crap." Tiago shrugged. "I mean, obviously hell and Satan can't exist, as such. A loving God wouldn't allow them to. They were made up by man to control other men. But when I was a student I loved Jesus for his unconditional love, and I loved my creator. For his forgiveness, I suppose." He nodded. "His forgiveness of my imperfections. Like you said yesterday, I made God in my image. I'm good at forgiving."

"But you shouldn't need to ask forgiveness from a real loving father." Raphael looked up.

Tiago was looking away. "You're right, of course. But being forgiven can be a very sweet sensation."

"I know. I've had to ask for forgiveness once or twice."

"Why doesn't that surprise me?"

"And reconciliation is good." Raphael waved more smoke away. "Well, I'm good at it. But then I've had a lot of practice."

"Again, not surprising. But I'm pleased to hear it. I suspect we'll be doing quite a lot of it."

A pigeon landed near Raphael's foot, pecked at some crumbs, some of his cigarette ash. "But is god's forgiveness like that? Like the relief of make up sex, that sense of being allowed back into someone's arms?" Raphael sipped his coffee. "I wonder what it's like being god. Having to forgive all those people."

Tiago nodded. "Difficult, I guess. Whenever I have to forgive someone it's like I'm giving part of my heart away, or tying a string to it that connects to them. It's only a matter of time before they pull on it again." He sighed. "You're never free. That's why god's heart bleeds for us. He's always forgiving us, giving us another chance. You've got to love him for that."

Raphael gazed at him, seeing the priest for the first time. "But surely it's better than being us. We have to be grateful. That costs a lot of pride."

"Like when you knelt to me on Friday. Did that cost you your pride?"

"God yes. And am I tied to your heart?"

"Yes. With steel cables." Tiago rubbed his eyes. "And now my mind's gone blank."

"You were a beautiful young virginal student, loving Jesus with mystical devotion." Raphael bit his lip; too flippant maybe.

But Tiago was unfazed. "Ah yes. So I was. I was a freak really. Some nights I would pray to him and I could almost believe he was with me. I think I even dreamt he was my lover. In fact, I know I dreamt that some nights."

Raphael shook his head. "I can't hack that competition."

Tiago touched his arm and smiled, words unnecessary for a few moments. "Anyway, I would wake up in the morning knowing that I longed to serve him, to be his vessel, his creature. That was the only passion I knew, that Jesuit zeal of the Counter Reformation, that intense longing." He sipped his tea. "Though of course my love for Jesus was never a proxy for loving a man. My love for him and my love for you are two separate things. Two separate beautiful gifts from God." He put his cup down. "As I told you in bed yesterday afternoon."

"Indeed you did." Raphael tried not to smile too knowingly. Lots of young men and women probably fell in love with Jesus and called themselves Christians. And given the loss of his parents at such a young age, it was unsurprising that Tiago had found comfort in a faith that held that suffering was meaningful and sacrifice was noble. Raphael knew different, but for all his faults he was gallant, and loving, and would never belittle his new lover's deepest beliefs; well, maybe just a bit.

"But you said you lost your faith when you discovered sex."

"Did I?"

"I think so. Something about mistaking the surface of the sea for the sea itself."

"Ah yes." Tiago winced. "I suppose there was a time when I thought I'd misread everything, that it was all just carnal ecstasy. But I was wrong. Jesus' love is infallible, and unconditional." He smiled and shrugged and picked up his tea cup. "Infallible. Unlike us."

Raphael looked for the waiter. "Would you like some more tea?"

"Please." Tiago nodded. "Look. There's nothing to be afraid of. He brought us together. He blesses us. It's not weird. There's no need to be scared."

"I'm not scared."

"You look scared. You look fucking terrified. Don't be. I'm not going to sing Kumbaya. Lighten up."

"I'm sorry." Raphael looked for words; he didn't want to hurt, but he wouldn't concede. "I'm just getting used to it. I'm getting used to the strength of your faith, the way you talk."

"But there's nothing to fear if you don't believe in god. Be logical."

Raphael caught the waiter's eye. "It's just that you're so certain." He lit another cigarette and shook out the match. "It just takes some getting used to."

Tiago smiled at him. "Look. Jesus loves our love. He gave us to one another. That's it."

"Fine. As long as you're happy."

"Yes. I am. I'm very happy." Tiago leaned forward. "In fact I'm so happy I want to go home and fuck right now. That's how happy I am."

"Gentlemen."

"Same again please."

Raphael watched the waiter walk away. "Take the word for the deed."

"I will. Actually I should show you something. Somewhere in this bag I have something. Yes. Here it is." Tiago took out a battered paperback. "John. Just his gospel, not the weird hophead shit." He placed the book on the table and stared at it for a while.

Raphael frowned. "Do you always carry that round?"

Tiago shrugged. "Not always. Often."

Raphael looked at the book, unsure about touching it. "Do you want me to read it?"

"You don't have to. But it's beautifully written. He loved Jesus the way I did, with a perfect sense of being loved. And Jesus had a soft spot for him." Tiago pushed the book across the table. "You can touch it. You won't burst into flames."

Raphael opened the front cover. Tiago's name was written on the flyleaf, and *Parabens,* and *Deus e justo. Deus e amavel. Abracos, Rogerio.* Perfect love. He pointed.

"Rogerio?"

Tiago smiled and bit his lip. "Yes. It was a present. End of exams, finals."

The waiter brought their drinks and went away.

"You mentioned him the other night. Rogerio. Your first lover."

"My first lover makes it sound very grand. It wasn't really like that."

Raphael put sugar in his coffee. He didn't take sugar. It was just something to do. "What was it like?"

Tiago stared at the table for a few seconds. "Oh, I don't know." He looked at his nails. "He was studying at the seminary in Lisbon. They asked him to come and talk with me, to see if it was right for me. He was twenty-four, in his final year. I was just twenty-one, and I'd just inherited some family money. I'd bought my car, and my flat in Lisbon. I was independent." He covered his mouth and stifled a shallow yawn that was astonishingly unconvincing.

But Raphael was curious. "And you fell in love with him?"

"Of course I did. He was more gentle, and thoughtful, and kind than any man I'd ever met, at least any man outside my family, and we spent hours talking about the love of Jesus, and our love for Jesus. We drowned in it – Jesus, Jesus, Jesus. And one evening after dinner and a bottle of wine, or maybe two, I don't know, he asked if he could stay, and we prayed together, and we got into bed and slept like children. And in the morning a garbage truck woke us up." Tiago stared across the square at nothing. "He said my name and reached out for me." He paused. "And I suppose love came upon us. The way it does. And the next week he moved in. And then we played house while I revised for my finals." He looked at the book. "That was when he gave me this."

Raphael smiled. He was touched and relieved. It was teenage, and sweet, and unthreatening. "And it was wonderful."

"Did I tell you that?"

"No. It's in your eyes."

Tiago smiled and sat back. "Falling in love in Lisbon in May is pretty good. The days are warm, and the evenings stretch out, and the jacaranda blossom makes a purple carpet on the ground. During the day I'd study at the College library and Rogerio would work with homeless people. And in the evening we'd make love, have dinner together, and then talk about how lucky we were to have found one another in Jesus's love. And then we'd go to sleep in each other's arms. I was happy. I was home."

"It sounds idyllic."

"Completely. And it couldn't last, could it?" Another counterfeit yawn. "After six weeks or so the seminary kicked him out. He said he didn't care, that his life was about us. And then he went on a retreat. A kind of recovery mission, I guess." Tiago rubbed his eyes. "And after that things got very fucked up for a while. He called me and said he couldn't see me, he was thinking things through. All abject nonsense, to and fro." He covered his mouth and sieved the words through his fingers. "And finally, one shitty evening, he came round and told me he was going to join a mission near São Paulo 'to work with the Guarani and to get away from my influence'. Those were his exact words."

"For fuck's sake."

"And those were mine."

Raphael was stunned. He'd been prepared for something to be wrong. But not this; cathartic rejection by a first lover whose latest postcard was still pinned above the fucking kettle. And dismissal for the sake of a god he still worshipped. No wonder he knew all about forgiveness. "Jesus."

Tiago had covered his eyes. "Oh no. This had nothing to do with him." He sighed. "And there was other stuff. About disease, and dying, and god's judgement. All that shit. Shit that idiots used to come out with, still come out with."

Raphael caught his breath. He'd dodged the hail of bullets that Fate had aimed at his generation; an abstemious and shy teenager, a non-joiner-in, he'd never nursed a dying friend or lover. But Martin had, and he'd born the scars with pride; he had been the activist, the undergraduate running errands for his sick and dying elders, bringing them youth and beauty and macrobiotic food, reading them poetry in a soft voice when their sight had failed. It had become His Cause, and he still rose to furious indignation at the prejudice, and the injustice, and the deep buried grief of survivors like Ben, his first tutor at Oxford.

He nursed Paul for two years, and he was lucky, they let him stay with him, let him cry on his ruined carcase while it was still warm, let him go to the funeral. Big of them, wasn't it? Gulping down red wine. *But he wasn't that lucky, because he's survived, hasn't he, like a single blackened stump after a forest fire. He was twenty-five when Paul died, and he's still alone, of course. How could you love again, want sex again, after it did that to you?*

And Martin would weep, and bite his blue lips, and be angry with Raphael for the unfeeling way he wore a smart red ribbon to the fundraising events but never quite succeeded in crying as hard as Martin thought he should.

But Martin had been wrong. Raphael wasn't unfeeling. Cruelty and the people that dished it out didn't make him cry; they made him furious and vengeful. He looked down at his hands now, watching them form fists, knowing he really wanted to punch someone; Rogerio, probably.

"But it was fine." Tiago wiped his eyes with the heels of his hands. "I sat up all that night reading sixteenth century Portuguese poetry. As one does." He cast a look of vapid optimism towards Raphael. "Good if you like that kind of thing."

"Right." Raphael gazed at him, wanting to comfort him. Not here. Maybe there would be time to go back to the flat before they went to Rob's.

Tiago sniffed. "Of course, he never went on to become a priest. I actually think he would have been the worst priest of all time." He sipped his tea. "He's a stonemason now, doing restoration work mainly. He told me last Christmas that one day every stone angel in Lisbon will have my face. Well, my mouth. Apparently I have an angel's mouth."

Raphael's heart moved sideways. "But he's in Brazil?"

"No. Lisbon. I saw him at Christmas. I saw him a few times last year." Looking away.

"You saw him?"

"Yes. We smoked a few joints. And then we went to bed. Five or six times. He's my oldest friend." Looking back. "So now you know. Happy now?"

"Not really." Raphael looked around, lowered his voice. "Look, I don't mean to be possessive."

Tiago nodded slowly. "But you are going to be."

"Yes. Yes I admit it, I am. But he can't be good for you."

Tiago gave him a steady look. "Raphael. Do not be a stupid cretinous cunt."

Raphael sat up straight. "What?"

"Don't talk about shit you don't understand. All right?"

Raphael looked round. People were looking at them. "Okay. Take it easy."

"He saved my fucking life. He's the best friend I ever had. Don't you dare criticise him."

"I'm sorry." Raphael shook his head, tried to turn Tiago towards him. "Look at me. Don't be angry. It just didn't sound like he was right for you. Tiago. Look at me."

But Tiago was looking away. "Raphael. There are things I can't tell you. He helped me, that's all. Don't be jealous." He looked at Raphael, narrowed his eyes. "You can't believe me, can you? Jesus, you are so fucking cold." He stuffed the books in his bag and walked away.

Raphael watched him go. "Fucking brilliant. Well done." He put his head in his hands and wondered why he was always the one walked away from. He knew about devotion, and he knew about forgiveness, but like many strong men he could bear infinitely more insult to himself than he could to the people he loved. He lit another cigarette and took out his old phone. The picture he had taken that morning was on the screen; a head and shoulders shot of a knowing, smiling, unshaven Tiago in a white shirt; perfection. Raphael gazed without hope; he could text, but he was crap at it and it took forever. He could call, but he doubted Tiago would answer. The plans for a weekend ahead lay in shreds; no introducing Tiago to Rob, no chance to edge Tiago's life closer to his own. It was all in ruins. He lit a cigarette and looked heavy-hearted at the smiling boy on the screen, the empty cups on the table.

There was a gentle hand on his shoulder. "Beautiful boy. Looks high maintenance though."

Raphael touched the hand with his lips. "I'm so sorry."

"You don't need to be. I'm sorry for swearing and walking off. That was unforgivable." Tiago sat down. "I have a bad temper. A cruel temper." He rubbed his eyes. "I'm a son of Thunder, remember?"

Raphael did remember; the words and the comfort of the night before, the sense of knowing he didn't want to live without it. He ate crow. "It was my fault. I'm jealous. And I get angry too quickly."

"No." Tiago shook his head. "No."

"Like last week, I had to recite a sixteen digit number into the phone to a computer that couldn't understand my accent. And get this. The phone had a digitised keypad?"

Tiago frowned. "Morons. I hope you told that computer to fuck right off."

"I did. It's probably reported me to a supervisor for training purposes." Raphael got the required response and put his phone away. "You have a beautiful smile baby."

"You mean this?" Tiago beamed at him.

"Yes. And your look of furious defiance is incredibly arousing." Raphael smiled. This was better, but he should explain himself. "The thing is I'm not actually very experienced."

"You've only ever lived with Tomas Paul, and then Martin?"

Raphael drew on his cigarette. "I never really lived with

Tomas Paul." Best to get this all out. "And he needed to see other people." He looked away, not wanting to see the look on Tiago's face, fearful that in these enlightened days his younger self might be judged to have got the fuzzy end of the lollipop.

But Tiago's tone was level. "You had some kind of open relationship with him?"

"Yes." Raphael shrugged and explained; it hadn't made him jealous, Tomas Paul had been seeing two women, one of them had been Mel, now the mother of his kids. He'd always been quite open about it. "I felt at the time that made it okay." He looked at his cigarette. "Some people wouldn't agree."

A hideous scaly pigeon jumped up onto the table. Tiago shooed it away. "I think when people are open about it, then it's sort of okay." He knew about lots of people that lived like that, stayed together, like that. It worked for them, he supposed.

Raphael nodded slowly at the *sort of.* He'd heard this kind of remark from Tiago a few times now, and suspected it was a smokescreen that concealed a deeply-held, opposing view. He wouldn't let it go. He took Tiago's arm. "It worked for me then. But i\t wouldn't now. Not with you. I want us to be enough for each other Tiago."

Tiago smiled. "We are. We will be. We'll get there." He moved Raphael's hand away, placed it on the table. "I suppose you'd better know the rest." As well as Rogerio, there was Jason, a partner in a venture capital firm in London, and Florian, a junior Trade Consul in Santiago, in Chile. They were just friends, company. Tiago rubbed his eyes. "They both know about you. They've always known. And they know that things have changed. I texted them yesterday." He shrugged. "Florian's cool, Jason isn't." Jason wanted them to get married. He would get over it.

"He's going to have to." Raphael nodded. True, Tiago was too beautiful to sleep alone, a sad bookworm in a forgotten volume; so it was good that these guys had called him beautiful, and comforted him. But it was better that they never would again. It was strange that you could feel so sure of someone, so quickly. Well, almost sure. "So there was no one in Paris?"

"You were in Paris."

Raphael ran out of suitable words. Had they been alone he would have said that that nothing else mattered in space and time but the two of them, and their love for each other, and their future together. But he was too dignified to do that in a public space, so he looked down at his hand on the table, longing for the reassurance of touch.

"I know how you feel." Tiago covered Raphael's hand with his own. "I do know."

Raphael held the hand and found some words. "Bed for you the moment we get to Rob's."

"Too fucking right."

...

It was a pleasant afternoon but Tomas Paul got back to Athelstan Mews pretty cheesed off. Why did all the good people have to die? And why did all the boring drones go on for ever?

For the sake of something to do he went down to the study in his lovely new basement and looked about in a trunk full of unfiled memories until he found the business card.

What a very long name it was. And what a very small world.

His phone vibrated, still on silent. It was the normal weird shit from Amelia.

Leander fine thanks. Been fishing, catching sticklebacks and used condoms, mainly. N&S.

He'd been about to reply when the second message came through.

Raphael Emmanuel Davide for Triploid.

And the third.

Rich, vain, currently playing fuck my neighbour. Good match, good timing. Know him?

Tomas Paul sat back in his chair, feet on the desk, looking at the card, thinking back to the nineteenth Annual International Thrust Symposium, Lisbon, January 2007. The already inebriated boy he'd met in the hotel bar had introduced himself as *Nuno* though that wasn't what was written down here. They'd started on differential calculus but they'd hit the margaritas pretty hard and by ten o'clock they were onto gods and destiny; and by midnight Nuno was giving him big eyes and suggesting they went somewhere quieter. Of course, when they'd got to the room Nuno had slid down the door like melting cheese, but he'd let himself be laid down on the bed. And then he'd killed it all dead.

"Jesu."

It was close, but no cigar.

Tomas Paul had watched Nuno sleep it off. In the morning he'd left him some foreign money he didn't need any more and gone without waking him, wondering why so many young people led such aimless lives.

Tomas Paul put the business card down. So much for the flawless lover; Tiago was nothing but a whited sepulchre. And now Clara was dying. It could all spell disaster for Raphael. And Tomas Paul only had two years left in which to do anything about it.

He went to the desk and retrieved a manila envelope. There was no need to open it. He knew perfectly well what it contained; a black and white photograph of two boys and a cello, and the last hand written letter he'd ever received, sent over ten years ago. He studied the address for a few moments, knowing that the elegant black writing on the envelope that made his name beautiful was nothing to the handful of words inside that made him immortal. And for the first time in his life, Tomas Paul knew exactly what he had to do.

So he called Amelia.

CHAPTER 14

THE BRUTAL TRUTH

Late on Sunday morning the sun was out.

Tiago stopped just inside the park gates and looked out at the city laid out for miles below him. Wandy was whimpering at his feet, pawing the grass, wanting to run.

"Wait." Tiago unfastened the dog's lead. Wandy looked up. "Go on then."

Nothing.

Tiago nodded. "You want some work? Okay." He picked up a stick and threw it. "Fetch."

Wandy careered off, wonky-legged but fast, nose to the ground, ears flapping.

Tiago watched him and grinned. It was a proper city park, not very big but natural and unkempt, with lots of old trees and hedges and few signs telling you what you couldn't do. Near the gate it was mostly grassy uneven heath, with narrow runners' paths bisecting hundreds of mossy anthills. A few hundred yards ahead of him the land plunged steeply downhill towards a small lake and some mixed woodland. Two lads in Barca shirts were kicking a football around near the lake. One turned and waved.

Tiago waved back. He could get used to this new life, walking the well behaved family dog in a quiet park on a Sunday morning. He looked at his watch. Raphael and Rob would just be starting their run now. He put his hands in his pockets and looked up at an aeroplane making a steep turn. Your life could change just like that.

Wandy came back, dropped the stick an inconvenient distance from Tiago's feet, and sat back, tongue lolling. Tiago pointed at the ground directly in front of him. "No, here."

Wandy picked up the stick and dropped it four centimetres closer.

"No. Here."

Wandy dropped the stick on Tiago's shoes.

"Fair enough." Tiago patted the dog's head and picked up the stick, which was now delightfully covered in moss and spaniel spit. "Oh, thank you Wandy. Again?"

Wandy barked.

Tiago threw the stick further. Wandy watched it fly through the air and looked back at him.

"What? Oh yeah. Englishman's dog." Tiago pointed. "Fetch."

Wandy shot off and Tiago grinned; Raphael had agreed they could have a spaniel, but really you needed two. He walked down the hill thinking about names that might appeal to Raphael; Hero and Leander, Dido and Aeneas, Sergius and Bacchus.

After five minutes he reached a rough path that led to the woodland and a scruffy bench. Tiago sat down, stared into space and let himself think about last night, the best Saturday night of his life. And now it was the best Sunday morning. The sun was shining on his face, but he closed his eyes, happy to shut the beauty of the morning out; the joy inside him was enough. Life couldn't get any better. Loneliness and delusion were banished, and the days of love and heroism he'd longed for were here. He was adored, he had a quest for justice, and his story was about to start. Spring was bursting out all over. Zephyrus was on his way. Tiago smiled and thought about Monteverdi. *Zefiro torna, e di soavi accenti l'aer fa grato e'il pié discioglie a l'onde e, mormoranda tra le verdi fronde, fa danzar al bel suon su'l prato i fiori.*

His phone buzzed in his pocket. He took it out and looked at the screen.

amadea.strini@ortygia.gr
To: tiagojosegpdasilva@creditdijonnais.fr
Subject: AMOR VINCIT OMNIA
Attachments: 130412 0800.jpeg (250 KB), 130412 0810.jpeg (235 KB)

Tiago opened the two photographs. The first showed him and Raphael embracing in the open doorway to the apartment, their long, unwilling goodbye. The second was Raphael in the front seat of his car, head back, eyes closed, smiling, ecstatic.

Tiago looked at it. Someone's idea of a joke. He had a lot of colleagues in Saint-Germain-en-Laye. "Sure. Knock yourself out guys."

The phone buzzed again.

amadea.strini@ortygia.gr
To: tiagojosegpdasilva@creditdijonnais.fr

Subject: Re: AMOR VINCIT OMNIA
Attachments: 140412 1600.jpeg (260 KB)

Tiago opened the file. It was another image, this time they were in the café in the Jardin du Palais Royal. He was standing with his hand on Raphael's shoulder. "Right." Tiago remembered the argument and shifted on the bench. "Okay, so? You're getting off on this? Good for you." Someone at work, their idea of a joke. Someone who didn't like him. That narrowed it down to a shortlist of about a hundred people. But who would call himself Amadea? Or, for that matter, had ever heard of Ortygia?

Wandy emerged from the woodland.

"Something weird's happening Wandy."

The dog came over and rested his head on Tiago's knee.

"Some creep is following uncle Tiago. Go and find him. Go and bite his bollocks off."

Buzz.

amadea.strini@ortygia.gr
To: tiagojosegpdasilva@creditdijonnais.fr
Subject: VITA BREVIS EST

"Undoubtedly." Tiago frowned. The email opened itself and shot through to a weblink:

DEATHS: Peacefully, after a brief illness, in his 85th year, businessman and philanthropist Raphael da Silva Davide, dearly loved husband of Tiago, devoted father of...

Tiago threw down the phone. "What the fuck? You sick fuck. You sick fucking troll." His mind raced; it couldn't be someone at work. They'd never have heard of Raphael.

The phone buzzed in the long grass like a trapped bee.

"Fuck off. Fuck you." But he had to look down at the screen.

amadea.strini@ortygia.gr
To: tiagojosegpdasilva@creditdijonnais.fr
Subject: Re: Re: AMOR VINCIT OMNIA
Attachments: 2106181630.jpeg (1 KB)

Tiago steeled himself, picked the phone up and opened the file. The screen flooded with colour; Raphael, handsome and very much alive, sitting on a bench in a sharp linen suit, in dappled sunshine, with his arms around two beautiful children, three years old maybe; a boy with a toy sports car, a girl with a golden toy kitten. The boy was dreamy with a high forehead, the girl dark and intense.

Tiago looked at the date, numbed, unable to compute.

Buzz.

amadea.strini@ortygia.gr
To: tiagojosegpdasilva@creditdijonnais.fr
Subject: Re: VITA BREVIS EST
Another weblink.

DEATHS: At home, after a long illness, Clara Davide, beloved wife of Robert and sister of Raphael, in her 43rd year

Tiago winced.

Buzz.

amadea.strini@ortygia.gr
To: tiagojosegpdasilva@creditdijonnais.fr
Subject: Re: Re: VITA BREVIS EST
THIS PROBABLY CANNOT BE STOPPED.
SORRY ☹

Tiago stared at the screen, hoping there would be more. But there wasn't. He put the phone down on the bench. He needed to think, and for that he needed to be calm. He sat back with closed eyes. *Utqueant laxis, Resonare fibris, Mira gestorum, Famuli tuorum, Solve pollute, Labis reatum, Sancte Johannes.*

He felt Wandy's cold snout push into his hand, and heard the phone buzz again, rattling on the wooden slats. He glanced down at the phone, unwilling to touch it.

amadea.strini@ortygia.gr
To: tiagojosegpdasilva@creditdijonnais.fr
Subject: Re: Re: Re: AMOR VINCIT OMNIA
LOVE IS MORE THAN THE GLORY AND SPLENDOUR OF SEDUCTION.

"You're fucking telling me."

amadea.strini@ortygia.gr
To: tiagojosegpdasilva@creditdijonnais.fr
 Subject: Re: Re: Re: Re: AMOR VINCIT OMNIA

YOU MUST BE STRONG.

Tiago sighed. "The story of my fucking life."

amadea.strini@ortygia.gr
To: tiagojosegpdasilva@creditdijonnais.fr
 Subject: VERITAS VOS LIBERABIT
EXACTLY. YOU MUST TELL HIM THE STORY OF YOUR FUCKING LIFE.
EVERYTHING, TODAY TIAGO.

Tiago covered his mouth. "Oh fuck."

He wasn't being trolled, or stalked. He was being blackmailed. And he had been hung out to dry. This was punishment for the lecture he'd given Raphael yesterday; for hubris. Any benign power watching over him had judged him proud, and deserted him. Dark forces were closing in. He hadn't been forgiven; the recent rise in his fortunes had just been a cruel trick to make his fall more spectacular. Raphael would drop him. All that lay ahead was loneliness and misery.

Buzz.

amadea.strini@ortygia.gr
To: tiagojosegpdasilva@creditdijonnais.fr
 Subject: Re: Re: VERITAS VOS LIBERABIT
HE WON'T MIND.
PROBABLY. ☺

Tiago shook his head. "Oh I think he will."

amadea.strini@ortygia.gr
To: tiagojosegpdasilva@creditdijonnais.fr
Subject: Re: Re: Re: VERITAS VOS LIBERABIT
CHEER UP. LIFE IS ABOUT THE FUTURE, AND YOURS IS BRIGHT.
PROBABLY.
NUNC ET SEMPER.

The screen cleared and went back to the picture of Raphael and the children. Tiago gazed at it for a few moments, then heard a plane above him. He looked up and watched it, moving, noisy and normal in the sky. The boys were shouting down by the lake. Wandy was yawning.

Tiago saw a sudden movement and looked back at the screen. The picture had turned into a video. There was no sound, but Raphael was laughing, and the children were climbing around on him, and dropping their toys, and getting their arms and legs tangled up, and prattling. He watched the clip again, trying to read Raphael's lips and solve the puzzle, when the clip turned into anther film in grainy black and white. This time there was no mistaking who the two people were, and what they were saying, because you could hear them.

Tiago watched the videos six times, then got up and walked back to Clara's, mostly oblivious to the dog padding along beside him, and the park, and the sun, and the traffic, wondering who Amadea was, and what the hell was going on, and how on earth he was going to get through the next few hours.

CHAPTER 15

OPEN

Robert Wayland Nelson had always sought to correct the adulterous and tragic warp in Life's Rich Tapestry that had spat him out by finding a wife he could love with total fidelity and intense devotion. It had turned out to be easy. Clara's dark, knowing looks had hooked him in a heartbeat. Her quick wit had tightened the line in less than an hour; and days later, when she'd taken him to bed and showed how much sensual pleasure her lissom body could give and take, he'd been happy to be reeled in. That children hadn't come hadn't mattered, because love hadn't gone, but grown, soon enveloping even the brother his wife adored. But though she and Raphael were like twins in appearance, they were opposites in essence; Raphael was brittle where Clara was tough, touchy where she was sanguine, fragile where she was resilient, and Rob knew which one of them needed more looking after. Although Rob took pride in his self-appointed role of guardian angel to both, he was no romantic. He was practical, and decent, and realistic in equal measure: he saw things clearly and called a spade *a fucking shovel* unless there were women or children present; he placed flowers on the grave of the mother he never knew; and he knew that it was okay that he would lay down his life for his best friend, while loving his own brother out of obligation.

And frankly, these days, he'd been missing that brother rather less than he felt he should have. Rob worked hard, and he'd always liked Sundays for the lie-in, and the chance to make unhurried love with Clara before going running or playing football with Raphael. But he'd enjoyed Sundays a lot more since Martin had gone back to England, leaving the contented three to spend the tail end of the weekend in peace. The new arrangement was working, and as an engineer Rob knew that when things were working, you didn't change them.

Today however things had clearly changed, and not for the better. Raphael's dignity had gone for a start: he was glued to Tiago; maybe he thought that if he let go he'd flop forward like a sad fifties robot with a flat battery. This morning, keen to be nice, he'd taken them coffee in bed and been met with the sight of Raphael sitting up, *clearly naked,* reading. *God thanks Rob.* Touching Tiago's bare, shoulder. *Hey sleepy, Rob's made coffee.* Rob had seen Raphael naked many times, but only in a shower, after sport. He'd had to look away and talk about the weather; though Wandy, rather less awkward in this situation, had jumped on the bed and tunnelled under the quilt.

This afternoon Raphael was lying with his head in Tiago's lap like a spoilt pet leopard. Rob watched and sighed quietly. It was a shame, but Raphael had made a poor choice. Tiago had seemed lively enough the night before, but now there was nothing to him; he seemed washed out, vapid, cradling Raphael like a child holds a teddy bear. It was a sex thing. Raphael would chew him up and spit him out, nobody would profit by the experience, and they'd all be back to square one.

Right now Raphael was sniggering at the thought of past glories. "Remember extreme Frisbee Rob?" He looked up at Tiago. "You made a wonderful lunch. That you didn't eat."

"Not that hungry." Tiago smiled. "Extreme Frisbee?" His voice was deeper than last night.

Rob decided to be guarded; Tiago might not be around that long. "I suppose it was fifteen years ago, ninety-seven?" He looked at Clara. She looked tired after the early train back from London.

She nodded. "Ninety-seven."

Raphael filled in the story; Tomas Paul had found it, a wooden panel, an encaustic wax painting, Apollo and Hyacinthus, all ending in tears with the jealous Zephyrus throwing the discus, hitting the boy, killing him.

Tiago nodded. "Poor Jacinto." His voice was sad and broken, rather different to last night's commanding tone heard through the wall. *Ride me Raphael. Ride me, and break me. Ride me till daybreak.* Rob sipped his wine. He was open-minded, but it had been like listening to someone else's porn movie in a cheap hotel. And it had kept him awake. For two hours.

"Indeed. Poor Hyacinthus. Poor little lambkin." Raphael nuzzled against Tiago's belly. "And Apollo turned the blood of his tragic beloved into flowers. And the bourgeois legatees of that story of the destructive power of divine desire and spite are now *Hyacinthus orientalis*, grown in glass bowls, by schoolgirls, and spinsters."

"Spinsters." Clara shook her head. "And you're wrong. It's the

English bluebell, *Hyacinthoides non scripta*." She put her head on one side. "All droopy."

Rob smiled. "She's right Raph. The English bluebell works better. You get huge drifts in the spring. You've just never seen them. English bluebell woods, beautiful."

"I've seen them, all right?" Raphael sat up. "I've seen fucking millions of English bluebells. I know exactly what the fuckers look like for fuck's sake."

"Tell me about the picture." Tiago stroked Raphael's hair. It was masterly lion taming, and Rob shared a smile with Clara while Raphael murmured. Tomas Paul had been shown the picture after a recital. It had been nailed into the back of the altar in a church near Regensburg; hidden away, even though it was pagan, because it was beautiful. Raphael balanced his wine glass on his breast. "Tomas Paul dated it first to fourth century, same as the ones in Egypt. But the fact that it's scenes from a story makes it unique." He yawned. "It's very vivid, great faces. I've got photographs of it at home. I'll show you later. It went to an orphanage in Namibia. It's in an office there, on the wall."

Tiago frowned at Rob. "But that was just a kind act. It wasn't complicated."

Clara shook her head. "It bloody was. Art only moves from the poor world to the rich world."

Raphael drained his glass. "That panel doesn't exist. No one knows about it, its value, other than us and Stephan, the priest. When we're ready, Clara will plant an on-line provenance for it." He turned to Tiago. "And the dating will back it up, and hey, it's been discovered. And then we plant a credible backstory to do with Germans in Southern Africa, and then some poor people are a lot better off. Because it's finders keepers."

And Raphael went on about the others, stuff Rob would have left out; the bronzes, the portraits, the drawings. Of course, he already knew about the girl on her way to Ontario. She was important, because it was the first thing they could easily copy. "Because we have the right materials. And I can draw."

Tiago looked down at Raphael. "Shall I tell them about Lux?"

Raphael frowned. "Not yet." He sat up. "Too soon."

"What's Lux?" Clara looked at Rob. "Something new?"

Raphael shook his head. "It's just an idea." He drew Tiago to him and spoke in a placating voice Rob hadn't heard before. "It's too early."

Tiago looked at him for a moment, then looked away, shrugged. "Okay."

Rob shook his head. "Fakes are difficult. The set up takes ages. And it makes people cross."

But it didn't matter. Raphael was standing up, holding his hand out to Tiago. "Let me show you some pictures." He turned to Rob. "Where's the key?"

"Norwegian Blue."

...

Rob and Clara kept their cars on the street and their garage was now pathologically tidy. Bikes, tack, wet suits, and garden tools hung on racks on the right hand wall; everything was pristine, ready to be used. Along the left hand wall were three filing cabinets and a large white chest freezer with a clean blackboard above it. Tiago gazed in envy at the orderliness of it. It wasn't dissimilar to part of a life that just hours ago had seemed within his reach; a quiet, contented existence of materialistic, urban-surburban coupledom. But that life appeared to be largely in pieces now.

"You okay?" Raphael was standing by the freezer, looking back at him.

"Sure." Tiago walked over to him. "Just tired. Show me." Maybe something amazing and beautiful would show him the way forward. But, thanks to Amadea, it was just two animal carcasses, lurid with frozen blood, four large frozen fish that looked rather surprised to be there, and a horrid looking rigid mass of frozen feathers in a bag. "Lamb from Rob's grandma, salmon from his dad." Raphael picked up the feathery mess and whacked it against the side of the fridge. "And an inedible pheasant Wandy chewed up last winter. Stupid fucking dog. He's meant to have a soft mouth." Raphael opened the bag, took out a small plastic package, and shook out a key. "My brother in law has a highly developed sense of mystery." He went over to a filing cabinet and unlocked a drawer. "Come and see this."

The three drawings were in plastic wallets in a folder marked "HMRC Tax Returns 2006-2010". Two of them were the same as the girl in the office. The third was a sketch of a plain boy with dark wings growing from his shoulders. Raphael drawled contentedly; the girl was Meladroni, and the boy was Cecco, the teenager Caravaggio loved and painted again and again, as Amor, as John the Baptist, as Bacchus, as an angel with Saint Francis. The feathers must have stunk, and Cecco probably stank too, but that wouldn't have bothered Caravaggio; everyone stank in those days. Raphael put the drawings down on top of the freezer, and stood behind Tiago with his arms around him like a dodgy golf pro. "Of course, Caravaggio was unlucky, because Cecco was boot-faced and stocky and squalid." Whereas Tiago would have made a much better angel, because he was beautiful and slender, and unspoilt.

Tiago heard it, but he wasn't listening. He was just looking at the girl, feeling himself drawn into her eyes, wishing he'd been dead for four hundred years like her, and only vaguely aware of Raphael's voice saying that, of course, everything in that garage was a fake.

...

Clara sent Raphael and Tiago home at five and took her husband to bed. Her lunch with Tomas Paul and a sense of taking control had made her happy to be back in her lovely skin, and after an hour of going at each other like knives, she and Rob began, appropriately, dicing Tiago into little pieces. It was obviously, said Rob, a sex thing. There was nothing to him. "I thought you said he was clever?"

Clara sighed. "He was when we met on Friday. Maybe he was intimidated."

"He's a commodities trader. He should be fucking bomb-proof." Rob tightened his arms around Clara's waist and bit her shoulder. "No. It's a sex thing. For most of last night I had my head under the pillow like Scooby fucking Doo. And this morning at breakfast, Jesus! Tiago comes into the kitchen in jeans and Raphael's shirt, the "I belong to this guy" look, and Raph just sits there with this stupid "look at me I'm getting fucked silly" grin on his face. If I'd turned my back they'd have been doing it on the kitchen table."

"You like doing it on the kitchen table."

"It's my kitchen table." Rob kissed her neck. "Actually I should give them a call later."

"Why?"

"I'm worried Tiago won't make it through the night."

"What on earth are you talking about?"

"I can see the headlines: **Portuguese city boy shagged to death; local businessman held**."

Clara slapped him. "Don't be horrid."

"Raphael Davide, pillar of the community, offered no plea."

Another slap. "Shut the fuck up." She turned. "You are jealous."

"I'm not." Rob shook his head; he gave it six weeks. Raphael had said on their run that morning that there was a boy in Lisbon. "Sky pilot, an old friend, you know. Not so old, sounds like." But there was some good news. Raphael was taking the Retreat off the market until Tiago had seen it. "Apparently he's always wanted somewhere like that near the city."

"Ah, he's such a nature boy, so unspoilt."

"An unlikely description given the comprehensive shafting I heard him getting last night."

"Don't be coarse about my brother's lover."

"You didn't have to listen to them." Rob kissed her. "No, if Tiago likes the place Raph wants me to help him put in a summer house and a deck next to the orchard. Tiago needs the sun. Though I can't imagine he's getting much daylight at the moment."

Clara smiled. "Ah. He's so madly in love, isn't he, my brother?"

"Yeah, right."

"What?"

Rob nuzzled her neck. "Well. It's going to be a shag pad, isn't it?"

"Don't be crude."

Rob's voice rose in indignation. "It'll be a shag pad. They'll be sunbathing, nude probably, on the deck, nice bottle of wine, then going inside and fucking like little rabbits." He closed his eyes and made a face like a little rabbit fucking.

"Don't be vile."

Robert put on a bad accent. "Oh Raphael. Oh angel. Ride me hard. That's. So. Good."

"Don't. Be. Horrid." Clara slapped him on the nose three times.

"All fucking night, last night. Little rabbits." Rob made the face again.

Clara laughed. "Stop it. You only say that because that's what you'd use it for."

"Absolutely. That's exactly what I'd use it for."

...

At eleven that night Tiago cooked supper while Raphael packed a case for the morning. The flat on Rue Vivienne had a good kitchen, all new and shiny, and cooking was better than worrying, because at least there was food at the end of it. Take today for example. It had been an unmitigated disaster, his dreams were in shreds, but lookey there; two perfect omelettes in the pan. Tiago poked at them diffidently with the slice and felt maudlin. Today he'd made the first two meals he'd ever cook for Raphael. What would the last two meals be? What would a dying Raphael be able to eat? What would he feed him in bed?

His tragic musings were cut short when Raphael breezed in.

"That looks amazing. Is it some gorgeous exotic Portuguese thing?"

"It's an omelette."

"Marvellous." Raphael opened a bottle of wine and they sat down.

Tiago pushed his food around. "You were going to show me that picture."

"I was. Excuse me." Raphael left the table and came back with three A4 photographs; three scenes in vibrant mineral colours on a pale background; golden, powerful Apollo, dark, slender, Hyacinthus, first fishing, then throwing the discus, then a dying Hyacinthus in Apollo's arms while Zephyrus looked on.

Tiago stroked the glossy faces. "Their expressions are so modern."

"Yes, though of course desire and remorse aren't exclusively modern sentiments."

"You think that's remorse, for Zephyrus?"

Raphael put his head on one side. "Maybe. Maybe I'm reading too much into it. I'd feel remorseful if I'd destroyed something beautiful just because I couldn't have it."

Tiago stared at his plate. "He's not a thing. He's a young man, Jacinto."

"Yes. Of course." Raphael poured more wine for them both. "You're still not hungry?"

"No." Tiago drank the wine down, three gulps. Better. "But this wine is good."

"It's a Margaux." Raphael looked at the empty glass, the untouched plate. "You didn't eat your lunch either. You'll starve to death." He shook his head. "You need some serious looking after."

Tiago covered his face with his hands.

"Jesus." Raphael got up, went round the table to him. "What is it? Tell me Tiago."

A shake of the head. "Nothing." He felt Raphael's arms around him, heard the sigh, knew what was coming. *No, please.*

"Come to bed baby."

"No." But he let Raphael lead him upstairs, sit him on the bed, kiss his hair. "Oh Tiago, oh Darling. Let me love you. I'll be gentle, I'll make it all better, I promise." He heard the longing in Raphael's voice; why the hell not? At least this way someone would be happy.

"Okay." He dialled up an old fantasy and zoned out, giving way to the touch and the loving words *Oh baby. So perfect. And see how much you want me.* Letting desire flow, letting the night air kiss his skin, automatic words falling off his tongue. *I do. I do want you. Now.* He let himself be eased back and closed his eyes, filtering out everything except Raphael's gentle commands. *Don't fight me baby. Show me you want me. Say my name.*

A few minutes later they lay together in darkness. Raphael pulled the cover over them. "Now. For the love of fucking god, will you please tell me what is fucking wrong."

Nothing.

Raphael sighed. "Tiago, baby. Listen. Nothing can affect the way I feel."

"Sure." Tiago nodded and buried his face in Raphael's breast. "Sure."

They were quiet together for a while.

"This street is so quiet."

"It's Sunday night. This city is dead on Sunday night."

The city is dead. Hell, why the fuck not. Why shouldn't the city be dead? Tiago turned his face away from Raphael's breast. "I'm so sorry Raphael. I'm so fucking useless."

"It's all right. Take your time."

A distant clock struck one. And then quarter past.

"That's enough time. Now tell me."

Tiago closed his eyes. "I thought I could make them come back. I never cried. People called me 'O corajoso Tiaginho'. Brave little Tiago." He rested a hand on Raphael's neck and told him the rest of it; he'd thought they were hiding, playing a game that he could puzzle out if he was smart enough. He'd invented codes, turned their names into a phone number, and stolen down to his aunt's phone late at night to call them, but the phone was never answered.

At the time of course, he had been hopeful, full of plans. "Everyone said my parents were with the angels, and there's a neighbourhood in Lisbon called *dos Anjos*." He pushed a hand into Raphael's collar. "Every year on my birthday I wrote them a long letter, my exam results, grades in music, sports awards. I learned the names of dinosaurs, the Linnaean names of birds, things that were hard for a child to learn, things that would show

how good and clever I was. I put them in the letters, so they would want me, and stop hiding, and come and get me." He took a deep breath. "And one day, when I was about ten, I just decided to go to dos Anjos, and find them." He closed his eyes and thought about the hot afternoon, the winding streets, the orange trees coming out, the skinny boy in the school uniform with the big satchel, the kind people stopping him to ask if he was all right. "I told people I was going home. But the street was long, and I was only little, so I sat on a doorstep to think about a better way of doing it. A lady came out and asked me if I was okay. She was in charge of the post office, and she was just closing up. I told her my parents' names and the address I was looking for, and she asked me to come inside." He put his head against Raphael's shoulder. The clock in the street struck the half hour.

Raphael spoke in a broken voice. "And she had all your letters."

Tiago sighed. "She had all my letters. They were pristine, unopened, my best handwriting on the envelopes, my drawings on the back, dinosaurs, blue magpies, the latin names."

Raphael pulled the counterpane up. "You're getting cold."

Tiago looked up at him, saw the tears, pressed on; not much more now. "She gave me Kia-Ora, asked me where I lived, and called home. João came to get me. He held my hand all the way home. He told me he was leaving for the army in a few months and that I should write to him, which I did. And he wrote back."

"I like the sound of João."

"Oh you'll love João. Decent, warm, loving. Not a fucked-up freak like me."

"You're not a freak." Raphael kissed him. "You're strong."

"No. I'm a freak." Tiago rubbed his eyes. "As I got older I got bitter. I couldn't understand why it had happened to me. My aunt and uncle told me to keep it all secret – I stood to inherit when I was twenty-one. They thought people might take advantage." He shrugged. "Of course they were right in a way, but they made me wary, and lonely. And I made it worse. I didn't want people's pity." He shook his head. "So I closed in on myself, went crazy with numbers, and mathematics, and ciphers, and Rubik's cubes, all that obsessive, insular stuff. And then I found Jesus, or rather I thought I did, and I became odd, morbid. I forgot what life was for. Sometimes I just wanted to be in another world. Even to be dead like my parents. To be with them again."

"Jesus."

"I don't anymore, but I did then. You see, when you don't have parents, the problem is not that no one loves you; it's that no one's obliged to let you love them. You don't belong to anyone."

There was a short silence.

Raphael coughed. "But that problem is solved now." And another silence. "Because now you can belong to me."

"Done."

But Tiago wasn't done, not really. There were more words fighting their way to the surface, but they were just a child's words; that his parents would have been proud of him, that he would have made them so fucking proud. They were the words of someone wishing for something he couldn't have, someone sentimental and weak, and therefore he wasn't going to give them air.

But fortunately he was in bed with the right man.

"They would have been so proud of you darling. Of course they would. But you're my pride and joy now. My beautiful, remarkable, strong Tiago."

Raphael's embrace was tighter than death, and Tiago let it soothe him. The rest of the story would have to wait. Right now, he needed comfort. So he ran through the movie until sleep came.

A stick thin young man in a dark suit arrives at a lively party in a gallery. He studies the invitation in his hand and looks around, shy and uncertain, hovering near a large clock, pretending to be interested in it.

A dark young man in a grey suit is watching this from the top of a staircase. He checks his watch, walks quickly down the stairs, lifts two glasses of champagne from a tray and goes up to the thin young man.

"Hello."

"Oh hello."

"I'm Raphael Davide. I own the gallery. Would you like some of this?"

"Thank you. I am Tiago Jose Gamito Pereira da Silva." The thin young man shrugs. "I'm sorry, I know it's a very long name but they all are in Portugal."

The dark young man in grey grins and turns his head to one side. "I'm sorry. I'm afraid I didn't quite catch very much of that. Well, any of it really."

"I am Tiago da Silva."

The dark young man in grey smiles warmly and nods, and they exchange cards. *"Tiago da Silva. How do you do? I'm Raphael Davide."*

They shake hands.

"Thank you so much for coming tonight. Especially as it's such a rotten night."

"Thank you for inviting me. I'm afraid I don't know anybody here. I just arrived from Lisbon this week. I don't know anybody in Paris. I work at Credit Dijonnais. I'm new."

The dark young man in grey smiles and shakes his head slowly. "I'm sorry, you'll think I'm a complete idiot but I really didn't get any of that either."

The thin young man looks completely crestfallen. The dark young man in grey touches his arm gently. "It is awfully noisy in here. It's a terrible place for a party."

The thin young man shakes his head. "No, it's my accent. It's terrible. No one understands me."

He looks up and the dark young man in grey nods slowly, sipping champagne.

"Why don't we go outside? I think it's snowing but it's quieter there."

"Snowing? I don't have a coat."

"That's all right. You can borrow mine."

He goes and gets his overcoat, and puts it round the thin young man's shoulders, and leads him out onto the terrace, where they drink champagne with snowflakes in it.

...

Tiago dreamt, and Amelia shivered in a dark doorway across the street. As a bird watcher she was used to waiting a long time for nothing to happen, but hiding in the park yesterday and skulking around this morning were more like seeing whether an experiment had worked.

She hadn't been entirely happy about what Tomas Paul had asked her to do. Targeting Tiago rather than Raphael felt imprecise, and scaring the bejeebers out of her nice new neighbour in the park had left her feeling decidedly guilty, but Tomas Paul said the direct approach was the one thing that would work; sending the files, playing to Tiago's dreams, and getting him to be open and tell Raphael the truth – that he'd been deeply, obsessively in love with him for years – would quickly win an old-fashioned Romantic like Raphael over. And a happy, deeply in love Raphael was more likely to give her the money.

Amelia huffed on her fingertips. It was certainly an odd coincidence that Tomas Paul had known Raphael and Clara at university – and odder still that he could be so sure Clara was ill; but Tomas Paul probably knew quite a few oncologists, and academics could be indiscreet…but then, who was she to judge? Tomas Paul had told her not to mention Clara in the emails, to forget all of that, that it wouldn't help *Triploid*. But Amelia was smarter than that. She'd known right away she had to mention it. That way, Tiago would break it to Raphael, and then Raphael would be able to take care of Clara, and she would get better. And alluding to Raphael's own death was the perfect way in. Tomas Paul had said *just get his attention, show him you know what's going on.* Amelia rubbed her eyes; this creativity thing was hard work.

...

At five Raphael came out onto the balcony and lit a cigarette. He looked pretty perky. After a few moments he turned back and spoke softly to someone inside. *Go back to bed wolfcub. It's much too early for you to be up.*

Wolfcub? Amelia shrank back into the doorway. *Wolfcub?* Raphael didn't sound spooked. Pet names were the first thing to go. Tiago had played a blinder. Her money was in the bank.

A few minutes later Raphael came out of the front door and walked smartly down the street, whistling softly, making light of the heavy leather holdall slung over his shoulder.

Everything was fine.

Amelia watched him walk away and called Tomas Paul.

PART THREE

HARVEST

CHAPTER 16

THE GADARENE SWINEHERD

Birds were singing, bees were buzzing. Early apple buds were nosing out. It really was a lovely April morning to be in a walled garden in northern Burgundy. And it really was way too early on a Saturday for Tiago. But he was putting a brave face on it, lying back on a lichen-covered steamer chair, in a smoky overcoat, his eyes closed behind dark glasses. Arms in his sleeves like a Mandarin, he was in his element. He was plotting.

Not against Raphael; not as such. Raphael was good; eight out of ten. The charming, sexy man of Tiago's dreams was turning out to be decent and kind, quietly solicitous in public; *I'll get that. Let me drop you off. I'll go, it's raining.* And affectionate in private. Okay, Raphael had a temper, but Tiago knew his was worse. It wasn't a deal breaker, not when there was so much love on the table, and playing to lose could be so rewarding. As it had, for example, on the Feast of The Second Saturday After.

I think you should move in here. I think you should move in this week. Tonight, actually. Why don't we go and get your stuff tonight?

It had been a sunny afternoon in the flat on Rue Vivienne.

Right, sure. Great idea. I'll see if that Russian hooker outside the florist wants to rent my flat.

And it had been quite a long, liquid, lunch.

I'm serious. You belong here, with me. Come here. Let me show you how nice it could be.

It was flattering, but it needed consideration, discussion. *Raphael. Let's talk it over.*

But Raphael preferred other forms of persuasion, and Tiago, eager to please and a bit pissed, had let Raphael take him to bed, and have his way, and enjoyed it, and said *yes okay then, okay, I'll move in.* And that night Raphael had swooped on the flat in Saint-Germain-en-Laye, noodling bluesy standards on the piano while Tiago packed clothes and books into an expensive leather holdall Raphael had got him as a moving in present. The next day there'd been a long lie-in, and *Tiago hash 2: We Love Sundays. Rue Vivienne, April 21st 2012. RED.* Tiago, asleep in his skin, and now framed in silver over the bed, to be pointed at like an item on a Chinese menu. *Bring me that beautiful boy.*

They'd play acted, Tyrant Raphael and Proud Tiago, and laughed themselves stupid. Yes; that had been a good battle to lose, as were the early morning skirmishes, waking under Raphael's wing to sounds from the city streets and turning to Raphael, and saying what he wanted, and making a move, but Raphael making a stronger one *On your back darling, do as you're told. You're a guest in our great city, remember?* And making unmeant sulky protests at liberties taken. *Jesus. Who named you after a fucking angel?* And pressing drowsy words into Raphael's hair, thanking the sun for the day ahead, the day that was starting like this, stolen back from Mammon.

Tiago arched his spine, a happy cat. They made love every day, twice, sometimes more, a photosynthesis that fixed touch and words in real time into less volatile matter, the new thing, *them*; and although Tiago knew he wasn't the world's greatest lover, being still too eager to lose himself to last long, Raphael was always kind about it, saying it would be useful if they ever lost their egg timer, and coming quickly wasn't a problem compared with some things you heard, about people who couldn't come with a lover's touch or tongue, but needed rough towels, or a nutmeg grater, or even an avocado slicer, a first world problem if ever there were one. And Raphael was an inventive, talkative lover, with a penchant for the third person that turned Tiago on more than he thought it should have. *Oh my sweet Tiago, my Antoninus. Tiago loves his Raphael, doesn't he? He loves being fucked deep. He loves it so much.* No, spending all day in bed whenever they could, wasn't a problem.

The problems arose when they were out of bed. One Sunday morning Raphael had ruined breakfast by admitting, when pressed, that well, frankly, no, he didn't like *Lux*; it was a good concept, it was elegant, but it was too ambitious, too risky. Tiago had protested, you had to take risk to have an impact. Doing small things took too long. If philanthropy really worked it would have worked by now. Charity, sponsoring kids, sending money, that was all chickenshit; to really help the poor you had to deal with the evil rich that created them and kept them down. But even then Raphael had smiled, and taken his hand. *You know what? I think we've reached the end of this conversation.* And led him up the stairs. *Bed for you, Saint Tiago.*

Tiago frowned. Maybe he'd given too much ground, been too easily swayed with sex and domestic comfort, and companionship.

He'd certainly let himself be slotted into Raphael's life, made a piece of his puzzle. But Raphael had made concessions too, big ones; like putting up with Bloomberg at breakfast (*An insult to the senses*) and broadband (*Great, the even more rapid dissemination of vulgarity*), and eating highly poisonous foods (*I've never touched fucking broccoli darling and I don't intend to start now.*) Tiago was sure that, with the right strategy, he would bring Raphael round to *Lux*.

One good thing was that Amadea now seemed to be at bay. There'd been no further attack, and even if there had been Tiago would not have panicked; because he saw now that Amadea was Martin Nelson. Tiago was ashamed he'd been so slow to work it out. On sober reflection it was easy to piece together means and motivation, Martin getting CCTV footage from the gallery, and sending it out of spite to show he'd always had his suspicions. And the film of Raphael and the children was clearly from some family occasion, sent to show that Raphael had a complex past and that Tiago was irrelevant. And as for the web links, Martin was a sick puppy, easily twisted enough to send those creepy obits. So there was no mystery. Amadea had Martin's theatrical paw print – the clincher, Ortygia, Ovid's term for Delos, birthplace of Diana and Apollo. Precisely the kind of pretentious crap a twisted classicist like Martin would delight in. But the joke was on Martin. He was the world's worst sniper; on target, but firing blanks. As far as Raphael was concerned, Martin was an un-person. Any mail for him was torn in half and thrown away, civil enquiries after him from Raphael's friends or neighbours were met with a shrug; *Fucked if I know. Fucked if I care.* One evening Tiago had asked Raphael about how things had ended; the first response had been an irritated shake of the head, *Don't ask.* So he'd given it a couple of seconds. *Why not?* And there'd been silence, the turn of a page, more silence, and then Raphael had read something out from his book as if Tiago had said nothing.

It was tricky; as long as Martin was a bad dream in Raphael's life, Tiago knew he was safe from Amadea. But as long as those half told truths remained – the secret of his own grubby past, and whatever dark betrayal Raphael was hiding – their love could still fly into a million pieces even without threatening texts. Only truth could toughen their bond, and make it resilient; and they both needed shaking up to tell it.

So that morning when Raphael had drawn him close with the usual priapic endearments, he'd turned to him *Not here angel.*

Okay. Shall I run a bath? Raphael loved making love in the bath.

No. The Retreat.

Raphael had taken some persuading, but eventually he'd given in to Tiago's Lysistratan tactics, and within an hour they'd found themselves sitting in the car, looking through chained gates at an avenue of bare beech trees and the house beyond.

"Right." Raphael had opened the window and stared out, narrating over the birdsong. It was strange, he hadn't been there since November, he'd given Rob the keys. If it felt wrong he was going to sell it.

Tiago shrugged. "Okay."

They got out and walked up the track to the house. The

property looked sad and quiet, the shutters closed, the front garden confused by neglect, fresh green shoots on the trees like spring, dead leaves on the path like autumn. Raphael kicked leaves aside and picked up fallen branches with gloved hands. Tiago let the silence run, trying the odd word, getting some back. *Owls? Yes. Bats? Yes.*

They reached the old porch and Raphael took out some heavy keys. "Loads of fucking bats."

Tiago tried a sentence. "You can't have too many bats Raphael."

Raphael looked at him while he unlocked the padlock. "You can't have too many bats."

They walked through two chilly reception rooms that smelt of coal and wood smoke, Raphael opening dusty shutters, pulling down cobwebs, touching wooden posts and beams, pointing out the blindingly obvious; fireplaces, cornicing, other older features. In the dark kitchen he leaned back against the range. "Right." His voice was brisk but cold air betrayed a long sigh. "Do you want to see upstairs?"

"Sure."

The stairs and landing creaked. "Some of these rooms are still part furnished. Rob thought it would be sensible. In case he or I needed to come and fix anything."

Raphael opened a door and smiled for the first time. "Actually you'll like this room. Let me open the shutters." There were pale green walls, a fireplace, a door leading to an en-suite bathroom, and in the centre of the room, an oak bed under a heavy sage green bedspread. The windows looked over poplars, a small village in the distance, a dumpy church. Raphael stared out the window. "It's spring."

Tiago watched him. "You okay?"

Raphael turned, gloved hands in pockets, hunched, apprehensive. "Sure." He sighed. "Well? Do you like it? Will it do?"

"I think it's lovely. I didn't think it would be so beautiful, so old."

Raphael stared back out of the window. "The place is full of ghosts."

"I don't mind ghosts."

"That's good, because there are fucking millions of them." He went to the chimney, peered up it, spoke to the cold grate. "I know it's cold in here but it's okay with the fire lit. This chimney draws well. And we've got plenty of wood." He picked up a poker, stared at it. "There's central heating too. Rob and I put it in."

Tiago came over, took the poker from him, put it down. "Hey."

"I could put the heating on, if you're cold."

"I'm fine."

Raphael frowned. "I'll find you a coat. And I'll make you some coffee."

...

Tiago heard Raphael's footsteps, a rattling tray set down. He felt cold; Raphael was leaning over him, blocking the little sun there was.

"Are you awake?"

Tiago opened his eyes. "Not really." He reached up and stroked Raphael's hair. "This is a nice coat. It smells of bonfires."

They drank their coffee and listened to the birds for a while.

"I've found something of yours in this coat."

Raphael looked over the rim of the coffee cup. "Really?"

"Close your eyes and put out your hand." Tiago handed him the Marlboro, the gold lighter.

Raphael opened his eyes. "Ah. Yes." Shreds of tobacco fell into his palm. "Right."

"It says "Fire for my fiery angel." Are you the fiery angel?"

"Yes." Raphael nodded slowly, put the cigarettes on the table. "A present. From years ago, before we had money." He turned the lighter over with his thumb. "Later he said I was gold outside, flint inside. Much later. In a poem." A slow nod. "Not a terribly good poem."

Tiago put his arms around him. "Please tell me what happened."

Instant. "No." Raphael put the lighter on the tray. "Is that what this is about?"

"Yes. That's what this is about."

Raphael pursed his lips. "I can't."

Tiago pressed his brow into Raphael's neck. "Tell me. Then bed. I promise."

"I can't tell you."

"Tell me."

Raphael looked up at him. "And then bed?"

Tiago kissed Raphael's hair. "Yes. The best we ever had. I swear."

Raphael bit his lip. "What did I tell you before?"

"That you grew apart."

"Well, that's true." Raphael closed his eyes and drew back. "It must be true." He looked at the lighter for a few moments. "Had we not grown apart, I wouldn't have been surprised to come home and find him in our bed with one of his researchers."

"Oh fuck." Tiago tried to draw Raphael close again, but Raphael resisted.

"I had no idea. I thought he was happy. I thought I was enough for him." A face of flint. "It was utterly and profoundly annihilating."

"Yes."

They kept still, holding hands, the strengthening sunlight warming them.

After a while Raphael stood up. "Right. Are we done here? I mean, are we finished here?"

Tiago sat up. "Sure." He got up and let Raphael take him into the house, up the stairs, through the dusty shafts of sunlight, to the pale green bedroom. This was where their future would be born, today, in this bedroom, in this bed. He had got the truth out of Raphael, and now they would make love, and afterwards he would tell Raphael his own secrets, all of them, and they would be able to start afresh.

It was one hell of a plan.

They kicked off their shoes, threw off their coats, and got into bed with their clothes on.

Tiago shivered. "These sheets are so fucking cold and damp."

"Don't complain. You wanted to come here." Raphael held

him close. "We'll soon get a sweat on you baby." And gripped him tight. "But first we need to strip you down."

So it was going to be like that. "Okay. So shut the fuck up and make love to me."

"You're not sufficiently biddable at the moment." Raphael pulled Tiago's sweater and T shirt off in one movement and threw them on the floor. "That's a lot better."

"Very masterful today, aren't you?"

"And you don't like my mastery of you?" Raphael unzipped him, and grasped him, rougher than usual. "You seem to like it."

"I do." Tiago looked into Raphael's eyes, unsure. "But Raphael. Be loving."

"I will." Raphael turned Tiago away from him, pushed fingers inside him, not quite as gentle as usual, but not rough; not really. "Oh my velvet darling. My silky wolfcub."

Tiago tried a purr. "Slow and sweet darling."

"You'll get what you're fucking given."

Ah.

Tiago turned back to see Raphael's face, and saw a total stranger. One of two things was about to happen, neither of which would particularly improve the shining hour; rape, or a massive argument. Tiago thought for a second, decided he might win the argument, and pushed Raphael away. But Raphael pulled him back. "Come on. We both know you want it rough."

There was nothing for it. Tiago jabbed his elbow into Raphael's belly and punched him in the throat. The move doubled Raphael up and he fell on the floor with a satisfying bump.

"Raphael, you sick fucking fuck." Tiago grabbed his clothes, darted into the bathroom and bolted the door, and few seconds later he heard the landing and stairs creaking; more ghosts in the house. Nice shiny new ones.

He put his clothes on and washed his face in ice cold water. Was first fuck to first punishment fuck in three weeks a record? Probably not. Had he brought it on himself? Definitely not. On the plus side, an easy decision lay ahead of him. If Raphael showed no remorse, he'd demand to be driven home, and have his stuff sent round, and make it clear he never wanted to see him again. It was a bit binary, but indignation had puffed up Tiago's pride; if Raphael wasn't good enough for him, it would be better to cut his losses now and get out. Wasting six years living in hope may have been foolish, but wasting another forty living in fear of a violent man would be reprehensible. Of course, if Raphael was sorry, it would be different. But if not, they were through. He would get back to work, and back to *Lux*, and back to Lisbon.

The kitchen door was open. Tiago followed a cinder path through the walled garden to a large secluded pond fringed with tall reeds and ornamental grasses. He chose the elevator voice. "Raphael?"

"Here." He was sitting on moss at the pond's edge, skulking in the long grass, pulling up dead reeds and chucking them onto the water. He was a picture of misery.

Steel cables tugged at Tiago's heart. He sighed and decided to pull his punches. Mostly.

...

Tomas Paul could normally find something worthwhile to do at the weekend, like doing a hatchet job on someone else's research proposal, or transcribing a piece of lute music so that only Yoda could play it, or encouraging the twins to shout *fascist cunt* at the tops of their shrill voices whenever Zhanik was in the garden. But today when he got back from Bushy Park he was gloomy. He went down to his study, took the envelope out of the desk drawer, and reminded himself of what the letter inside it said.

Tomas Paul,

This is very hard to write, so I'll keep it short.

Tomas Paul lit a cigarette and pondered how far his plans had gone awry. He'd been confident that when Tiago fessed up to his shameful past of cheap thrills, Raphael would drop him like a maggoty apple and go into one of his sulks; and then, desolate and longing for companionship, maybe he'd be open to the prospect of rekindling the good times before Martin Nelson had turned his head with hollow, unmeant, promises of domestic contentment.

Tomas Paul peered at Raphael's words; but though they were beautiful, and touching, and a paean to his perfection, he couldn't resist the academic urge to evaluate.

Two months ago I met someone. He's come to Paris to be with me.

"A tawdry gesture."

I want to be with him. I want what he wants – a shared life, intimacy, a home.

"He wanted to play house, bourgeois domesticity. You fell for it. And he got bored with it."

You don't. I don't think you ever will.

"Too right."

I can't wait to see you next month. But it will be the last time we ever meet as lovers.

"Well let's see, shall we?"

I've loved every moment I've spent in your arms.

I swear I'll never let you down.

R

Tomas Paul smiled. This was just what he needed. It wasn't going to be a fling, as such. Only cheap people had them. No, it would be more like the beautiful echo of a sweet refrain, two years of stolen weekends and nights, on which they would return to their true love.

He couldn't blame Amelia. But he was going to have to do the rest of this himself.

He would make a new start at Raphael's fortieth birthday party next month. Odd that his invitation hadn't arrived yet.

...

At three-thirty Raphael surveyed his bonfire with satisfaction. It had taken him two hours to build it, but only because he was dragging it out. After their rapprochement by the pond he'd driven Tiago into town to get food and wine, and now he was leaving him to sleep off a liquid lunch upstairs. He'd go up to the bedroom soon and light the fire; that would take the edge off the damp evening, and other things.

But it was too damp outside to light the bonfire, so Raphael went into the orchard to look for bugs, reading the oxidising copper labels in Martin's terrible spidery writing; Dabinett, Kingston Black, White Beech, Orleans Reinette, Laxton's Superb, Ribston Pippin, Sops in Wine. They'd put the orchard in about a month after Raphael's father had died; Martin's idea, inspired and poetic, as always. *Something to remember him by darling. Something that will grow.* Martin knew about apples, and he'd chosen the mixture of varieties, and with Rob's help they'd planted seventy-six trees, one for every year of Andre Davide's life. But though Martin had originated the orchard, Raphael knew that Rob had saved it; by mulching it, and by putting in the irrigation system that got it through three dry Burgundian summers, and by stopping Raphael torching it last Autumn. *Come off it Raphael. Burning trees? That's nazi psycho stuff mate. Have a word with yourself.*

Have a word with yourself. Raphael lit a cigarette. Tiago had had a number of words with him that morning, by the pond; quietly spoken, perfectly clear words. Apparently what he had just tried to do was completely fucking horrible. Now, Tiago was not a martyr, and he was not going to milk it, but if he (a finger lightly placed on Raphael's chest) ever tried anything like it again, then he (Tiago indicating himself with the thumb of the same hand) would leave the same day. And that was it. They were done. And then there'd been a kiss on the forehead, a full stop, and they'd sat in the drizzle, listening to the birdsong. Raphael had wanted to explain without excusing; that it had happened because Tiago had tried to control him with sex, like Martin had, and that Martin had come to love it rough, very rough, and that he'd never refused Martin whatever he wanted. But he'd said nothing, just looked away, towards the doghouse, hoping the lesson would soon be over, and it had nearly worked; there'd been only one more thing. Tiago knew about grief, you see. You needed time to get over loss. Apparently it was a month for every year, grieving. And Raphael had had ten months, hadn't he? And if he couldn't get over Martin, maybe they were better off alone.

It had been a short lecture, but effective; especially the last line. Raphael knew the answer to that one. He lit another cigarette, knowing it was his last chance to think alone for a while. In the last year he'd come to hope he'd never again allow himself to be controlled by a lover; so much for that. But all the same, Tiago wasn't going to have it all his own way; he wasn't going to sleep all evening, for a start. Raphael went indoors and walked silently upstairs to the bedroom. Tiago was making rather a cute little lump under the covers.

Raphael shook Tiago's shoulder gently. "Time to wake up, wolfcub."

Tiago took a deep breath, rubbed his eyes. "What's the time?"

"Four."

Tiago snaked a hand out from under the covers and took Raphael's hand in his. "I'm sorry for what I said. I was brutal."

Raphael let the silence run. As he'd expected, Tiago was soon filling it; he'd been shocked. He hadn't meant it. They weren't better off alone. They were made for each other. Et cetera.

But Raphael had a PhD in Reconciliation Studies. Words hadn't got them into this mess, and words wouldn't get them out. He silenced Tiago with a kiss and spent the next hour showing him how sorry he was.

...

By evening they were propped up on cushions against the bed, sharing a second bottle of wine by the fire, wrapped up in blankets. Tiago watched the wet wood crackle and spit in the grate while

Raphael drawled on about what they might do with the apples they'd get from the orchard that summer. "Cider, calvados. We could ask Amelia. She knows about that stuff, apparently."

Tiago looked up at Raphael's mouth, the odd tall yellow flame making the front teeth bronze. He'd got his script ready, about frailty, the stupid things people did, and after this morning he thought Raphael would be particularly understanding. He placed a few words like jackstraws. "You know, it was my fault this morning. I tried to control you. This is all still so new to me. Sex, I mean."

Raphael smiled and shrugged. "Oh, it'll come darling." He wasn't to worry. Sex was a minefield. And technique would come with experience, with trust. They loved each other deeply, enough to forgive one another, and that deep love would get them through the tough times. But when love wasn't deep, when it died, then all that was left was comfort. And that wasn't always enough. Raphael rubbed his eyes. "I suppose that's what happened to us."

Tiago flinched. "To us?"

"To me and Marty. I guess it happened a few years ago. Comfort wasn't enough for him." Raphael yawned and knelt forward to put another log on the fire. "Fair enough, I suppose."

Tiago gave up. The perfect opening was gone, and he didn't intend to spend the evening listening to Raphael excusing Martin. He snuggled up. "We should tell stories."

Raphael stared into the fire for a few moments. "Okay. How about the Ruined Maid?" He was a man of few words, and he told a dark story well; the proud mother, the headstrong daughter, the seduction, the shabby death in the bedsit, the kind wife who raised the orphan boy alongside her baby son, and the half-brothers who grew up loving each other, but not liking each other much.

At the end Raphael sipped his wine. "Rob took me to Yorkshire in January. He showed me Rosamund's grave. She was eighteen when she died. Eighteen. We stayed with his grandmother Elinor, rode her neighbour's horses, five days in the snow. We sat by the fire at night talking about anything and everything. Elinor's a remarkable woman. You would never think she'd lost her only child." He lit a cigarette, lay down with his head in Tiago's lap, and closed his eyes. "Right. Your turn."

Tiago composed himself. He had his own version of the seduction tale, The Lost Boy, but frankly he'd had enough for one weekend. "Okay. This is about the King and Queen of Portugal." How they met, and fell in love, and got married; how his handsome father took him on the scooter and drove him screaming over the sand dunes. How one afternoon the white stork flew low over the house, bringing death, not life, spooking his aunt and the two young traffic cops, tearful behind their aviator sunglasses; and how João, just eleven, swept him up, and carried him to their campsite among the orange groves, showed him how to trap salamanders in jars and light a fire, and pointed out which stars his parents were now living on, and how to pray to them. And how the burnt cork trees stank, and the plastic dolls in the crappy shrine on the bend in the road scared him, and how the white marble tomb shone that afternoon in the quiet, walled, village cemetery by the water tower; and how the people of the village still crossed themselves when they saw him. He stroked

Raphael's hair back from his face. "So, unsurprisingly, I don't go back there."

Raphael took his hand and kissed it. "You are so strong."

"I have no choice."

...

The bedroom was pitch black. Tiago sat up in bed, woken by a trill of rapid divisions and long notes; *Troglodytes troglodytes*. A moment later came a cadence, real music. *Erythacus rubecula*.

Raphael reached for him. "Sleep darling. It's too early."

"I want to see the dawn." Tiago put the overcoat round his shoulders, went to the window and eased open the shutters. The rising sun was deep pink, peeping out behind skinny poplars beyond the church. The wren was on the garden wall, steam rising from its tiny beak. The robin was hiding. A sudden volley of swifts screamed overhead.

Raphael sighed. "Those fucking birds make the most terrible racket imaginable."

Tiago turned. "Swifts fly here all the way from Africa, Raphael."

"To crap all over my house."

"It's not personal." Tiago went back to the bed, sat down. "What's the church like?"

Raphael shrugged. Everyone who went to that church was a hundred years old. They rang the fucking bell at eight. It was cracked, and tuneless, and it went on forever. He licked his lips. "Do you want to go?"

Tiago took the coat off. "Not really."

They woke at ten and Tiago went downstairs to make coffee. He watched the kettle boil and gave the weekend six out of ten; the rest would have to wait for Lisbon.

...

No-one was supposed to be in the lab on Sunday, but Amelia often was, and it was fine, because no one ever saw her in there, because you weren't supposed to be in the lab on Sunday. She arrived at six in the evening, pulled down the blinds and peered at the sequencer; the samples had been running since Friday night. Ideally she'd need a few more days, but if she was pushed to it she could pull off the reads later today.

She needed to settle in for the next few hours, so she put some music on; Corelli, to help her think straight and react appropriately to the disappointment she fully expected. She'd done a bit of research since her foray into Tiago's apartment, checking out erotic fiction, porn movies and chat rooms, and she was pretty convinced that unless Tiago was the most fastidious lover in the history of mankind, all three samples she'd collected would turn out to be Raphael's.

At midnight she interrupted the run and checked the reads. All three were identical. She was going to have to try harder to get two pollinators for *Triploid*.

"Bollocks." Amelia copied the files, deleted the run history on the sequencer, and went home.

CHAPTER 17

VERITAS VOS LIBERABIT. (HONEST.)

It was early, and the terminal was quiet, and Tiago was gazing up at the departure boards with a cheerful grin. He had a lovely surprise in store for Raphael, an early birthday weekend away in Lisbon at the stylish hotel Chopin, a crazy night out at some of his favourite bars and clubs in Bairro Alto, and a big family lunch on Sunday where he'd introduce him to João, and Inês, and his aunt and uncle, and Tiaginho. There'd been Halcyon days since the weekend at the Retreat; at work he'd got two projects sanctioned and recruited two little Mini-him modellers, Aurora and Colin, who thought he was god. And at home he and Raphael were going through a serious nesting phase, having made the two vital decisions that the new range for the Retreat would be a four oven, enamelled cast iron job (in navy blue) and the puppies would be spaniels (in black and gold). The pressures he felt so acutely in previous weeks had disappeared. Amadea's continued silence had assured him that the past of which he was ashamed would not come back to haunt him. Clara, whom he now knew well, was smart enough to take very good care of herself; people like her didn't die of curable diseases. And *Lux*, now improved beyond measure, was ready for launch at Raphael's birthday in a few days. He was on the front foot, and things were looking good. Even the flight was on time.

"I got coffee Oh Secretive One." Raphael was walking towards him with two paper cups, smiling despite the early start. "It's probably filth. So. Are you going to tell me where we're going?"

"You'll have to be patient." Tiago looked up at the flight information, took Raphael's arm. "This way."

They walked along and stopped at the first gate. Tiago looked at the cards. "Frankfurt. No." He turned to Raphael, clicked his heels, and raised an admonishing finger. "Frankfurt. Nein." He walked on and called over his shoulder. "Come on. Don't want to miss it."

Raphael stood and watched him. "Are you going to do that at every fucking gate?"

"I might do. Why? Is it annoying?"

"Moderately." Raphael walked over to him. "At least, it's sufficiently annoying that there may be consequences for you later on."

"Do you mean you're going to pretend to get all strict with me?"

Raphael nodded. "Precisely. And you're going to pretend to be outraged."

"Prima." Tiago walked on.

Raphael walked after him. "Nobody says "Prima" any more."

"Shame." The next gate was Moscow. "Moscow. No. Moskva. Niet."

Raphael took Tiago's arm. "You're going to get such a fucking seeing to."

"Sweet." They walked on together, more slowly. "You don't need to know where we're going. I've taken care of everything." Tiago stopped at the next gate. "Here."

Raphael looked at the flight details and smiled. "Perfect."

...

It was a cheerful hotel room, with fresh yellow walls, a yellow sofa, blue and white azulejo designs on the wall; a beautiful room to get dumped in. Tiago stood in the doorway and looked around, regretting the naïve optimism with which he'd planned this trip. They'd had a great flight, and he'd asked the taxi driver to take them to Chiado via Saint Apollonia so Raphael could see the Tagus, and the two bridges, and Cristo Re. In fact everything had gone swimmingly until they'd walked into the lobby, and the receptionist had looked up and winked at him.

Tiago sat on the sofa and frowned. The receptionist had been a barman at the Sofitel a few years back, but he wasn't the only person in Lisbon who might recognise him. Amadea be damned; there were dozens of people here who might remember the kind of life he used to lead, possibly better than he did himself. At least he'd bought flexible flights home so they could travel back quickly, or separately, or quickly and separately.

Raphael went over to the balcony and opened the doors. Warm sunlight poured down and street sounds rose up; voices, music, squeaky trams on rusty rails.

"This is amazing."

Tiago went over and gazed over the rooftops towards the river. "Yes." He wasn't very good in situations like this, when events were rushing towards him. He closed his eyes, tried to think tactically.

"It's glorious. Why on earth did you leave?" Raphael stood behind him, resting his chin on Tiago's shoulder. And then he started, and pointed. "Hey look there. Tall ships. Three caravels out on the water, going under the bridge. There's a cross of Christ on the sails." He tutted. "I got the crosses too small on mine."

Tiago opened his eyes and saw the ships; they were in full sail, about half a mile away, coming in from the ocean, the three crosses of Christ blood red on the white background. It was his first omen for weeks. *Get on with it.*

He turned to Raphael. "Raphael. There's something I need to tell you."

Raphael nodded. "Right."

"Best if we sit down."

"Sure."

The two of them sat quietly, their heads bowed. Down on the street a dog yapped, and a car drove up outside playing samba music. A boy shouted *Aren't you ready yet?* and a girl shouted back *Of course, you're late* and there was laughter, the car door slamming and the car speeding away, and more doggy yapping. Raphael kissed Tiago's hands. "Right. Enough. Now talk to me."

"I'm thinking what to say."

Raphael sighed. "Jesus. You are so maddening sometimes." He rubbed Tiago's shoulders and went into checklist voice mode, a soothing tone he used for working out what was wrong with the central heating, or where his car keys were, or more usually, calming Tiago after a rough day at work, or a bad dream. It was a voice designed to take the drama out of things, to turn Tiago's disaster scenarios into bite-sized problems that could easily be solved. Was he ill? Was someone else ill? Family? Inês? A friend? Was it work? Had he, Tiago, done something stupid? Was he, Tiago, going to get fired? Did he need money?

Tiago said no to everything, knowing that in a moment he would be hearing it couldn't be that bad, and it would all look brighter if they went to bed, and then talked it through. He looked at the pristine bed; a bed they may never mess up now.

"Raphael. This might end things between us."

Raphael shook his head, put his arms around Tiago's waist. "Nothing will change. I swear it. How bad can it be?"

How bad? Tiago looked up, looked down. "I love Lisbon. I was twenty-three when I had to leave. But it wasn't work. It was life. My life was unbearable."

Raphael rested his hand on Tiago's knee. "You had a bad love affair?" A squeeze. "Was it a Lusitanian love triangle? You, Rogerio and the Grand Inquisitor?" He frowned. "You didn't shag the Grand Inquisitor did you? I think that's strictly against the rules. Even these days."

Tiago slumped. This was very unhelpful, a playful, flippant Raphael that didn't pay attention, and had to be told everything at least twice. He shook his head. "No. Not a triangle." He closed his eyes and forced the words out, the drinking, the men, going to their rooms, making his way out in the darkness afterwards, and going home, and scrubbing his hands with a nail brush. "Mostly here in Lisbon, sometimes when I was working abroad. For two years. I don't know why." He stopped, sick and dizzy, feeling his heart beating hard.

There was a long silence in the room. A distant tram rattled downhill over old rails. When Raphael finally spoke his voice was soft. "So when was all this?"

"Just after my finals. It started when I was twenty-one."

"Why?" Raphael took Tiago's hand in his, ran his thumb over the back. "Why on earth did you behave like that?"

Tiago shook his head and smiled. The caravels had got it right. Raphael accepted him. Raphael loved him, didn't care about these things. "Don't know." A seagull mocked him from the balcony *You were mad, mad, mad* and chattered *idiot idiot idiot* and beat its wings hard, and flew away, and Tiago closed his eyes, and felt his hand being lifted up and kissed.

"Listen. I'm so sorry it hurt you. I'm sorry it made you feel bad about yourself. But everyone fucks up. The only person you hurt was yourself. All that matters is who you are now."

"Yes."

They were quiet for a while.

"Did it start after Rogerio left for Brazil?"

Tiago shook his head. "I suppose so. But it wasn't his fault. I didn't have to react like that, did I?" He frowned: maybe Raphael hadn't appreciated the full facts. "The thing is, there were so many of them."

"It doesn't matter Tiago." Raphael kissed his hand again. "Look. You were lost. The past is full of shit, you know that. But it's in the past, and you leave it there. We say "Fuck the past.""

don't we? We say, we go on." He sighed. "You know this honey. We've talked about this."

Tiago nodded, hardly listening. "I kept count. I wrote their names down, at least what they called themselves. I called myself Nuno. No idea why." He went over to the bed, wrote on the notepad, tore off the page and brought it over. "Here." He stuck his arm out straight, holding the number away from himself.

Raphael shook his head. "I don't care Tiago."

"Read it." Tiago pushed the piece of paper forward. "Read it Raphael."

"No, baby." Raphael pushed it away, deflected it. "It doesn't matter to me."

"Thirteen."

Raphael took the paper and looked at it, nodded slowly. "Thirteen?" It was a voice of wood. He got up and walked out onto the balcony and stood there with his head down, his back turned, white sunlight streaming over his shoulders.

"Fuck."

Tiago covered his face; it was his fault for keeping it secret for so long, letting Raphael believe the fantasy. *Flawless.* Well, that was smashed, now.

"Tiago. Come here." Raphael was beckoning him out, with a hand, his back still turned. "Come out here." A sigh. "Come on Tiago. Come outside."

Tiago went out onto the balcony. The sunlight was dazzling and he stumbled. Raphael took him in his arms and kissed him on the forehead. "Hey. Wolfcub."

There was a whistle from the street below. Two huge blonde

girls with rucksacks were walking past, laughing, waving up at them. "Caught you!" Australians.

Tiago waved back from Raphael's embrace, his head on Raphael's shoulder. "Jesus."

Raphael murmured into Tiago's hair. "Better now?"

A nod.

"Good." Raphael took the lighter from his pocket and handed it to Tiago. "Shall we?"

Tiago lit the corner of the page and they watched the fragments disperse in the street below.

...

Half an hour later they were lying on the bed, down to the dregs of a bottle of red wine. The streets outside were getting quieter, emptying of people, filling with the humid air of noon.

Tiago was light-headed and light-hearted; he'd drunk more than half the wine.

Raphael lit a cigarette. "So how did it stop?"

"My salvation?" Tiago was chirpy, and unpractised, and unguarded. It had been at the Sofitel down the road, with Torsten, a German professor, tall and handsome. He wasn't sure what had happened but he'd fallen asleep in Torsten's arms and woken up alone with all his clothes on; so, nothing, probably. Maybe he'd just wanted someone to talk to. Tiago stretched. "When I woke up there were two one hundred dollar bills on the pillow." He looked down and drained his glass. "For services rendered, or not rendered. I went out the fire escape and onto Liberdade, a big boulevard. It was cold, January, and the homeless people were on the benches, waiting for coffee and food from the outreach workers. They stared at me." He'd sat on a bench, wondering if he should give them the money, and then he'd heard his name. His real name. Tiago rubbed his eyes. "It was Rogerio."

Raphael stirred for the first time. "Your Rogerio?"

Tiago smiled. "Yes, mine. He gave me coffee in a plastic cup, asked what I was doing there."

There were squeaky car brakes outside, and there was music on a radio, and then the car was starting up again and driving away. The querulous tones of two American women echoed in the corridor, *Jeez, the humiddidy,* and the sound of the door of the next room being unlocked, opened, closed.

"Go on."

Tiago scratched his head. "Rogerio asked me to wait for him while he finished with the homeless guys. He had a van." He frowned, not sure where to start the story again. Raphael wouldn't need to know that the van Rogerio was driving had smelt of cigarettes and old clothes, that there'd been two plastic rosaries and a wooden crucifix hanging down from the rear view mirror.

Raphael touched him on the arm. "So where did he take you?"

"Prazeres. It means Pleasures."

"What is it? A park?"

"No. It's a cemetery."

"A cemetery." Raphael sat up. "Of course." He shook his head. "Where else?"

Tiago looked at him. *Be loving, be grateful, hold back words you can't unsay.* He took a deep breath. "He showed me a stone angel there, a boy, with tattered wings, and a book open on his lap. They'd found a dead guy there the week before, lying at the foot of this angel."

"Right." Raphael stubbed his cigarette out half-smoked, stared at him. "And?"

Tiago shrugged. "Well Rogerio had seen the angel, and thought about me." He rubbed his eyes. "I suppose it was the book."

"Unbelievable." Raphael shook his head. "Fucking unbelievable, these people."

Tiago looked away. "You don't understand."

"Oh I understand all right."

"Actually you don't." Tiago shook his head. "He was trying to help me, Raphael. He was trying to show me something beautiful, to show me hope, that Jesus's love is unconditional."

"Yeah, right." Raphael sat up, drained his glass and put it down. "What he was actually trying to do was manipulate you. He was trying to get back into your bed."

"No." Tiago got off the bed and walked across to the window. "No."

"But he did. I bet he fucking did." Raphael stood up. "Deny that he did. You can't, can you? Because he did, didn't he?"

"Because that's what you would have done?" Tiago bowed his head.

But if Raphael was wounded he didn't show it. "This isn't about me. It's about him." He pointed out the window at a past outrage. "He fucked you up to start with, then he fucked off. He should have stayed and loved you."

"Yes, he should." Tiago turned to face him. "But he wasn't strong enough. Have you never been too weak to do the right thing?"

"You were in danger. He put you there, helpless, and drunk, with all those fucking men. Any one of them could have hurt you. It would only have taken one. He was directly responsible for that. Can't you fucking see it?" Raphael came over, stopped a foot away. "Because I fucking can. And I'll never forgive him, as long as I live. And if I had my way I'd never let you go near him again."

"He doesn't need your forgiveness. And I don't need your fucking permission. It was my choice, not his fault." Tiago shook his head but couldn't shake his fury off. "Didn't Martin hurt you? And didn't you go fucking crazy?"

"Yes." Raphael seized Tiago by the shoulders and shook him. "What a fucking stupid question. You know I went out of my mind, for months."

Tiago knocked Raphael's arms away and pushed him back. "Right. And was that his fault or yours?" He was cocky, so sure of his reasoning, his supreme logic. "Truly Raphael? Couldn't you have handled it better? I mean, if you had done something really stupid, if you had fucking killed yourself, would it have been his fault?"

"If I had killed myself?" Raphael's voice was soft. He closed his eyes.

"Yes, killed yourself. Like a fucking idiot, in one of your alpha male fucking rages."

Raphael's silence was louder than his shouts had been.

"I thought about it, in October. I was about to do it. Clara stopped me."

"You were about to do it?"

The room span, and someone kicked the ladder away, and Tiago fell. It was the short drop, the cruel one, not fast or far enough to break his neck, but enough to leave him breathless on the floor, helpless at the thought of the devastating email that totally missed the point.

Hey Tiago, did you hear about Raphael Davide L... man, he was so beautiful, so hot.

But after a few slow seconds Raphael was kneeling beside him, apologising – not for the big thing, but the little thing – saying *he was sorry, so sorry, for shouting.*

The floor seemed a good place to be; so they sat there for half an hour, leaning against the sofa, watching the shafts of sunlight track across the carpet, and Raphael told him how things got better, and Tiago made him swear he'd never hurt himself again, and they went back to the bed to hold one another, to soothe old and new wounds. Raphael's voice was cracked from the shouting.

"You're right. It wouldn't have been Martin's fault. It would have been mine. We're not a bunch of fucking puppets. We must take responsibility for our lives." He kissed Tiago's hair. "But I can be rational about my own pain. I can't be rational about yours." He sighed and asked if there were any more to tell.

Tiago sniffed. It seemed mostly trivial now, given what Raphael had been through, but he closed his eyes and rattled through the rest. "He took me home, and we spent the day together, and he said he was sorry for what he'd said, and done. And yes, we did go to bed. We needed the comfort. And on the Monday I asked for a transfer, and on the Tuesday I was accepted, and a month later I went to Paris."

"And last year in Lisbon?"

"I told you before."

"Tell me again."

"And last year in Lisbon, like I told you before, I told him about you, and that my heart was broken, and we smoked a few joints and made love as friends a few times."

"You smoked a few joints and made love as friends few times."

"Maybe seven or eight." Maybe twenty or thirty. Tiago omitted this irrelevant detail and stroked Raphael's face. "And then he told me to come back to Paris and get you."

...

They had an excellent lunch at outside tables in a stylish, traditional restaurant on Rossio that Raphael pronounced *pleasingly French*, and afterwards they moseyed through sultry, breezeless backstreets. The mid-afternoon air was oppressive, but they were happy; Tiago relieved, and Raphael being superior in the French manner; he hadn't expected so much weird Kabbalah stuff.

Tiago smiled at him. "I told you. We're Celts. Simple people, living close to the ground. Not sophisticated, rational northern Europeans. We're dreamers, and poets, and weavers of spells."

"Don't I know it? You ensnared me with your sorcery."

"I did." Tiago tripped; the tiles were very level. "The streets are very uneven you know."

"You're very uneven. Let's get you back."

Tiago drew Raphael close and gave him a very specific instruction.

...

Tiago opened the balcony door and looked out over the quiet rooftops, the river, silent and silver, beyond them. "Everyone's gone in. Everyone's asleep."

"Everyone's got the right idea. It's damn hot." Raphael took off his jacket and shirt and threw them onto a chair. "I can't remember why you wanted to come back, but I'm going to take a shower." He kicked off his loafers, unbuckled his belt, stripped off, slow and casual.

"Join me?"

"Maybe."

"He says maybe." Raphael stalked naked into the bathroom.

Tiago went out onto the balcony and leaned on the iron rail, squinting up into the blinding blue sky, and then peering down at the peaceful, stultified city, the rows of small, shadowy, stone terraced houses nearby where people were now, presumably, sleeping it off.

He smiled at the swifts, not in handfuls, but in squadrons, corkscrewing down the narrow streets between the houses, skimming the roofs, screaming in an ecstasy of spiralling acceleration. *You are free, free, free.* He was, and he was sharing their weightlessness, racing fearless into the future, because he had been strong, and determined. And he had chosen the right guy. He gripped the balcony rail, white-knuckled, clinging to reality, and wanting as much of it as he could get. Starting now.

He went back inside, undressed, and walked into the bathroom. "Hi."

Raphael smiled at him from the shower. "You'd better come in here."

Tiago did. "I'm so sorry for all the fucking drama."

"Oh baby. So am I." Raphael held Tiago close, guiding water over his head, down his back. "We're starting again. I'm baptising you into the Church of Christ Economist, the Church of Saint Raphael and Saint Tiago. It's a very exclusive church. It's just for us."

Tiago smiled. "Maybe a dove will fly in and land on my head."

"Maybe it will." Raphael smoothed Tiago's hair back, and kissed his mouth, and massaged the flesh between his shoulder blades, pushing gently against the vertebrae.

"You're perfect."

"I wanted you to think that." Tiago shook his head. "But you know how cracked I am."

But Raphael drew him closer and put him right. A pearl started with a flaw, didn't it? And that's what Tiago was. A lustrous pearl. He kissed Tiago's throat.

"My amazing Tiago."

Tiago tightened his arms around Raphael's neck. "More."

"My treasure."

"More."

"Not in here." Raphael stopped the shower, and took Tiago to the bedroom, and the still quiet of the afternoon was enhanced by the tender sounds and quaint vocabulary of human lovers.

...

Not long afterwards Tiago heard chairs being dragged out onto the balcony next door.

"Jesus. I forgot the doors were open."

Raphael drew him close. "So what? They already think Europeans are sex-crazed libertines." He yawned. "It'll give them something to talk about back in Stuffed Squaw Montana."

"At least they didn't bang on the wall."

"They did actually."

"I thought it was the headboard banging."

"Well, it did a bit." Raphael kissed him. "My angel. Beautiful baby. So hot and hungry."

Tiago had lovely manners, so he asked Raphael if he wanted anything, and Raphael said *later*, and pulled the covers over them. They lay quietly for a while, until it was *later*, and then they slept until six, when Raphael's phone bleeped.

"Shall we be decadent?"

"Oh yes."

They ordered room service and had a quiet night in; after all, they'd be coming back.

...

It wasn't a terrific Saturday night for the service sector in Paris either. Rob and Clara were eating a hearty beef casserole, one of Rob's signature dishes. It required half a bottle of red wine, so he used a whole one. "I made this the night Raphael and Tiago stayed."

Clara nodded. "Did you text him?"

"Yes." Rob smiled at Clara; she'd been sleeping better, eating more in recent weeks. "How did you get on this afternoon?"

"I've got the outline. But it's only an inaugural lecture, for thick people."

Mel was away with the twins, so Tomas Paul was living the dream in London, eating a takeaway curry from its container on the kitchen table. He scrolled up and down the screen of his laptop, bemused. The invitation still wasn't there. Maybe his email had spammed it.

...

"How thick?" Rob made a face. "This thick?"

"Slightly more cretinous. Yes, exactly like that."

Rob's phone chimed. "Raph." He picked the phone up. "Lisbon is "awesome" apparently."

"Awesome is a Tiago word." Clara smiled. "I'm glad they're having a lovely time." She pointed her fork in the academic manner. "And I knew you'd come round to Tiago."

Rob shrugged. "I like running with him. He gets on with it." He didn't mind being wrong if it meant life was turning out to be better than he'd hoped.

...

About a mile away Amelia sat on Tiago's bed, eating nothing, not even an apple. She'd come hunting tonight, but it was apparent that her plan had been too successful. Love had taken hold too quickly, and Tiago had moved out and taken all his surplus cells with him. It was what they called an unintended consequence. And it was a complete pain in the arse.

But all was not lost. Sitting on Tiago's bed had given Amelia several new ideas, all of which had some merit. Being passive wasn't going to work. She could play the huntress, study and track her prey over days, or weeks, or months, until she got a clear shot. Or she could set a trap, and lure him to her. Or she could get him drunk, and rig something up with electrodes. Or maybe she could try a bit of all three.

She took one last look round the bedroom and knew at once what she would do next.

CHAPTER 18

IF YOU'RE STRONG ENOUGH

The fine weather stayed, and on Sunday evening the hotel room was old gold with tired sunlight, a deep, waxy amber, like old paint. Sunday lunch had ended about four, goodbyes had taken an hour, and Tiago had wanted to come back the long way, so they had wandered through Baixa to the waterfront, then made their way slowly back to the hotel.

"How bad was it?"

"How bad was what?" Raphael was extremely mellow. Everything was under control. Tiago's saga of loveless sex hadn't worried him; it was such an old story, the confused boy in the Hall of Mirrors, looking for his own image in the faces of strangers. He wasn't even sure he believed a word of it. Tiago didn't lie, not as such, but his imagination was powerful. Talking to a stranger in a bar and thinking about having sex with him could easily have been recorded later as sex, the writing down making it somehow true. And even if it were true, Tiago's view of decadent abandon was comically modest; thirteen men in two years was hardly an army of lovers. It wasn't even a platoon. Raphael smiled contentedly to himself; hand jobs, for god's sake. It was schoolboy stuff. He'd expected at least head, especially given Tiago's aptitude for it.

"Raphael?"

"Sorry darling, miles away." You really had to wonder where thirteen had come from.

"How bad was it?"

"How bad was what?" Five was probably nearer the mark, plus seven or eight others sprung from Tiago's kaleidoscopic mind – Sporting Lisbon players, TV weathermen, George Clooney; that would make it thirteen.

"You know."

"I know what?" Raphael smiled; a German called Torsten. Honestly. Why not a Swede called Sven, or an Italian called Antonio. He yawned and stretched. Yes; it had been a good weekend. Even the row made sense to him now. Raphael had come to see himself as Tiago's protector, and he'd been unhappy that in Tiago's mind Rogerio had got there first. But even that was fine, because Rogerio wasn't up to the job; he was a confused young loser, not a real man, a caring man, at ease with himself. Tiago would never find his way back to Rogerio's bed. "I have absolutely no idea what you're talking about." And the argument had forced him to tell Tiago about what had happened last year. Raphael sniffed and smiled. Suicide. What a stupid thing that would have been to have done. He could hardly believe it of himself now.

Tiago pinched him and told him not to be annoying.

"I'm not being annoying." And Tiago's family liked him. And the sex had been fantastic. It was all good.

He looked up. Tiago was grinning.

"You know."

Raphael gazed. "I don't know anything. How bad was what?"

"The third degree from João. You were talking for nearly an hour out there."

Raphael yawned. "Oh, he was fine. He wanted to know what I did, where I lived, what car I drove." But that wasn't all. At first João had asked those questions; but at the end he'd wanted to know if Raphael would take the unopened envelopes he'd kept for nearly twenty years, and if Raphael would take Tiago to the cemetery in São Placido that summer, and stand by him while he placed the letters in the glass-fronted marble tomb above the grave where they belonged, with the dead. *Please take them from me Raphael. They need burying.* João was a strong man, so he'd cried buckets, remembering the child, *O carajoso Tiaginho,* and Raphael was too, so he'd put an arm round him. "He wanted to know whether I was rich enough for you."

"Fuck off."

"Did I say rich? I meant "good." He wanted to know whether I was good enough for you." He'd said *yes of course* about the letters; so maybe that meant he was.

"I would have thought yes. He told me yes when we left."

"Really?"

"Yes. He told me you were a good man and for god's sake not to fuck it up."

"Touching sentiment." Raphael wondered what the grave would be like. "Your little namesake's very charming."

"Yes, he liked you. I thought he would."

"He did seem to take a shine to me, once he'd stopped hiding behind you."

"He's shy. But he did stop hiding. He shook your hand. That's a first. João took a picture."

"Look forward to that." Raphael smiled; why did children always have sticky hands?

"I think that's the first time anyone's offered him a handshake. I thought he did very well."

"He did." Raphael always treated children like adults, and it always worked. But now he was tired, and so although he loved nothing more than tales of childhood inanity, he closed his eyes, and only half-listened to the marvels Tiago was recounting. Tiaginho loved the little paper boat Raphael had made for him. And Jacinta thought Raphael was very handsome. Raphael nodded, seeing Tiago carrying one child, leading the other by the hand, knowing what he was meant to feel – *Suits me, doesn't it?* – but feeling it anyway, and happy to.

"Yes. Well, she's a very beautiful little girl. Lovely grey eyes. Apple green dress." He kissed Tiago's forehead. "Why don't you get some sleep?"

But Tiago wasn't sleepy. He got off the bed and went over to the window. "I need a bath." He walked through into the bathroom, unbuttoning his shirt, humming a tune the musicians had been playing in the street.

Raphael heard the taps running and called through. "Did you say we were going out tonight?"

"Yes. The concert. It doesn't start till ten though."

Raphael counted to five, called again. "I think you may need to get some sleep honey."

"Sure."

That meant no chance. Raphael got off the bed, went over to the window and looked out across the rooftops and down into the streets below. People were getting up, making tea, getting ready for the evening. Over the road a woman opened tatty blue shutters and waved at him. He smiled and waved back. He liked this city. The people were relaxed, and friendly. They got on with life, moved things on gradually, doing their best; and when they fucked things up, they tried again. They had a quiet dignity. He could learn something from them.

After ten minutes he went through to the bathroom.

Tiago smiled up at him from deep white foam. "This is lovely."

"Good." Raphael walked across and knelt down, put a hand into the bubbles and blobbed Tiago's nose. "Pongo."

Tiago brushed his nose like a dog would. "You can be so fucking annoying."

Raphael sat back on his heels. "So this concert starts at ten?"

"Yes. But I was hoping we might meet one more person before that."

•••

At seven they walked down the hill to the waterfront and turned right towards the delicate filigree bridge. The tired, custard yellow light of the setting sun caught the mood of a weekend on its last legs, the city shrugging its shoulders. *Sure. You can still squeeze some pleasure out of Sunday night if you feel so inclined. Knock yourself out.*

Raphael looked across. Tiago still looked dreamy and self-absorbed, as he had since lunch. "Hey." He put an arm around Tiago's shoulders, making one big shadow with two heads and four legs. That would annoy the gods. "Okay?"

Tiago stopped. "Sure." He pointed across the water. "Cristo Rei. When I was a kid I thought that was really Jesus watching over us. Every child in Lisbon does." He turned back and looked up at Raphael. "It's impossible not to. I mean, there he is."

Raphael nodded. "Indeed. No faith required."

"None at all." Tiago shook his head. "But it's a fascist statue. Salazar built it."

"But it's still beautiful."

Tiago smiled. "Thanks. I think so."

They broke apart gently and walked along again, separate, but connected by affection. After ten minutes Tiago pointed to metal tables glinting in the sun ahead. "I think he said meet here, at this one. He's usually late." Tiago's phone rang and he turned away, and waved. "He says he can see us."

Raphael looked across to the tables. A young man was standing up, waving; he was in jeans and a black hooded top, with dark, shoulder length hair, and sunglasses, naturally. Raphael nodded. "Is that him, in black?" He wondered what kind of figures they cut, the two of them walking close together; how that would look if you were Rogerio.

"Yes. That's him." Tiago turned to him. "God. His hair's grown."

"Go and say Hi." Raphael nodded. "Go on, I'll catch you up."

"No, it's fine. We'll meet him together."

They walked on and Rogerio walked towards them, hands in his pockets.

...

Chopin usually made Tiago soulful and tactile, but tonight he was celebrating, so they had fun scaling the steep cobbled streets of Bairro Alto, and slumming it, drinking cheap strong cocktails full of sugar and icy slush, getting high and laughing about the tourists. They went to a club in Principe Real and danced for a while to distorted music among skinny girls with laddered tights, and grinning boys in skinny jeans and tight T shirts, but after ten minutes they gave up and sat at the bar watching the dancers, feeling superior and antique.

Raphael pointed to a slim, dark-haired, serious-faced boy. "Was that you?"

"Of course not. I was tucked up in bed with St Thomas Aquinas." Tiago poked at the green slush in his glass with a tasteful pink stirrer in the shape of a pneumatic Perspex angel.

"She's got a tray of tits. Like Inês."

He leaned forward and slipped off the barstool and Raphael decided it was time to go back.

...

At two the cool night air from the estuary was drifting into their room.

"Your love is deep and gentle as the sea." Tiago caught sight of the shadows on the wall beside them. "Oh, I'm so close baby. Look at us. Look what you've done to me."

Raphael kissed his mouth, holding him close until he called out. And then they talked about love until Tiago fell asleep.

Raphael held him contentedly, wondering why he'd once been so wary of Rogerio; he was just a kid, a softly-spoken hoodie with a struggling beard, and a Renault 4, and Jesus on his shoulder, confusing him. It seemed incredible that such a non-entity could ever have broken Tiago's heart.

Raphael went to sleep with the smug satisfaction of a man deeply loved, and the sore throat of a man unused to the company of small children, and consequently prone to their ailments.

CHAPTER 19

THE END OF AMBITION

Soon after landing back in Paris, Raphael became spectacularly ill very quickly. By Monday night he had a temperature, and on Tuesday morning spots showed up, deep red and itchy as hell.

Tiago had called João, and been told Tiaginho had chicken pox, and as there were only a dozen spots, and they were hardly disfiguring, the patient had quickly decided that chicken pox in a forty-year old was a ridiculous rather than a dangerous predicament, and that he would behave, directing his anger at the virus, and enjoying being nursed in his own home. Tiago had cool hands, and a soft voice, and infinite patience, and cooked great food, and ran soothing baths, and smoothed calamine lotion onto Raphael's mostly unblemished skin. Raphael rallied quickly. On Thursday afternoon he sat up in bed sketching images the fever had planted; weird motifs for Tiago, and himself, Clara, Rob, and Tomas Paul, five strange illuminated letters with odd imagery and Latin inscriptions. Tiago loved them, pronounced them *absinthe drawings,* and had them framed and put on the hallway wall.

On Friday morning Raphael woke up without any trace of fever to hear Tiago taking work phone calls downstairs, mostly in languages he couldn't understand, but not always. *Yes. No. Very definitely no. Aurora, I told you, that is Paul's job. That is what he's paid for. If you do his job, who is going to do yours? Don't be a pushover. If you start your career acting like that you'll never get out of it.*

There was silence, and then Tiago's footfall on the stairs, and then Tiago's face round the door.

Raphael smiled at him. "Hello angel."

"Hi." Tiago came in, a letter in his hand. "Post. This came for you."

It was from Amelia, an invitation to a concert at her house in England, the last weekend in June, after Midsummer; a chance to see the temple, and what needed doing.

"Kitminster Episcopi." Raphael smiled and scratched his head. He'd always told Tiago that Amelia had come to see him in the shop, and pitched the project to him there. He wasn't about to admit Amelia's role in getting their love over its stuttering start. "Shall we do this?"

"Don't scratch." Tiago took Raphael's hand in his own. "It's her temple thing, isn't it? Her project. She told me about it the night we met." He read the card. "I think it sounds good." He frowned. "You know she wants money?"

"Everyone wants money. But some people deserve it more than others." Raphael smiled. "Don't you think it would be great to restore a temple? Just think of all that karma."

Tiago shrugged. "Sure. But I think we need to know more about it."

"So ask her over for Sunday night. I'll be bored by then." Raphael patted the bed. "And I'm feeling a lot better you know."

"I'll tell you when you're well enough for that, Raphael Emmanuel Davide."

Tiago went back downstairs with a smile on his face. He was a terrific nurse; Raphael was recovering faster from chickenpox than anyone you read about on the internet. And he was a terrific manager. Aurora had proved to be razor sharp and perfectly capable – which was just as well now she was taking his place at the conference in Cusco. He put the kettle on and stared at his reflection in its sloping steel side. He'd meant to work up *Lux* in Cusco, but now he knew for certain that *Lux* would never happen.

And he knew for certain that it didn't need to. Tiago smiled and put tea into the pot; this was what happened to everyone, in a way. You started out with dreams, but then you found a lover, and settled down, and looked after one another, and had a home, and a family, and that became your mission. Beauty and love flowed from everyone's everyday life, and it would be the same for them. Raphael would draw, and they would play music, and their children would be beautiful, because all children were; and love would grow as together they reaped the joys and overcame the disappointments of parenthood. And as for justice? Well, they would carry on with the pictures, and do what they could with petitions, and voting for the right people, and making generous donations to charity.

He called Amelia and asked her round to discuss the project on Sunday night.

...

Amelia liked to big herself up, but she knew she was just a

bench monkey, part of the poor bloody infantry on the front line trenches of science, digging herself deeper every day into the claggy expertise that made her less employable with every year that passed. Of course, it wasn't all that esoteric; apples were interesting to everyone. She'd loved them since she was little, running into grandfather's orchard before breakfast to pick them and eat them still warm from the sun, the first ones of the season, dewy and tart, the later ones sweeter but defiled with the escape tunnels of codling moths. She'd lost her virginity under a Laxton's Superb, though that had hardly been the best adjective for the occasion, and as a teenage girl she'd quickly concluded that variety and quality mattered more than quantity, and that there was a lot more to life than Cox.

Her great inspiration had come at nineteen; waiting in the misty, pre-dawn orchard for *Sitta europea*, she had accidentally focused her zoom lens on two desperate, car-less doggers.

Come on Lee Ann, let's do it here.

Oh Stanislaus, I wish I'd met you twenty years ago.

A touching scene, that stolen clinch; but Amelia wasn't thinking about the new Europe. She was looking at big-boned, long-limbed, Stanislaus, thrusting like a hydraulic ram; he would make a great apple tree, one that would withstand high winds, and dry summers, and dry rocky terrain. She'd collected the condom and spent the day alone in the greenhouse, potting on.

Those trees were six years old now, her seven Stanislaus whips. They'd turned out tall and resilient, but not that different to her control group, so it was inconclusive. But that had been more metaphysics than science. Science had moved on since then, and so had she; now she knew exactly what she was doing. And with the right funds, her perfect *Triploid* trees would soon be springing up in the orchard; not simply restored varieties, but improved ones.

Amelia rang the bell for the apartment and turned back to stare at the doorway over the road. Her cold stakeout had worked out well. She might even get her cheque tonight.

Tiago opened the door, smiling and proprietorial. "Hello Amelia. You look lovely." He kissed her three times, and Amelia breathed in the lemongrass and sandalwood in his hair, the bitter incense on his neck, a smoker's recent nibble. "Raphael's in the shower."

"How is he?"

"Lots better thanks." Tiago shook his head. "Poor guy. He's going out of his mind. I think tonight will really cheer him up though."

Amelia smiled. Still madly in love. Good. She asked the usual questions; how did he get it, how was he feeling, was he watching out for post-viral conditions, they could be dreadful, worse than the actual disease, but really she needed to be sure the virus would be gone by Midsummer.

Tiago's answers were reassuring but when Raphael came into the lounge Amelia was more than satisfied; true, he seemed thinner than the man she'd met, but he was bright-eyed and his smile was sincere. If he'd been a dog his tail would have been wagging. He kissed her with real warmth. "Amelia. How nice to see you again."

The doorbell rang and Tiago went to get it. Raphael smiled at Amelia. "Okay?"

"Sure. You?"

"Never better." He nodded towards the hallway. "Rob's my brother-in-law. He's a civil engineer, and he's actually done a few restoration jobs. We thought if Rob were here we could make the decision tonight."

Amelia nodded. "Sure." She hoped Rob wasn't too keen on detail.

...

They ate heartily and chatted in the unconsciously pretentious way liberal people do about films, and books, and places they'd stayed or would like to stay, and hobbies; music, sports, photography. Amelia put down her glass and took out a tiny, battered phone. "I don't mean this. I mean a proper camera for taking pictures. I have zoom lenses too. All that old crap that no one has anymore." She took the folder from her bag. "I took these with it actually, though you could probably do as well on a smartphone now."

"Hmm." Raphael poured more wine and nodded towards the folder. "So what have we got here?" So what have we got here?"

Amelia picked up the folder. "So. It's a folly, a temple to Diana and Apollo, on my grandfather's land in England, at Kitminster in Devon. I'm going turn it into a centre for music, for children. Children who otherwise wouldn't get the chance, deprived children." She laid out the photographs, the original eighteenth century drawings, plans and elevations, the new plans for the restored structure, speaking slowly and clearly about her Georgian ancestor, the original builder, a sugar magnate and a slave trader, and how the place was in a mess, but in a beautiful spot, in an old orchard on the river Kit.

"I've always wanted to restore the temple, and restore the orchard, put a pig or two in it maybe, but I've never had the money." She pulled back; maybe she was being too presumptuous. "Of course, you don't need to decide now. You can see it at Midsummer, and decide then, if you like."

Raphael had been picking up the documents one by one, glancing at them, handing them on to Rob and Tiago. "A slave trader, you say?"

Rob frowned. "Most commodities people were back then, I guess?" He looked at Tiago. "At least I suppose they were?"

Tiago shrugged. "Probably." He pointed to the plans. "And in a way, this redeems that, I suppose."

Raphael looked at Tiago, nodded, and turned to Amelia. "So how much would you need?"

"Seventy thousand euros would fund the whole thing." Amelia handed a page to Raphael who gave it to Rob. "Here's the breakdown." She sipped her wine and sat quietly, giving the men the silence they needed for thinking.

Rob went down the page line by line. "It's so expensive getting projects done in England."

Tiago turned to Raphael. "Diana and Apollo. We like them."

Raphael smiled at Amelia. "We do like them. We're the last pagans in Europe." He looked at Tiago. "Coffee?"

Tiago got up. "I'll make it."

Raphael stood. "I'll help you." He went out, his hand in the small of Tiago's back.

Amelia watched the kitchen door close behind them. Rob turned to her and rubbed his hands together. "So then. Why apples?"

She smiled, but not too much. There was no need to flirt; Rob had married an intelligent woman, and so intelligence would probably be enough to win him over. She explained how her grandfather had given her an interest in the old varieties, and how she alone among her four sisters had got the science bug, and wanted to go do Science at Turing.

"Turing? I'm Turing too. Civ Eng, 1991."

"Really? That's amazing."

There was a series of loud bumps from the kitchen; the sound of crockery and cutlery shaking, like an aircraft encountering heavy turbulence. It didn't sound a lot like people making coffee.

Rob picked up the documents and turned to her. "The lounge is nice."

They went next door. "Kitminster Hall? Isn't that the Rockingham place?"

Amelia shrank, but only a little. A small, tactical confession might be a good move. "Okay. Technically, I'm an Honourable. But I ditched all that. I ditched the aristocracy for the meritocracy. I'm not a landowner. I'm a brain owner."

Rob nodded. "That's slick."

It was slick. It was also Beethoven. Amelia smiled. "I joined the coalition of the purposeful. I had to. My father is Lord Rockingham. He doesn't approve of what I do. What he really likes to do is put on a Tyvek suit and roll around on perfectly good crops. Like a great big prat."

"So you're the Honourable Amelia Rockingham?" Rob gave her a clean cut "I quite fancy you but I'm perfectly harmless" smile that made her rather homesick.

Amelia held up a hand. "Worse. I was christened Thalia. She being the Muse of comedy. Awful isn't it? But now I'm Amelia."

"And Postthridge?"

"My grandmother was Elsie Postthridge."

"Really?" Rob was impressed. "And the genetics?"

"Don't know. But I do have two parents and three older sisters I can't stand."

"Interesting. I have a half brother like that." Rob grinned and looked away. "He was Raphael's partner. It was pretty awkward. Especially when it all went to ratshit last year."

Amelia frowned, trying to remember what she did and didn't know. "Shame."

"Not really. They drove each other mad." Rob looked over at her for a few seconds. "Look, Amelia. One thing, before they come back. They want to do it. And they've got the money." He waved the page at her. "But what's all this crap about Tittlebats?"

Amelia shrugged. "They're a kind of bat. They're very rare."

"Right." Rob rubbed his eyes. "Look. Just because I'm an engineer it doesn't mean I've never read a book."

Amelia bit her lip. "It's contingency."

Rob nodded. "Sure. And I won't let on. But don't push your luck Amelia. I don't know why you need all this sandbagging. But I won't let anyone rip Raphael off." He squeezed her shoulder. "It's not the money. They've got stacks of it, between them. But

I won't have Raphael's feelings hurt. He doesn't take that well. Okay?"

Amelia nodded; it was an odd warning, and a strange way to put it, but she liked Rob more for it. He would be a good man to have on your side if you could win him over. And she had. She shrugged. "You're a project manager. You know that anything could happen."

"Yes, well." Rob touched her arm. "Sorry to get hard on you. You're having a go. I like that. I bet you get away with a lot of things. But just watch yourself on this"

Tiago came in with a tray of coffee. "You're in here." He put the tray down and stared at it. "I'm sorry. I couldn't find the milk." He frowned. There was a long pause. "And Raphael's making a phone call."

Raphael came through the doorway. "Sorry about that. I couldn't find my lighter."

They chatted for a while over the coffee but Amelia had English manners and knew that once the hosts have started having sex in the kitchen the evening is pretty much over. After five minutes she got up to leave. "I must be off. Busy day in the lab tomorrow."

Tiago and Rob kissed her goodbye and Raphael saw her into the hallway. "Thanks so much for coming. You're our first non-family guest."

"I'm honoured." She looked over his shoulder. There were five drawings on the wall, five illuminated letters; T, R, R, C, TP, Latin inscriptions. "What are they?"

Raphael looked, smiled. "Oh those. They're my absinthe

drawings. I got a virus, and a fever. Tiago likes them." He turned back and drew on his cigar. "I'm very grateful Amelia. For what you did for me that night."

Amelia shrugged. "I didn't really do anything."

"Still." Raphael put his hand on her shoulder. "And we'd like to go ahead with the project."

Amelia kissed him. "That's wonderful. Thanks. I hoped you would. Can you come for the Midsummer party? We'll have music."

"We wouldn't miss it for the world."

The door closed behind her but Raphael's *Very good* followed her out onto the street.

...

Raphael's birthday dawned sunny and hot. Tiago woke early, pushed back the sheets, and watched the metronomic fish gill blink of Rapahel's heart, thinking about the gruesome reality under the skin; the sinew, the sticky crimson flowing in and frothing carmine pouring out, a red rapids. He timed the ticking beats and did the arithmetic; seventy billion gone, and seventy billion to go, if they were lucky. It sounded a lot but it was still a finite number, and therefore far too few were left to waste on arguments.

Last night they'd gone to bed separately for the first time, Tiago commandeering their bedroom, opening the slammed door only to rain pillows and colourful Portuguese insults down on Raphael at the foot of the stairs, the argument seeming as fatal as it was unexpected, starting, as these things often do, after a beautiful dinner, and a second bottle of wine, and an ill-judged gift in a plain envelope.

"What's this?"

Tiago smiled. "It's for the business. An investment. I've got enough money, like you said."

"Oh no." Raphael's smile was all wrong. "That's so kind, but it wouldn't be right." He handed the cheque back. "We don't need your money."

"Why not?" Tiago took the envelope and stared at it blankly, shocked at the pronoun that made him an outsider into bitterness made his tongue sharp. "Right. This is fucking Tomas Paul, isn't it?"

"Don't Tiago."

Tiago shook his head. He hated this stern, cold Raphael. "Manipulative fucker."

"Enough, now, Tiago." Some danger in the voice.

But not enough. "You used to let him swan in and fuck you whenever he wanted."

Raphael got up, walked over to the door, lit a cigarette, and took a long, very slow drag. When he did finally speak he sounded rather bored. "Actually, we didn't fuck."

"You didn't even fuck."

"I suppose that having come late to penetrative sex it's unsurprising you should have a tendency to exaggerate its importance in a relationship."

"They didn't even fuck." Tiago got up, walked to the window, looked out at the street below, feeling trapped, ashamed of himself, out of control. He lowered his eyes and spoke to the glass. "Who pays the bills Raphael? Who pays the lease on the shop? How do you cover the cost? Not by selling. I know about selling. You're not a salesman. Salesmen talk about what they sell. You haven't mentioned one sale since we've been together." He turned back. "Who pays for our food, and drink, and our tickets to the opera, and the clothes on your back? He does, doesn't he? He fucking keeps you."

Raphael was fresh out of charm. "Nonsense."

"Not nonsense. Truth. He owns this flat. Doesn't he?"

"No. I do."

"He gave it to you. He must have. You could never have afforded it. Not then, not now." Tiago crossed his arms.

Raphael looked at his cigarette as if he'd never seen one before. "It was his sister's flat. She left it to him. He sold it to me."

Tiago sucked a lemon. "For how much?"

"That is nothing to do with you." Raphael's voice was icy. "Don't be jealous. Anger doesn't suit you darling."

"I'm not your fucking darling. You won't fuck me into submission like you did Martin."

"I can assure you that fucking you is the furthest thing from my mind right now."

"Oh really?" Tiago argued rather well when he was winning, but tonight he was no match for Raphael, so he just let rip; Raphael thought he was such a fucking charmer, but actually he was completely fucking selfish – too lazy to pick his clothes up off the floor, or buy a pint of milk, for fuck's sake – and so fucking stubborn, stuck in his ways, like an old man, a weak man, too weak even to quit smoking, too weak and stupid to do the one thing that would stop him dying of cancer like his father had, a vain man in the middle of a midlife crisis, terrified of aging, a masochist in thrall to a creep of an ex-boyfriend who'd seduced him, and used him, and still treated him like dirt. Maybe Tiago should treat him like dirt. Maybe Raphael would think more of him if he did. Was that what he wanted? To be treated like dirt?

Raphael eyed Tiago steadily for a few seconds. "Are we all done now?"

And Tiago had exited upstage left, squirting out repulsive valedictory abuse like a skunk; but at three he'd relented, and come downstairs to collect Raphael, and there'd been sufficient reconciliation to let them sleep in the same bed.

And now it was morning and Raphael was waking up.

"Hey, darling?" He stoked Tiago's face. "Why so sad honey?"

"Just thinking about last night."

"Oh honey. I didn't even know you existed."

"I know. But it hurts me that you take his money. It hurts my pride."

"It doesn't hurt mine. It shouldn't matter to you. He means nothing to me now. How can he, when you mean everything?"

They had a late breakfast and took a taxi to Clara's house. Raphael sat back, eyes closed, murmuring sweet nothings *You know, I used to run along here all the time with Rob, and all that time you were here, so near to me.* And Tiago let his hand be taken, and looked out the window at the regrowing trees along the river, wishing the days and nights of Raphael's past could be swept into bags and carted away like so many dead leaves.

Clara was happy to see them. She kissed Raphael and he embraced her. "You okay? You look tired."

"I'm fine. I'm just tired. I'm always tired these days." She put her arms around Tiago. "Good morning my beautiful, good and deserving baby brother-in-law-type-thing-person."

It was like hugging a xylophone. Tiago forced a smile. "Hi. Lots to do?"

"Nothing. It's all done. Help yourself to beer."

Raphael took two beers, lobbed one to Tiago. "Are we first?"

"Yes."

The dog barked, voices sounded in the hallway, and the kitchen door opened; it was Rob.

"Hey Raphael. Happy Birthday, you poor old sod." He came in, took Raphael's hand and shook it hard. "Forty eh? You poor old fucking bastard."

"Thanks."

Rob put an arm round Tiago, making them a ring of three. "Hey Tiago, he's looking good. You must be taking good care of the miserable old git."

"I'm doing my best."

The dog ran in and informed them there was a stranger in the hallway. Raphael knelt down and messed with Wandy's ears. "We're getting two dogs, apparently."

Rob nodded. "You can have that one for starters. He chewed up one of my running shoes last night." He took a beer from the fridge and opened the bottle with his thumb. "I have to keep you in here for a bit. Tomas Paul and Clara are putting your present next door."

"No they're not." A tall, fair haired man was standing in the doorway; black coat, black sweater, blue jeans, black framed glasses.

Tiago stared. It was Apollo.

"Hey." Raphael went over to Tomas Paul, and embraced him the way old lovers do when new lovers are pretending not to watch. "Good to see you."

Tiago gave his hand and a polite smile, and told Tomas Paul he was very like his portrait.

...

It wasn't a bad start, but three hours later Tiago was sulking on his own in the kitchen. He'd offered to go and make coffee, good coffee, Portuguese, but now he felt too bitter for that. You couldn't beat the past. You had to live with it. But it was a problem when there was so fucking much of it, and it owned the house you lived in.

He went to the sink and turned the taps on and off, trying to sluice the day down the plughole. Lunch had been an utter disaster due to Tomas Paul. First he'd presented Raphael with a ridiculously ostentatious present, a breath-taking seven course lute with a cherry wood back, a spruce soundboard, the Fermilab design inlaid in ivory in the back of the ebony neck, *the best present of all time*, a show stopper. And then he'd told some bullshit magical realist story about the second world war, and angry gods, and the mercy of Jesus, that had triggered a cavalcade of in-jokes, with Raphael and Clara saying that Tomas Paul had dropped too much acid in the nineties, and Tomas Paul squabbling with Rob about the name of Churchill's parrot, and Churchill's cat, and making Raphael laugh as if it were all completely hilarious. And throughout the whole meal Tomas Paul had fired little barbs at Tiago; "What does our charming Tiago think of that?" "Where did our talented young friend go to University?" and, possibly the worst, "What would our gifted young Iberian economist do?" clearly the most thinly veiled of insults.

Tiago hadn't wanted to spoil the party, but like all people who don't want to spoil the party, he had, by tipping wine down his throat until Raphael had put a hand over his glass (humiliating) and made excuses for him *Tired, aren't you darling?* (worse), and then getting so drunk he'd blurted out his *Lux* pitch and blown it, walking them through it like a clown on stilts, erratic, leaving too much unsaid, so that afterwards Clara had frowned, and Rob had said *Pardoner's Tale, right?* and nodded too fast, and Tomas Paul had smirked and described it as "promising and ingenious." He hadn't been able to see Raphael's reaction, because he was sitting beside him; but the arm snaking around his waist and drawing him close had been a gesture of comfort, not congratulation.

The kitchen was boiling. Tiago opened the top sash of the window. The back door banged shut and Raphael and Tomas Paul walked out into the garden.

Oh great.

Tiago pulled the blind down.

"Well, congratulations Raphael. He's really something."

"Thanks. Where are you staying?"

"Your favourite hotel. Your favourite room. It's okay, but the bed's too big."

There was a pause. "You never fucking give up, do you?"

"What?"

"It's been thirteen years. I've moved on."

"I haven't. You ended it, not me. You're still beautiful to me."

"Good. You can find even more beauty in my fidelity to my new lover."

"Good put down."

"I've been working on it."

Tiago put his head back, eyes closed.

"I'm sorry. I'm sorry I was so angry."

"No. I understand, Raphael. You still have this fidelity thing."

"Just leave it Tomas Paul." A few moments of silence. "Sorry. But you can be so fucking annoying."

"Yes. I went bad after you dumped me."

A pigeon cooed up on a gutter. *Froo-frooo-froo.*

"But it's not too late, is it?"

Froo-frooo-froo.

"I'm afraid it is." There was another long silence. "Look. I need this cigarette. And I won't smoke in Clara's house. If you want to talk, let's talk about something else."

"Okay. So, the inlay on your lute is Siberian mammoth tusk ivory, about ten thousand years old. There's a lot of it around these days because the permafrost is melting."

Raphael laughed. "Has anyone ever told you you talk shit, Tomas Paul?"

"Everyone does. Ceaselessly."

Tiago turned his back to the window.

"Well. We may as well smoke."

"That's what I came out here to do."

There was a metallic scrape; flint.

"Jesus. Wasn't that from Martin? How did it survive the great conflagration?"

Raphael laughed. "It hid in a coat pocket. Tiago found it. He insisted I started using it again."

"He's quite something."

"Yes, he is. He's brave and very determined. He's had to be."

"Clara said."

A plane went over, drowning out the conversation for a while, and then Raphael's words emerged, telling Tiago's story; the car crash, the seminary, Rogerio, the loss of self, and now their life together in Paris, their plans for the future. He made it sound beautiful, hopeful, perfect, a story of two people finding redemption, and coming home.

"Sounds like a happy ending."

"Yes."

There was a long exhalation, someone blowing smoke. "Do you remember your bad dreams when we were students?"

"God, yes. Holocaust dreams."

"I would hold you until your heart had stopped racing."

"I'd forgotten."

"I never will. Do you remember that time in Milan? You were nearly in the street when I caught you. You were butt naked."

"Fuck, yes."

There was laughter. Tiago folded his arms.

"Funny how you wind up happy by accident." Raphael coughed. "I just hope I can keep him that way. He's so much younger."

Smoke drifted into the kitchen.

"You're happy enough now though, aren't you? And the smile says yes. "

"Now, Tomas Paul." There was a long pause. "Some things are private."

"You don't need to tell me about it. I can imagine you in bed together. I have imagined it."

"Leave it Tomas Paul."

But Tomas Paul didn't leave it. "He goes up to bed first, while you put out the lights and lock up. And in bed he's so soulful in your arms, so loving and passionate. It must be rather charming. He probably prays before and after you fuck. Possibly even during."

Another plane went over, but it was a big one, and it was five seconds before Tiago could hear again. A slightly raised voice, Tomas Paul's.

"Just remember Raphael. When you want a real man again, you know where I am."

"If you'd been a real man, Tomas Paul, I would have been enough for you."

The back door slammed, the kitchen door opened and Rob came in.

"Hey Tiago. What's so funny?"

"Nothing."

"Did you find the coffee?" Rob reached into a cupboard above Tiago's head and handed him a sealed coffee container with a Union Jack on it. "The plan's good you know. Lux, I mean. It's just a big stretch. I'm sure we could do it someday."

Tiago shrugged. "It's fine. It's just a thought experiment." He meant it. It was no problem. Nothing was ever going to be a problem again. He was still feeling pretty contented when Clara came in and suggested they all went out into the garden for some nice cold and rain.

Tiago resisted this inviting offer, made the coffee and took the tray through to the sitting room. The lute was on the sofa. He picked it up, detuned to a guitar tuning and found the notes he needed. *Ut queant laxis, Resonare fibris, Mira gestorum, Famuli tuorum, Solve pollute, Labis reatum, Sancte Iohannes*

"Very nice." Tomas Paul was standing in front of him, arms folded.

"Thanks." Tiago put the instrument down, got up and walked over to the window to stare out of it. It was a magnificent suburban vista of absolutely nothing to look at, but he wasn't going to turn round, because this way he could better pretend that Tomas Paul no longer existed. From the tone of Raphael's voice in the garden that was very possibly true, although oddly he could still see a mirage reflected in the window; Tomas Paul sitting down, lighting a blue and yellow cigarette. "Where are they all, Tiago?"

"Outside. Looking at slugs." Tiago focused on the pavement over the road. A couple of kids were walking past, a young boy and a girl, eighteen, nineteen. The girl had a violin case, the boy had a rucksack and a couple of shopping bags from a cheap supermarket. The girl dropped a glove on the floor, and it fell into the wet gutter. The boy bent down, picked it up, put it in his pocket. They kissed and walked on, a picture of sweet, simple tenderness. Tiago smiled; yesterday this would have upset him, this spectre of young love, like the glamorous student romance of two beautiful boys sticking pins in the map of Europe that marked the footprint of their love, a love story with its own classical music soundtrack, an impossible act to follow. It was amazing how quickly things changed. Or had they? Tomas Paul was still sounding pretty chirpy, droning boringly on about Guido d'Arezzo and the Hexachord. Raphael had rejected him, and how; but maybe their spat would blow over, and maybe it should. Tiago looked at Tomas Paul, and felt magnanimous; a good person, a loving person, would never seek to change a lover's happy memories of a former lover, but would want them to remain, immutable, like a bowl of golden apples. A good person would never want to excise the beauty of lost love from their lover's life. A good person would be big about his lover's ex-lovers; especially when he'd heard them being ground into the dirt.

Tiago was good. He turned, planning to say something nice about the lute.

But the door opened and Raphael came in.

"Get your jacket honey." Ignoring Tomas Paul. "We're going."

"Going?"

Raphael came over and put an arm round him; he'd told Clara Tiago wasn't feeling great, that he was really tired. They were going, now. They would go to Tiago's place. It was time they checked it over. And it was only two kilometres. The walk would make him feel better.

Raphael led him into the hallway, fitting him into his jacket as if he were five years old. "Come on."

"What about the lute?"

"Fuck the lute. Come on."

"Wait." Tiago took the folded *Lux* drawing from his jacket pocket. "Let's see how smart he is."

CHAPTER 20

A PROPER JOB

Tomas Paul lit a cigarette while Clara and Rob pored over the runes. He'd recognised Tiago at once as the boy from Lisbon – some of his habits, like climbing into a bottle of wine, hadn't changed at all – but it was clear Tiago remembered him about as much as he liked him; which was to say, not at all. But then Tomas Paul hadn't gone out to be likeable, with the flashy present, and the "gifted young Iberian economist" line he'd rehearsed all the way from the airport. He sniffed. Given the inauspicious start, it was surprising how much Tiago had improved; Tomas Paul had expected a puppy-faced snub-nosed charmless wonk, but Tiago was clever, and proud, and swelled up with fuck-you-ness. It was unsurprising that Raphael wanted to make a go of it.

Rob pointed at the bottom right corner. "Six people, obviously."

Unsurprising, but very disappointing. Tomas Paul looked up at Clara. Yes, that was how he felt too, inside; open-mouthed, greenish, like a stuffed carp in a glass case.

"What, exactly, does the hanged man mean?" Clara frowned. "I mean, are we killing people now? How simply fucking marvellous."

Tomas Paul and Rob looked at her, then at each other. Put like that, it was a little extreme.

"I mean have you gone out of your fucking minds?"

Tomas Paul frowned and decided to play it straight. "You don't think we should kill people?"

"No I don't." She frowned deeper, not a thinking frown, an angry one. "Have you gone completely fucking crazy? Is everyone crazy except me?"

Tomas Paul smiled at Rob. "Do you think get the feeling she doesn't approve?"

"Shut up. It's not funny." Clara shook her head. "I can't believe I'm hearing this."

Tomas Paul wagged a finger. "You're spoiling Raphael's birthday. I admit it's academic, now he's walked out of his own party."

"No. You spoiled Raphael's birthday. Fucking showing off." Clara poked him hard in the chest. "And don't laugh at him Rob, don't encourage him. Fucking hell Tomas Paul. You've never been anything but trouble."

"Honey." Rob put his hand out to her; a total waste of time.

She knocked it away. "Don't you fucking honey me Robert Nelson." She shook her head and let it all out; did they want to wipe out every dodgy industrialist that ran a dirty factory? She was a philanthropist, not some kind of vigilante, obliterating people, scoring them out. She shook her head. "Unbelievable." She walked away and stood with her back to the room. "Whatever. Do what you fucking like. But you're on your own. Because I won't help you with this. We'll do the girl, the Meladroni, and that's it. No more." She put a hand to her side and took a deep breath, and the room was quiet for a few moments. Rob shrugged and gave Tomas Paul a *leave her alone* shake of the head, but Tomas Paul ignored it.

"Clara. With Tiago's plan we don't need to kill anyone."

Clara turned to him. "Well, that's pretty fucking big of you Tomas Paul."

"Don't you see Clara? He's going to make them kill each other."

•••

They looked up the grid reference on the rebus and fired up an old geological map, the beautiful patchwork of bright pinks, and greens and yellows, speckled and striped, with thick black fault lines; where the gold was. Or where it might be. Rob spoke in a quiet voice, puzzling it out.

"He's called it *Lux Aeterna*. It's a memorial to the dead. And he's done his homework. *Radix malorum est cupiditas* is Chaucer, the Pardoner's Tale. The story of the three villains. Death will take *Ut*. And then *Re, Mi and Fa* are lured to where the gold lies, or might lie." Rob smiled at Clara. "He would need you to make the gold fields appear, disappear."

"Geodesy." Clara nodded. "Of course you could easily plant something, or someone." She shook her head and smiled in a tired way. "It's an interesting concept. But it needs to stay just that. A concept." She rubbed her eyes. "He doesn't really intend to do it though, does he?" She looked at Rob. "Not for real?"

"Of course not darling. He's not that crazy."

"I mean if he does, someone needs to stop him."

Rob took her hand. "Don't worry honey. He's just showing us how smart he is."

But Tomas Paul looked at the rebus. He wasn't so sure.

•••

The half hour walk to Tiago's flat passed mostly in silence. Raphael was furious, but he was still too dignified to rant in the streets. Outside the apartment block his phone rang. It was Rob. "Give me five minutes."

"Sure." Tiago went through to the lounge to open the windows and let out the stale air.

Raphael came in and called for him.

"In here."

Raphael came in and walked over to him. "They said no, two and half against a half. Clara and Tomas Paul against, Rob maybe. They think it's too risky. I'm sorry."

Tiago smiled. "I'm inconsolable. But you can try your best."

•••

Afterwards they drank black tea in bed. "It's the first time we've been here for ages."

Raphael nodded. "Yes." He shook his head. "Tomas Paul was a complete cunt today."

"He's just jealous. He wishes you were still his lover."

"No he doesn't, not really."

Tiago had practised the line in his head and it came out well. "I fucking heard him Raphael." He took Raphael's hand. "Please don't cover for him."

Raphael looked down. "Right." He got out of bed and walked

over to the window, peered round a blind. "I wondered if you had."

And I wondered if you'd tell me. But Tiago had learned to let the silence run at times like this.

Raphael turned back. "You were right, last night. We have to cut him out. He's getting worse. I don't know why." He looked down at the floor and thought out loud. It wouldn't be easy. Tomas Paul wouldn't like it. He saw himself as a co-founder. He could make things very difficult. And Tomas Paul picked up quite few bills.

"So we're going to need some money."

"Money, we have."

...

The next morning at ten Tiago sat at his desk staring into a large expresso and reflecting on Raphael's powers of understatement; Tomas Paul picked up all the bills, and they were going to need a fuck of a lot of money. But although the situation was serious, it wasn't complicated. Two simple things could be fixed quickly. Raphael was not a partner in the business that bore his name, but an employee on a salary of "about a hundred thousand," which turned out to be nearer one forty. If he wanted to walk away from Tomas Paul he would have to get a job somewhere else, or set up on his own. It would be a big change, but it was unlikely it would be a problem in the short term; Tomas Paul would sue for peace, not wanting to lose his friend and figurehead, and it would be up to Raphael to carry on spending the money that poured into his account as long as he felt he could. If he didn't feel he could, then Tiago would willingly pay for everything, including the seventy thousand that Amelia needed; both of them regarded that as a done deal. More immediately, Raphael was determined never to spend another night in the Rue Vivienne apartment. They'd talked about living together in Saint-Germain-en-Laye, but Raphael wrinkled up his nose at that; he had a better idea. Tiago could swap his apartment for somewhere in the City, somewhere in the ninth maybe, and they would move there together with Raphael's stuff, and move Tiago's possessions out to The Retreat as Raphael owned The Retreat outright. He'd bought his share with a legacy from his father, and then taken over Martin's half after their split in lieu of his share of their investments.

It was a terrific plan, and by nine that morning Tiago had already called HR and asked them to set up viewings for the afternoon, when his phone rang. It was the São Paulo office. He listened, and felt the cross round his neck, and all of a sudden ironing out the wrinkles of domestic life didn't seem that much of a challenge. He made a few calls, and spoke to a few people, and got home rather late.

Raphael had seen the news. "Is that a Hexacorp operation?"

"Yes." Tiago sat down and told him everything the news organisations didn't know, things he'd learned from a priest in one of the missions, where they were bringing in the dead and the dying. It was chaos, there were fatalities and injuries, but no one knew how many. The press reports and the company's own reports were inaccurate; they'd said there were explosions and walkouts and riots, ruptured pipelines spilling chemicals, even guerrilla attacks from local groups. He looked into Raphael's eyes. "It's terrible, what's happening."

Raphael stared back at him. "What have you done?"

"Nothing really." At least nothing he was going to tell Raphael; but he had spoken to Fa, who'd taken time out to call the office for advice about his portfolio. He might activate that link in the future, he might not.

It was too late to help the people dying today, so he sipped the glass of wine Raphael had poured and looked at a few floor plans.

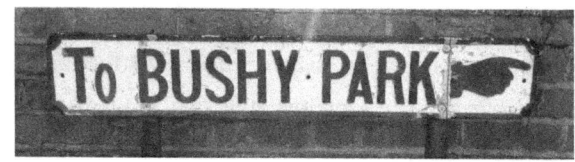

CHAPTER 21

THREE RAINY DAYS THAT DIDN'T SHAKE THE WORLD

It never rains on the Bushy Park Run. But sometimes it absolutely chucks it down.

Tomas Paul stood with the assembling park runners, gazing at the Bushy Park fountain. Like everyone else he was so wet he may as well have been standing under it; but unlike everyone else, he'd come to ask it for advice. It was hard from this angle. As ever, Diana was facing west, her back turned to the start line as if she wasn't interested in the runners' puny efforts. Why should she be? Tomas Paul knew she was swifter than any of them, sweeping the course to clear the deer from the path of the worried well in the time it took the stewards to make announcements. But today she didn't seem interested in him. He nodded; fair enough. He'd spilled the beans twice now, and she was sulking, pretending he didn't exist.

He'd suspected for a while his powers were waning. It had been raining since April, and today, with only days to go until Midsummer, the sun was nothing but a timid shimmer behind thick clouds. In a few hours it would be close to its zenith, floating above the black line Tomas Paul drew on an orange for enraptured schoolchildren on College Outreach days.

TROPIC OF CANCER. YOU ARE HERE.

But today he wasn't here.

He was on a rocky Adriatic headland with Raphael, the sun cooking them both through thin early nineties ozone, with bottled beer warming up and the transistor radio buzzing like a wasp beside them while they lay like demigods, the envy of mere mortals around them. *What do you think we'll be doing in twenty years Tomas Paul?* Raphael's voice dreamy, his eyes half closed, the cigarette smoke puffing out on *be* and *Paul. Do you think there'll be any jobs for musicians then? Do you think there'll be any orchestras? Or will it all be synthesisers?* And turning to him, propping himself up on one arm, his hip jutting up like a sand dune, his skin sweet and glistening with coconut oil. *Will we all be unemployed?* Tomas Paul had looked at him and found it impossible to say anything other than the question foremost in his mind. *Do you think we'll still be lovers?* And Raphael's smiling and kissing him and saying *Oh Tomas Paul, of course. We'll always be lovers. We'll always be friends. We'll never fight. And we'll never let each other down.* What a time. Youth. Sheer bodily bliss, and nothing else mattering except living to the full in every glorious moment. And now, what remained of it? Just a bad aftertaste, a bitter memory of days that would never come again. Because time was linear, and because they had fought, and because he had let Raphael down.

And because Raphael never forgave.

Tomas Paul glowered at the statue; there weren't enough golden statues in London. The British eschewed such gaudy monstrosities, and normally Tomas Paul's spirits were lifted by Diana's Rococo decadence. But today he merely envied her perpetual mineral inexistence. He was tired of human life. It was overrated. He should bugger off. His death would save Clara's skin, if anyone was paying attention.

He looked up at the statue. "Is that what you want?" Was she paying attention?

Was she buggery. But still, it wasn't a *no*. Tomas Paul frowned; if it was what she wanted, and Clara lived, then Raphael would be happy. His sacrifice would bind them in eternity.

"You want a sacrifice? How archaic."

A small herd of fallow deer were browsing fresh grass near the pond. They looked up and watched him, presenting their antlers in perfect synch like an array of telescopes. They would know everything; she told them everything.

"Is that what she's after?"

The deer dipped their heads to the wet grass and resumed their grazing. *Dunno, ask her.*

"I bloody will." Tomas Paul crossed the road, weaving between impatient cars, and climbed the bank towards the ornamental pond that fed the fountain beneath the statue. "That's it, isn't it?"

No answer. He needed to see her face.

He climbed over the low wall and let himself down into the pond. The water was waist deep, and freezing, and the bottom of the pool was slippery with goose shit, but Tomas Paul was sure-footed. "That's what you want, isn't it?"

It took him a while to wade to the fountain. He heard a couple of voices, the Park Run stewards on loud hailers *Who is that guy? Does anyone know that guy? The guy in the fountain?*

Are you all right mate? And a couple of swans took umbrage, until they recognised him, and retreated. But he pressed on and in two minutes he reached the stone plinth at the foot of the statue. The cascading water was deafening, so he stood under it for a few minutes with his eyes closed, letting the torrent slake the misery that had possessed him for weeks.

There were more voices, closer up; commanding voices "Are you all right Sir? *Sir?*" Tomas Paul opened his eyes. There were two big strong lads standing in front of him; two squaddies, the British Military Fitness lads.

Tomas Paul closed his eyes gave them peace signs. "Never better gentlemen. Don't mind me." He was better than all right. The drenching had purged his dismal mood and freed his mind. Disappearing wouldn't be enough; he had to dematerialise to leave behind the curse of human memory. But he saw it now, a new life, in a new shape, and freedom.

The squaddies looked him over. "Will you come with us sir?"

Tomas Paul nodded, and let himself be led, and gazed across at the comely does. They stared back, speckled and elegant on slender legs, gently defiant but still fluttering pale tails like fan dancers; and batting their beautiful eyelashes.

He would leave a letter for Raphael; he owed him one.

•••

On Sunday morning Rob, Raphael and Tiago went running like three big kids and Clara slept in. She woke at ten and stretched out like a starfish, turning her head right and left, hearing the little bones creak in her neck, waiting for the stab in her side.

Waiting.

She sat up and hugged herself. The pain had gone. She felt for it, probing stupidly, finding there was nothing, just the skin and flesh folding under her fingers.

"Promising."

She on the end of the bed and listened to the empty house. Two hours ago the men had crept around, getting breakfast as quietly as they could, bless them, but she'd still heard the feint *ting* of spoons on cereal bowls, and the *beeps* of running watches, and quiet voices talking about where they would run, and how muddy and wet it was, and how great their shoes were for these conditions.

She smiled sadly. At times this year she'd wondered if they'd get by without her. She'd known that of course they would, that they would have had to, that they would have had no choice. But the truth was that she was rather intrigued about the future the four of them might have, and she didn't want to miss it.

...

Early on Thursday morning, Rob looked at the surly girl behind the counter. You couldn't blame her. The train was packed and it probably went against her principles to sell coffee this bad.

"You're paying in euros?"

"Er, yes. Yes, please."

"Five euros."

"Thanks." Rob reached into his pocket, brought out a handful of silver and gold, picked through it. "Here."

The girl took the money, chucked it into the till and turned away.

Rob turned and mouthed a silent, pointless punch line. "In England, we say thank you." But he was still in a good mood. This was better than flying, and soon they'd be in England, and that afternoon he'd be hurtling like a madman over English gallops.

There was a sudden shift in the timbre of the background noise, a softening. Rob looked up at the blurry green mess outside the greasy window and smiled. "Hello Blighty."

He rode the rolling action of the train past rows of dozing passengers and found Raphael still sleeping, arms folded, a thick green scarf draped round his neck. Rob put the cups on the table, rearranged the scarf, and took his seat opposite. Was "sidekick" one word, or two?

"Is your friend always such a good sleeper?"

He looked up and saw the Chef de Train beside him. "Er, yes, He's pretty good."

She smiled at him and nodded at the coffee. "You look after him."

"Yes." Rob coughed. "How long is it now please?"

"Forty minutes only. You have connections?"

"No, we're fine thanks." Rob watched the girl's retreating form, admired her nice legs, thought they were like Clara's. He looked at his friend the good sleeper, and smiled at the tweed jacket, the unseasonal scarf, so damn stylish. The return of colour to Raphael's clothes since the spring had been a huge relief after the months of monochrome and navy, the creaseless, sharp shell he'd grown to disguise the collapsed man within. And someone whose opinion mattered had clearly told him that green suited him.

The train sounded its horn. Raphael breathed deeply and opened his eyes. "Where are we?"

"England." Rob waited for the cutting *apercu*, the Raphael take on things.

"I promised Tiago sunshine at Midsummer." Raphael looked at his watch. "Today."

"That was rash." Rob took the lid off Raphael's coffee. "This is the wettest June on record, with the least sunshine."

"Fascinating."

Rob flicked the sugar sachet. "I got you this. It's probably disgusting. I'm sorry."

Raphael looked down the aisle. "Who was the woman I heard?"

"Chef de Train." Rob poured the sugar and stirred Raphael's coffee. "She thinks I'm your tup." It was one of their favourite in-jokes, a line from one of Elinor's farmer neighbours after Sunday lunch in her local; the man had watched Rob shielding Raphael's match with his coat. *Frenchman is he? Looks like Pirlo. Your Rob'll be the tup, though?* Elinor had choked on her scotch telling them that.

Raphael settled into a smile and watched Rob stir. "I can't imagine why."

"You could do a lot worse than me mate."

"I certainly could do."

"You certainly have done." Rob grinned. He liked Tiago a lot and resented Martin's continued vitriol. *Vapid Jesuit boybot. Reptilian cyborg Pinocchio. In six months Raphael will be bored titless. Tell him from me.* But Rob decided to tell Raphael something else.

"Tiago called me last night actually. I'm to look after you." He blew a kiss.

"Fuck yourself Robert."

"He's good for you." Rob looked out of the window. "This could be the big one Raphael."

"Much too early to say." Raphael sipped his coffee. "We hardly know one another."

"You mean he's never seen you ripped to the tits on scotch?"

"Correct."

"Or dancing on bars? Or doing karaoke?"

"I only do Motown."

"Still." Rob had long ago decided not to tell Tiago how many times he'd put Raphael to bed, and turned out the light, and checked to make sure he hadn't choked on his own vomit. He wanted this to work. "Good stuff for my best man speech."

"Oh. Are you going to a wedding?" Raphael sipped his coffee and made a face. "Fuck that's awful." He put the cup down. "I'm sorry Rob. Thanks all the same. It's very thoughtful."

Rob brushed his short hair forwards. "I thought you needed it." He drummed the table, planned another sally, following his orders from Clara. *Talk him into it. This is the best offer he's ever had.* "But seriously though Raph. He's a really nice lad. Clara really likes him."

"I know she does." Raphael eyed him and took a deep breath. "And, possibly more importantly, I like him. But let's see." He drained the coffee cup and yawned. "Fuck. I'm completely fucking fucked."

"Raph." A mother and daughter were walking down the

aisle. Rob waited for them to pass. "I thought he was away last night."

Raphael shook his head. "He was away last night. He's working in London this week. I didn't sleep because we were arguing."

"Bad."

"By text message."

"Worse."

"And then I had a long sulk. In my tent." Raphael wrinkled up his nose, an expression he'd borrowed from Tiago. "It was entirely my fault. We'll make it up tonight though, at Amelia's." He ran a finger along the edge of the table, drawing a line under the drama. "And then things will be better than ever." He coughed. "He's not unreasonable."

Rob looked out at the rain and smiled.

SNAFU.

CHAPTER 22

WHO CAN FROM JOY
REFRAIN?

Though dinner was scheduled for eight o'clock and the concert for ten thirty, Raphael was dressed and assessing his reflection by seven o'clock. He needed to appear spectacularly smart; not to impress Amelia's friends, who were toffs, and musicians, immune to white tie, but because Tiago was more likely to cede if he beheld him in full mating plumage. Amelia had certainly given them a setting fit for a romantic reconciliation; their room was in the oldest part of the house, connected through an old orangery to the orchards, with walls the colour of pale coffee, and curtains, bedclothes and bolsters in ivory and old gold, and a carpet in barley wool with oriental swirls of peacock blue. The bed itself was too soft, and the bizarre crank key Raphael had found on the bedside table beside a chunky Lalique lamp had been only partially successful in increasing the tension of the mattress to something they might actually be able to sleep on, though he suspected they'd still roll together into the centre if Tiago didn't put a bolster between them.

Raphael frowned at the dozen white roses he'd bought in Kitminster Episcopi that afternoon. They might not be enough, even though it was possible the row hadn't been entirely his fault. He'd told Tiago so many times he hated phone conversations in noisy bars and restaurants; he hated repeating himself, and asking Tiago to repeat himself, trying to hear and be heard over chatter, and laughter, and background music, and people saying things like *Hey Tiago, yours is coming next angel.*

"Who was that?"

Say again Raphael?

Here you are beautiful.

"Who was that?"

Sorry honey, can't hear you.

"Who just called you angel? Who called you beautiful?"

Say again?

Here, get it down you Tiago. That's right. Good lad. Back of the fucking net.

"Who is that?"

A pause.

Oh, the barmaid.

He'd hung up in fury, switched off the phone, and switched it back on to send messages saying not to call. Tiago had texted him back to say that would not be a problem.

His phone buzzed.

Running late – see you before midnight hopefully. T x

Moderately encouraged by the x, Raphael stared forlornly at the roses, found himself getting wound up, and went out into the garden to pace away his frustration.

The scent of the evening was so good he didn't light up for fifteen seconds.

...

Tomas Paul had wanted to meet in a church, or a quiet city court, somewhere profound and auspicious; but they were stuck for time, so at seven fifteen he found himself in a horrible Leadenhall pub full of braying traders in Ted Baker. Tiago was sitting at a dark corner table between a stained glass window, a quiz machine and a soviet poster boy with blond, Spitfire pilot hair, a slate suit too tight across broad shoulders, and light grey eyes that looked Tomas Paul up and down, took him in and wrote him off in less than a heartbeat: *oldguy.*

"Hello." Tiago smiled and offered his hand without sincerity. "This is Jason Sadler."

"All right?" The accent was Poplar, veering to Limehouse, the tone of the owner of a nice flat on the Marina. Jason looked like the kind of financial professional Tomas Paul found it essential to avoid at parties; a preening spiv, slightly crumpled by this time of the evening, but still a real hotshot on something absolutely fascinating like the performance of the retail sector.

Tiago on the other hand, looked more like the well-tailored, callow, lethal quant that sat silent in Tomas Paul's investors' meetings for thirty minutes and then asked a one word question. "*Investability?*"They were an odd couple, if they were a couple.

Jason crushed Tomas Paul's hand with a three-sovereign-ring knuckle-duster, dropped it, downed half a pint of lager in three gulps and made to leave. "See you later then TJ?"

Tiago didn't look at him. "No. I already told you."

"Oh yeah. Seeing hubby tonight aren't we?" And Big Jase grinned, and ruffled Tiago's hair, and said *cheers,* and walked away.

Tiago straightened his hair with a graceful gesture that was like something Raphael would have done, then took out his phone and put it on the table, which wasn't.

Tomas Paul sat down. "Friend of yours?"

"Sort of." Tiago shrugged. "We're not as close as we used to be." He sipped his Coca Cola, put his glass down on a dirty beer mat, and studied the scratched tabletop. "I'm sorry I was rude. At the party."

Tomas Paul shrugged. "I started it."

"You did, rather." Tiago stared into his glass for a few moments, and Tomas Paul looked him over, mapping the trajectory of his descent. Six years had worked only subtle changes on Tiago; the face was longer, the cheeks narrower, the lips slightly thinner. In a few years Tiago would be unremarkable, a slightly more than averagely handsome man. Tiago looked up with an enquiring look. "What?"

Tomas Paul took a deep breath, "You don't remember me, do you?"

Tiago frowned, narrowed his eyes, wrinkled up his nose. "No. Should I?"

Tomas Paul shook his head and said not really, no.

...

Raphael surveyed the Kitminster grounds with a draughtsman's eye, glad of the strong evening sunlight that was creating strong contrasts and sharpening the shadows. The gardens might have been designed to look their best on a midsummer evening after a wet spring, or it might have been an accident, this being England. All that mattered right now was the setting would charm Tiago into a conciliatory mood; if he ever got there.

Raphael checked his watch, realising with some disappointment that Tiago's absence would also mean he had to spend dinner making small talk with one of the twenty or so other guests he'd seen arriving at the Hall that afternoon. He sighed and wandered over to a hedgerow, trying to remember the English names Martin would have used for the wild flowers that broke up the thick dark green. Ragged Robin was one, and Periwinkle, and Campion. And what was that very tall, lethal one? "They give it to people with heart problems?" He saw a lazy wet bee struggling to escape one of the bells, put out his sleeve to give it something to grip onto. "Come on bee. What do the English call the fucker?"

"We call it Foxglove."

Amelia was standing beside him, elegant as a damselfly, pretty and slender in a celadon green silk dress, her hair in a soft French plait. No jewellery, no make up; no need. "Still talking to yourself, I see."

"Only way I can get a sensible answer." He kissed her and told her she looked beautiful.

...

"This is yours, if you want it." Tiago took an envelope from his breast pocket. "Raphael drew it. When he was ill. He drew them for all of us." He smiled. "The crucial five."

Tomas Paul opened the envelope and took out an A6 piece of white card.

Tomas Paul nodded. It was like an invitation to his own funeral.

"Will you do Lux?"

"Don't know. Maybe. Part of it, slowly." Tiago looked at his drink. "Maybe."

He would. Tomas Paul took a deep breath. "Look, Tiago. Those emails."

Tiago smiled and nodded. "Yeah. I worked that out." He stared towards the quiz machine and unpicked nearly everything. The video was a clip shot at a wedding, something like that. "Your kids, I guess?"

"Yes."

Tiago nodded. "You're lucky. They're beautiful." He stifled a quiet yawn. "Oh yes. And the black and white film is CCTV from your gallery." He smiled, sipped his drink, checked his watch. "The photos could have been taken by anyone. I haven't worked them all out, but it wouldn't have been hard."

Tomas Paul nodded. "So if you know how, you know why?"

"Sure. You wanted to scare me off, because you were jealous." Tiago finished his coke and stared at the empty glass. "Because I know you still love him. I think you want him back. I guess it's a midlife crisis thing, like these school reunion affairs. But you know he needs me, not you. The future matters, the past less so."

It was cocky, and brutal, and very much as Tomas Paul would have done it. "Indeed."

Tiago got to his feet. "I need to go."

And Tomas Paul told him he needed to stay.

···

Raphael gave Amelia his arm and they walked towards a small formal pond just in front of the house.

"Just you?"

"I'm afraid Tiago won't be here till much later. I think he'll miss both the dinner and the concert. I'm sorry."

"Can't be helped." Amelia frowned, then brightened. "Actually we've got a few minutes till dinner. You can meet Leander. And do you like great crested newts?" She laughed and led him towards the pond, giggling like a much younger woman would have done. "And please don't say yes but you can't eat a whole one."

Raphael didn't say anything. He was too startled. He'd never seen a bird wearing a gold necklace before.

...

Tiago was studying the beer mat. "Say again?"

"I'm all done here. I'm out of here. This dump. I'm gone. I'm done. In two years from now. Think entropy. Bang, whoosh, splat, big mess, nothing left. Baikonur."

"Baikonur?" Tiago was staring, open mouthed, his assurance gone for the first time.

"Yeah." Tomas Paul checked his watch, let five seconds go by, took a pull on his pint, shrugged. "There mustn't be anything left." He stared at the blue and red stained glass in the window; the pigments had merged across the lead, making a small section veinous red. It was a botched job, not like his was going to be. His was going to be precise, an excision. "It'll be messy. But only my death can save Clara."

"Only your death can save Clara?" Tiago was frowning. "What are you talking about?"

Tomas Paul smiled. What the fuck was he talking about? He put the envelope in his pocket and explained that a sacrifice was needed to save Clara, that it had to be him because he'd broken the rules by spilling the beans, that when Tiago heard about the explosion he was to remember that Tomas Paul was okay, that he wouldn't feel pain, that he expected a good send off. "You know what I mean – seventy-six Pol Roger and Jaroussky singing *Alto Giove.*" He grinned. "You got that?"

"Sure." But it wasn't a convincing response. Tiago was staring spellbound at the space above Tomas Paul's head; big puppy eyes and white lips. "I've got all of it."

...

It was nearly midnight by the Tiago's taxi reached Kitminster Hall, but it hadn't taken him five hours to be certain that the words on the blackboard in the pub behind Tomas Paul's head had summed it up perfectly; crackers, nuts. Tomas Paul thought he was a god and he was going to top himself. It put last night's row with Raphael in the shade.

The taxi turned onto a torch-lined drive and Tiago glimpsed an elegant shape shimmering pale green in the dusk; Amelia, standing by a pond in an evening gown, pointing something out to someone out of view. The car straightened up and Tiago saw Raphael, looking impossibly dashing, waving a cigar in greeting, smiling sadly, pleased to see him.

...

By four in the morning most of the guests had gone to bed and the house was largely silent. In the low lit Games Room, Tiago was perched on a sideboard, playing quietly on one of Amelia's Baroque guitars, thinking up a form of words that wouldn't start an argument. *Did Tomas Paul drop a lot of acid in the nineties? I only ask because...*He frowned. No.

"How was the concert?"

Raphael was stalking round the billiard table, playing smug trick shots, sipping scotch. "It was lovely. Very chic. Purcell, mostly. A bit of Handel."

"Did you sing?"

"I did actually. Quite well." Raphael leaned on his cue and gazed at Tiago. "You know, the first time I saw you play guitar I thought you were out of my league."

Tiago smiled. "And what do you think now?"

"Oh, I still think you're out of my league. But now I just think I'm a lucky fucker."

Tiago nodded. *Does Tomas Paul have a history of psychosis? I only ask because…* No.

A clock in the hallway struck four, and left a comfortable silence. It was their silence, and Tiago didn't want to break it, so he let it run.

Raphael lined up a shot but then stood back. "You should be good at this. Why won't you give me another game?"

"I'd rather watch you. You look like James Bond."

Raphael lined up the shot again. "You used to want to be a priest and now you want to fuck James Bond." He played the shot. "That's progress."

Tiago nodded. It was a good line but he had a better one. *Would it surprise you to hear that Tomas Paul believes he is in fact the god Apollo, that his sister was the goddess Diana, and that when he blows himself to bits at Baikonur in two years he'll be reincarnated as a stag?* Definitely not. He sighed and stifled a yawn. "Sorry."

Raphael looked at his watch. "Bed for you I think."

Tiago put down the guitar and crossed his arms. "It sounds like a command."

Raphael put the cue away and came over to him. "It should do. Because it is one."

...

Amelia sat on her bed in her evening gown, reflecting on a successful day. The evening had been a triumph; all her funders were happy and the money was in the bank, which was good because she'd already had to start spending some of her *Tittlebats* contingency in Mothercare this morning. She'd got her a funny look, but that was just a question of nomenclature. They probably didn't get asked that often for *one of those things that bugs nurseries* but they knew what she wanted, and now it was all set up, the monitor hidden in the lamp by the bed.

She munched a water biscuit and sipped a glass of calvados; if Raphael and Tiago would only go to bed she could begin her observations.

...

Raphael smiled to himself while Tiago lead him a tortuous route through dark corridors to their bedroom. He was feeling mellow, and relieved, and looking forward to the final act of their reconciliation between the sheets. But when they reached the bedroom, Tiago turned to him.

"Can we go outside? I want to see the site of the temple. I want to see it at sunrise."

"Of course."

He followed Tiago out into the orchard, but though the sun was rising he soon lost sight of him in the early mist that had become trapped between the river and the house.

"Tiago?" Raphael wandered over to the nearest trees and leaned over to look at the bronze labels stuck into the ground beneath them. The orchard was the work of a tidy, productive mind, but it was still beautiful. Raphael nodded. Maybe his own orchard could be like this someday. He looked round for a second opinion.

"Darling?"

"Here."

Tiago emerged smiling from the mist, and then suddenly turned; a cormorant, wings churning the mist like jet engines, flew straight over his head, and made a last minute steep ascent to clear the roof of the house. Tiago pointed.

"The river must be over there. And the temple."

"Find it. I'll catch you up."

Raphael watched Tiago walk away; he wanted to check the labels on the tree trunks now, to see if they were the same varieties as his. It seemed that some were, but there were others he'd never seen before. Irish Peach, James Grieve, Laxton's Superb. Amelia had told him this was her grandfather's orchard; he'd been digging for victory, providing food and drink for the war effort. Raphael walked up and down the rows for a few minutes, noting names and planning improvements in his own orchards. He was impressed for the most part; the trees were mainly healthy and sturdy. But to his surprise the row of trees nearest the river was disappointing. Ten slight specimens, no more than whips a few years old, their labels red plastic, Dymo-embossed in white.

STANISLAUS

STANISLAUS CONTROL

Raphael frowned.

"What is it?" Tiago was standing beside him.

Rapahel shook his head. "These trees are younger."

Tiago shrugged. "Probably just Amelia's experiments." He pulled at Raphael's sleeve. "Hey, I found the really old orchard, where the temple was. It's a mess. Come with me."

Tiago was right; the really old orchard had been utterly neglected. The ground between the trees was waist high in nettles and ferns, ox eye daisies and bugle, ivy, and a few low shrubby trees that had either got there by self-seeding or with the assistance of squirrels; filbert, and hazel, the odd struggling horse chestnut. Many of the apple trees were dead. Those that had survived were gnarled from want of light, and grey-green with lichen. But they still had apples on them. Raphael picked one and bit it; it was sharp, but not inedible. He smiled.

"This hasn't been touched for decades."

But Tiago wasn't interested in apples. "Raphael." He kicked some of the brambles and ivy aside. "Look. One of the plinths."

Raphael looked over. Low shafts of sun were breaking through the muddle, shining on the forest floor, and on Tiago's hair, and on the plinth, and on something that shouldn't be there; a hand sticking up through the knotted ivy, black, like a heavy duty rubber glove. Raphael's stomach turned.

"Oh shit."

He went over to Tiago, put his hands on his shoulders, moving him back, shielding him. "Don't look."

Tiago looked over Raphael's shoulder. "It's just a statue." He knelt. "Oh Jesus. It's him."

It was hardly recognisable; a dark stone object, marbled with slime, covered in moss and starbursts of orange lichen. A very English Apollo, short-haired, strong-jawed, striding and purposeful, six-packed and athletic, the lyre resting on his left hip.

"Oh, poor god." Tiago brushed slugs from the corrupted hair

and looked up, tears welling in his eyes. "We have to save him Raphael."

"Sure." And Raphael smiled and held him close while the mist lifted, and wondered what on earth he was getting into.

...

They woke at six.

Tiago peered at the tray of tea things Amelia had left out and wrinkled up his nose; every now and then the English were just weird. "I'm sure Amelia has real coffee." He pulled on jeans and a sweater. "I'll go."

He found the kitchen empty, filled the kettle and put it on the range, and sat down at the kitchen table. He'd known from the state of her flat in Paris that Amelia was not a particularly tidy girl, but this was something else; the table was almost buried under old newspapers, and balls of twine, and garden implements. He picked up a newspaper and a sketch fell out; it was a coin, or a medal, an A, and a girl with a tree, and Ortygia in bold beneath it.

"Ortygia?" Tiago frowned, remembering Tomas Paul's admission in Leadenhall. Tomas Paul used Ortygia as an email address. Maybe his connections extended even further than he'd admitted. Tiago put down the sketch and dug deeper into the pile of newspapers. A small bunch of plastic labels scattered onto the floor, the kind of labels you used for labelling plants. Tiago got down on the floor and gathered them up.

STAR OF LISBON
DAVIDE'S DELIGHT

PARISIAN BEAU
DASILVA'S REINETTE

Star of Lisbon. Davide's Delight. DaSilva's Reinette. He chewed his lip. Was this some form of bizarre hero worship?

The kitchen door opened.

"Oh. You're up." Amelia was standing in the doorway. She looked as guilty as a mugshot, albeit a pretty funky mugshot, her pale green ballgown shimmering under a vast, shabby tweed coat. She came over and stood by the table and Tiago found himself staring down at a pair of elegant but muddy bare feet.

"I was making coffee Amelia." Still on his knees, he handed her the labels. "These fell on the floor."

"Thanks." Amelia took the labels from him and squirrelled them away in a drawer, her eyes on the sketch. "I do hope you both slept well?"

"Yes, thank you." Tiago got to his feet in a flurry of apology. They'd slept very well. It was a beautiful bed, a lovely bedroom. But they'd wanted fresh coffee, he hoped she didn't mind.

"Not in the slightest."

They sat in polite silence for a few moments.

Amelia nodded towards the sketch and coughed. "I saw the drawings at Raphael's apartment. I wanted to create my own."

"Yes. Yes, I like it." Tiago looked towards the window ledge. His attention had been caught by a moving image on a small screen; it was a blurry image, rather like the one he'd seen on the baby monitor they used for Tiaginho. But the image wasn't of a cot, but a bed; an ornate, rather rumpled, double bed. An athletic, naked man was getting into that bed, and pulling the covers over himself, and lighting a cigarette, and leaning back smiling into the pillows.

The kettle whistled and Amelia jumped up. "I'll do it. Do you like these kettles? I do. I know they're terribly expensive and old-fashioned but they last for years, you know." She put the kettle on a trivet, folded her arms, and stared at the floor.

A large dog barked somewhere.

Birds sang.

The man on the monitor started whistling Chopin.

Amelia let out a deep sigh. "Look, Tiago, it's not what you think. It's not something trivial. I'm not some kind of perv. I need your help. It's a matter of life or death."

Tiago looked back at the monitor. Raphael was grinning, and humming to himself, and blowing smoke rings, a picture of solitary contentment known only to those who were never lonely, because they knew they were truly loved. Tiago nodded. Seeing things in black and white could be instructive. You couldn't own someone, however much you loved them. All love brought was a set of responsibilities. And the greatest of those was to ensure that life didn't break your lover's heart. Maybe that did make it a matter of life and death.

He went over to Amelia and turned her towards him. "Life or death, you say?"

"Life, certainly." Amelia looked up at him with eyes of glacier blue. "Look. I'm sorry about the emails. They were Tomas Paul's idea."

Tiago's heart skipped a beat but he fought back the urge to interrupt.

"You see," Amelia shrugged, "I was trying to help." She put up a hand, played with a loose thread on his sweater. "You're not angry with me, are you?"

Tiago thought for a moment; no, he wasn't angry. There was no point getting angry with somebody who could be so very useful to him. But she wasn't going to get off scot free.

He put Amelia's slender fingers to his lips and made her an offer.

ALCINA FARADAY is a scientist, businesswoman and stepmother who writes literary fiction about the redeeming power of love and the disturbing possibilities of modern scientific reality.

Her Spiral Wound Trilogy "Beauty, Love and Justice", "These Modern Girls" and "The Commodity Fetish" follows a cultured rabble of unhinged, uncool, reality-averse GenX/Y outliers as they seek success and heroism, survive squalor and indignity, have a few laughs, and – mostly – emerge relatively unscathed from the moshpit of modern life in Paris, London and Lisbon.

Alcina lives in London and Devon with her engineer husband and a small colony of palmate newts.

Urbane Publications is dedicated to
developing new author voices, and publishing
fiction and non-fiction that challenges, thrills and
fascinates. From page-turning novels to innovative
reference books, our goal is to publish what
YOU want to read.

Find out more at

urbanepublications.com